Praise for

Islomanes of Cumerland Island

"Cumberland Island is a small landmass off the Georgia coast with a surprising history of decadence and ruin. In language as rhythmic of the sea, Bourke paints a portrait of one family's abiding attachment to the place, its natural beauty as well as its exotic history and ongoing controversy. A rich and rewarding read."
— **M. M. Buckner, author of** *Watermind* **and** *The Gravity Pilot*

"Islomanes of Cumberland Island explores the captivating world of a barrier island off the coast of Georgia. As rich in history as it is in rocks, minerals, and fossils—wild horses are the star attractions—it was first home to the industrialist Carnegies, who made it a retreat for the wealthy. But that was *then.* As Rita Welty Bourke takes us on lyrical trips around the island as it is today, delving out fascinating pieces of its history as we go, we see this Ozymandian canvas the Carnegies left behind as the ecosystem nature intended it to be."
— **Cathie Pelletier, author of** *The Funeral Makers,* *The Weight of Winter,*
and *Northeaster.*

"From the Timucuan Indians to Civil War heroes to steel magnates and beyond, the challenges and triumphs of the island come to life in page after page. From the Dungeness ruins to slave quarters to standing mansions, the story unfolds. *Islomanes of Cumberland Island* is an easy read and one to get lost in."
— **Barbara Ryan Harris, Publisher,** *St. Marys Magazine*

"An astonishing, richly drawn exploration of one family's journey back to their beloved Cumberland Island, intricately woven with the fascinating and sometimes tragic history of the area."
— **Sara J. Henry, author of** *Learning to Swim* **and** *A Cold and Lonely Place*

When I'm reading a book I really like, I find myself reading faster and faster. I have to stop and slow down so as not to do the author the disservice of skimming over carefully wrought prose. I had to slow down a lot reading this book. It's that good."
— **Cynthia Williams, author of** *Hidden History of Fort Myers*

"Bourke weaves the stories of the past and present together in a captivating way. A must-read for lovers of historical fiction, nature, and wildlife preservation."
— *Publisher's Weekly*

"Rita Welty Bourke, self-proclaimed islomane, draws from her many visits to Cumberland Island. Besides her family's adventures and their love for the island, she brings meticulous research to the pages. The history of the island includes little-known vignettes about its inhabitants, most notably Lucy Carnegie, who created a respite for her family that could not last."
— **Phyllis Gobbell, author of** *Pursuit in Provence* **and** *Secrets and Shamrocks*

"Bourke's observations cut through expectations as she leads you through powerful meditations on Cumberland Island, horses, nature, history, and family, all of which linger long after you've closed the book. I want to pack up and head to Cumberland Island, but this writer has already taken me there in ways greater and deeper than setting foot on the sand."
— **Corabel Shofner, author of** *Almost Paradise*

"Bourke's masterful storytelling reveals the enthralling history, environmental challenges, and enduring attraction of the island to all manner of travelers for over a century. This compelling and satisfying read is both a trip back in time and an eminent reminder of how we choose to live and love in the 21st century."
— **M.B. Dunn, author of** *Fate Havens*

Islomanes of

Cumberland Island

"*Somewhere among the notebooks of Gideon I found a list of diseases as yet unclassified by medical science, and among these occurred the word Islomania, which was described as a rare but by no means unknown affliction of spirit. There are people, Gideon used to say, by way of explanation, who find islands somehow irresistible. The mere knowledge that they are on an island, a little world surrounded by the sea, fills them with an indescribable intoxication.*"

"*…we all of us, by tacit admission, knew ourselves to be Islomanes.*"

— *Reflections on a Marine Venus*, Lawrence Durrell

Rita Welty Bourke

Islomanes of
Cumberland Island

Addison & Highsmith

Addison & Highsmith Publishers

Las Vegas ◊ Chicago ◊ Palm Beach

Published in the United States of America by
Histria Books
7181 N. Hualapai Way, Ste.130-86
Las Vegas, NV 89166 USA
HistriaBooks.com

Addison & Highsmith is an imprint of Histria Books. Titles published under the imprints of Histria Books are distributed worldwide.

Library of Congress Control Number: 2021937940

ISBN 978-0-9801164-5-8 (hardcover)
ISBN 978-1-59211-204-3 (softbound)
ISBN 978-1-59211-271-5 (eBook)

For my mom and dad who are gone,
but are with me every day.

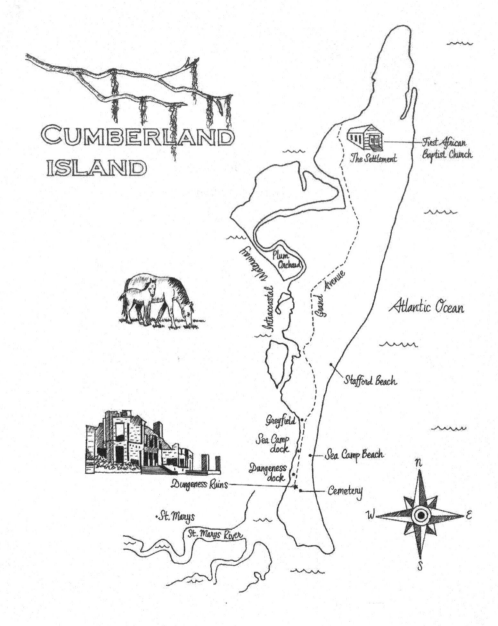

CUMBERLAND
ISLAND

The Settlement

First African
Baptist Church

Plum
Orchard

Intracoastal Waterway

Grand Avenue

Atlantic Ocean

Stafford Beach

Greyfield

Sea Camp
dock

Sea Camp Beach

Dungeness
dock

Dungeness Ruins

Cemetery

·St. Marys

St. Marys River

N

W   E

S

Map by Katherine Carpenter

Prologue

The General's wife came out onto the veranda of their Cumberland Island home one spring morning and called to her husband. "Shoot some of those birds out in the oak trees," she said. "I'll give them to the cook and we'll have them for dinner."

General William MacKay Davis, Civil War hero and cousin of Confederate President Jefferson Davis, summoned his son, Bernard, who had just the day before moved with his wife and children onto the island. The two men walked side by side into the yard. When they neared the trees, the younger man broke open the breech of his shotgun and inserted a shell. He closed the breech and as the barrel snapped into place, the gun went off. Bernard's five-year-old son, George Dewson Davis, fell from one of the trees.

Bernard ran to the spot where the boy lay. "Oh my God, Georgie, did I hit you? Are you hurt?"

"Yes, Papa," he said. And a paleness came over him.

Bernard saw blood on the boy's lips. "Where, my darling? In the mouth?"

"No, Papa, here," the child said, and he placed his hand on his side. "But you didn't mean to do it."

Bernard took his son into his arms, and as he did, a massive hemorrhage poured from the child's mouth. Within minutes, he was gone.

Nine months later, in December of 1880, Bernard, too, was dead, presumably by his own hand. Father and son are buried in unmarked graves in the Greene-Miller Cemetery on Cumberland Island, Georgia.

Adapted from accounts in *Songs of Three Islands*, by Millicent Monks, *Cumberland Island: A History*, by Mary Bullard, *Cumberland Island: Strong Women, Wild Horses*, by Charles Seabrook, *The Carnegies & Cumberland Island*, by Nancy Carnegie Rockefeller, newspaper articles and genealogical records in the George A. Smathers Library, University of Florida.

1

I t's dark when we drive onto the island. The four lanes of the Torras Causeway narrow down to two, the slant of the bridge over the Frederica River gives way to level ground, and the light reflected off the tidal creeks grows dim.

Rhamy, who's driving, slows to read the sign: *Welcome to St. Simons Island, Georgia.*

"We're here, Daddy," she says. "Wake up."

I look back at my husband. He stirs, but does not awaken. "Let him sleep," I tell Rhamy. "It's been a long day."

The road is like a tunnel, the branches of the live oaks reaching across, touching, intertwining. Lights from houses half-hidden among the trees pierce the darkness. The muted sounds of TVs, dishes, and cutlery are carried on warm breezes.

"It feels so different from being on the mainland," Rhamy says.

"I'm glad you decided to come," I tell her.

"I don't think I've ever been on an island before."

"Manhattan is an island."

"But not like this," she says. "It's so quiet, so peaceful."

I know what she means. If an island is as densely populated as Manhattan, it can't truly be called an island.

"Who was the King?" she asks.

It takes me a moment to make the connection; the road we're on is called King's Way. "There was a family named King who had a cotton plantation on the island. It was probably named for them. Or maybe for the man who built the hotel. He was a big, tall guy, well over six feet. He had a friend who was tiny. Every evening they'd go for a walk around the island. Locals began to call them 'the King and the Prince.'"

"So that's what they named their hotel."

"It's where Charlie and I stayed last year. We booked a two-bedroom suite, ocean view. I think you'll like it."

A car approaches, the headlights washing over us. It passes, and the night sounds resume.

"It feels like we're disconnected from the mainland," Rhamy says. "It's almost like being in another country."

"We're on an island," I answer.

During the night, the ocean kicks up, flowing into St. Simons Sound, washing up onto the beach outside our windows. I open the glass doors and step out onto the terrace. Waves tumble onto the shore, smashing against the Johnson rocks that protect the hotel complex.

A year ago I stood in nearly the same spot, listening to the same sounds, feeling the salt air brushing against my skin. It's good to be back.

We're on an island. There is water all around. We are in a place where life flows gently.

By morning the sun has risen bright over the water, the tide has gone out, and the beach has reappeared. Charlie and I are sitting in the breakfast room of the hotel. Rhamy has gone off to look at a group of paintings on display near the reception desk. There's Starbucks coffee in the lobby, dolphins playing in the waters outside the windows, and five gloriously empty days ahead of us. We'll have no trouble filling them. Our only worry is if five days will be enough.

Our table is littered with brochures that describe the lighthouse museum, ghost walks, trolley rides to historic island sites. Charter a deep sea fishing boat, swim in the pool at Neptune Park, picnic under live oak trees six hundred years old. Take a sunset cruise to a waterfront restaurant, visit Sapelo Island or Fernandina Beach, kayak through the marshes of Glynn. For the less adventuresome, there are coffee shops, restaurants, and a bookstore in the village.

I hand the Beachview Books flyer to Charlie; he always wants to check out local bookstores.

Rhamy comes back to our table with yet another brochure, this one called *The Wild Horses of Cumberland Island*. It describes the artwork, the artist, and the island that inspired the work. "How did we miss this when we checked in last night?" she asks. "There must be twenty paintings, all done by a local artist. There are scenes of horses running on the beach, grazing in the forest, drinking from a waterhole. There's one of a newborn colt I just love. It's kind of expensive." She tilts her head, considering.

About Cumberland Island, there is no hesitation. She wants to go. The thought of visiting an island with a human population of thirty and a wild horse population of nearly two hundred is a dream come true. She can't imagine that she's never heard of this place, never knew of the wild horses that live there. She has to go, has to see for herself what they look like, how healthy they are, and would it be possible to adopt one.

From the time she was a little girl, Rhamy has loved horses. Grown up now, still in love with horses, she takes a bite of toast, a sip of orange juice, and goes off to examine the paintings more closely. I watch her walk across the lobby and ascend the steps to the raised platform where the pictures are on exhibit. Sun hat hanging from her fingertips, she moves from painting to painting. The morning sun streaming through the skylight washes over her, so strong it fades to pastel the blue T-shirt and khaki shorts she's wearing.

The King and Prince is a grand hotel. Opened in 1935 as a seaside dance club, it began to accept guests six years later. A live band might once have played on the platform where Rhamy is standing. Charlie's grandparents could have danced to the music and sipped whiskey at the bar, had they visited here. Just three generations from the old country, they would not have been welcome at the elite Cloister Clubhouse on neighboring Sea Island. Membership at the Cloister was reserved for the wealthy and the well born. Shanty Irish, even after they'd moved up the social ladder to Lace Curtain Irish, were not accepted.

When Rhamy returns, she brings with her a painting of a white colt, pink nose, shiny black hooves. I take the picture from her to examine more closely. He's such a newborn, he's barely dry. If he tried to walk, his legs would be wobbly.

I pass it to Charlie.

"I couldn't resist," Rhamy says, pushing her blonde hair back from her face. "I'll have it framed when I get back to Portland. It'll be perfect over the couch in my den."

Perfect, I suspect, because it reminds her of the horse she owned for years and had to put down.

She tosses her sun hat onto a chair and she's off again, this time to talk to the concierge.

I go back to watching the dolphins. There are at least six of them, frolicking in the shallow waters by the shore.

"She's planning our trip to Cumberland Island," I tell Charlie.

He nods, but he's absorbed in one of the brochures, and I'm not sure he even heard me.

Rhamy has been a teacher in a private school in Portland, Oregon, for the last ten years. Taking charge comes easy for her. And she looks better in a hat, any hat, than anyone I've ever known. She loves hats, almost as much as she loves horses. Invite Rhamy and her husband to a wedding, and she has to have a new hat. One that matches her outfit, of course.

We love her hats and we love how she takes charge, but never oversteps. We love her spirit of adventure and her enthusiasm for travel. We even love the rivalry that exists between Rhamy and her sisters. It pleases us that she wants to spend her spring break with us on St. Simons Island. Kate and Madeleine are not invited. For these few days, Rhamy wants us all to herself.

It's not a hard sell. We love coming here. We love spending time on an island, being separated from the mainland, sheltered from its troubles by a body of water that's rich in nutrients from both land and sea, a playground for dolphins, habitat for sea turtles, breeding ground for all kinds of sea life.

"The 11:45 ferry tomorrow is full," Rhamy announces when she returns, "but there's room on the early one. It boards at 8:45 in the morning. We'd have to drive to St. Marys, about an hour south of here. The concierge can reserve seats for us. Too early?"

I look at Charlie. He's never been a morning person.

"If we wait another day and take the late ferry," Rhamy says, "we'll only be able to spend a few hours on the island. Please, Dad?"

When Rhamy was six months old and teething, Charlie didn't want me to give her zwieback toast, for fear she'd choke. When she was five, she fell off her bicycle and scraped her knee; he wanted to take her to the emergency room. A year later a Sunday School teacher frightened her with a vivid description of the final days; he took her out of the class. Which is not to say Charlie is overprotective. Just that this first-born child of ours is precious. The day she was born, he brought his guitar into my hospital room and played a song he'd written for her. Ten months later, it had been recorded and was climbing the country music charts.

"What time do we have to get up?" he asks, and I know we're going to Cumberland Island in the morning.

It's the Carnegie mansion that attracts him. He's always been interested in the robber baron era, the tycoons of the late nineteenth and early twentieth century and their attempts to create an American aristocracy that rivaled that of Europe.

One of the brochures tells the story of Thomas Carnegie, younger brother of Andrew Carnegie. Snubbed by industrialists who planned to build a members-only clubhouse on Jekyll Island, Thomas sailed his yacht to the next island in the chain. When he saw Cumberland, sparsely populated, her once prosperous cotton plantations reverting to the wild, feral horses inhabiting the island, he knew he'd found what he was looking for.

Thomas Carnegie's plan was to buy the entire island, and he very nearly succeeded. The Queen Anne style mansion he built was large and ornate, and it soared to the heavens. The gardens that surrounded it rivaled Eden in beauty and bounty.

If there's anything that would entice my Charlie to Cumberland Island, it's the Carnegie connection. He's not so excited about the amenities, or lack thereof, on the island: drinkable water not widely available, no restaurants, no place to buy sunblock or bug spray, roads of sand and shell, biting and stinging insects, prickly bushes, all under a sticky hot sun.

But Rhamy wants to go, and he's willing to suffer, at least for a day.

Though reluctantly. Charlie is not a man who would do well stranded in a wilderness. Or on a deserted island.

2

The concierge has promised to leave our ferry tickets with the desk clerk. We're to pick up box lunches from a bed and breakfast in St. Marys, Georgia.

"It's a 45-minute drive," the clerk tells us in the morning. "Go back across the Torras Causeway to the mainland, pick up I-95 in Brunswick, and head south. Get off at Kingsland, just before the Florida line, and take East King Avenue across to the St. Marys dock." He hands Charlie the tickets and a business card from the bed and breakfast.

"Spencer's," the clerk says. "They'll have your box lunches ready. Pick them up on your way to the dock. They do a wonderful job. I'm sure you'll be pleased. We send customers there all the time."

Ten minutes later, we've lost our way. Neither the concierge yesterday nor the desk clerk this morning mentioned road construction south of Brunswick, or the cloverleaf that was so confusing we somehow ended up going north on I-95 instead of south. We'd gone miles in the wrong direction before Charlie found a place to exit and get back on, heading in the right direction this time.

Rhamy, sitting in the back seat, takes the Cumberland Island brochure out of her purse and hands it to me. She looks worried.

Ferry check-in is required thirty (30) minutes prior to departure or the reservation will be canceled with no refund. Check-in takes place upstairs in the Cumberland Island National Seashore Visitor Center.

I hand it back to her without comment. I check the dashboard clock and the direction indicator in the rearview mirror. At least now we're heading south. I glance at the speedometer.

"Why don't you let me drive," I suggest.

Charlie accelerates to 65.

We pass the Port of Brunswick, and I look out over acres of land covered with thousands of cars. Some are coming into the United States: Jaguars, Kias, Mitsubishi, and Porsches. Others are headed for Europe or Asia: Fords, GMs, Mercedes, and BMWs. Ocean liners in the Brunswick River, empty of their cargo, look as if they are floating on air. Empty trains are queued up, ready to be loaded with auto racks that make it possible to carry double and triple layers of cars.

Charlie's first job, after we were married, was to trace lost railroad cars. If we're sitting at a railroad crossing, he likes to identify the different cars and the freight they might be carrying. Over the years I've learned about boxcars, flatcars, gondolas, and covered hoppers. He hated the job, but he loved the trains. I lower the window so we can hear the train whistles sound as the trains head out to dealerships in the East and beyond.

"Wouldn't you like to let me drive so you can see the scenery?"

He shakes his head, but he accelerates, and I watch the speedometer creep up to 70.

The thirty-minute deadline is not always enforced. We're late, but not too late to board the ferry. Spencer's boxed lunches in hand, we hurry down the gangplank and find seats along the starboard side of the boat.

Charlie is worried about the car. Because there was no time to find a space farther down St. Marys Street, he parked in a two-hour spot. What if the car is gone when we get back, towed to some distant lot? What kind of fine might we have to pay? How would we even pay a fine? He'd tossed his wallet in the trunk, Rhamy and I our purses, so we have no money for a cab, towing charges, or a fine.

Out on the river the wind picks up, and it whips across the water. None of us is prepared for how cold it is. This is the last week of March; it should be hot.

And it is, but not on the ferry. The cold spray hits us, and we decide to move inside, but all the booths are filled. We try upstairs, thinking that at least we'll be in the sun. But others have had the same thought; every seat is taken. We settle on trying to stay on whichever side of the boat seems more sheltered.

Forty-five minutes later, Rhamy sees her first Cumberland horses. She grabs my arm. "Look, Mom, there, on the beach."

Three horses are grazing at the edge of the marsh.

"Cumberland Island," she breathes. "We're here."

The ferry slows as we approach the dock.

"Look farther back," I tell her, "into the marsh. There are more. Six or seven, at least."

Other passengers join us at the railing, and another row behind them, until most of the passengers have migrated to the side of the ship closest to the island. I wonder if we're in danger of tipping. But this is the Cumberland Sound, not the ocean, and the water is shallow. We glide along, the ship's motor barely audible.

Five minutes later, the ferry pulls up to the dock and we disembark. A park ranger steps out from beneath the roofed area and greets us. When we are all assembled there, she runs through her prepared speech: "No feeding, touching, teasing, frightening, or disturbing the wildlife. Use common sense around the horses. The beach is on the other side of the island. It'll take you at least thirty minutes to get there, maybe more. You can collect shells and sharks' teeth, but everything else stays on the island."

She points out the restrooms, the Ice House Museum, and the road to the Dungeness mansion.

"Ice House?" someone asks.

"They used to bring chunks of ice over from the mainland for the Carnegies. That was before refrigeration. The Park Service turned it into a museum. I hope you brought water, but if you didn't, there's a faucet outside the building. You can use that. There's no place to buy food of any kind on the island. This is a wilderness area."

There are nearly seventy of us standing on the dock, and the sun is beating down on us. The ranger looks us over, as if trying to pick out the one who's going to cause problems, get bitten by a snake, kicked by a horse, carried out to sea by a rip current.

"You can catch either the 2:45 p.m. or the 4:45 p.m. ferry back to the mainland," she says. "Be here on the dock at least a half hour before departure. If you miss the last ferry, it'll cost you a hundred dollars for a boat ride back to the mainland. If you can find someone to take you. There'll be a guided tour of Dungeness in about an hour, but you're welcome to head out on your own."

She steps aside, and we're released. As we're stepping from the dock onto the sand, she calls out a final word of caution: "Watch out for the horse droppings."

3

General William MacKay Davis purchased the 4,000-acre plantation on Cumberland Island just three months before the death of his grandson. He planned to spend the rest of his life there. Now he wanted to leave. He recalled that Thomas Carnegie, brother of famed Andrew Carnegie, had, the previous summer, offered to buy the plantation for $25,000.

Lucy Coleman Carnegie, Thomas's wife, was anxious to find a winter home away from the polluted city of Pittsburgh with its coal-burning foundries, railroads, and steel mills. When she read an article in *Lippincott's Monthly Magazine* about the island, she wondered if that might be the place she was looking for. Cumberland had "the balmiest climate in the South" and "game in abundance." The author, Frederick A. Ober, described the live oak forest as "so difficult to pierce that the deer with which the forest swarms choose the old paths …in their walks from sleeping to feeding grounds." The article told of plantation owner Robert Stafford who burned the homes of his freed slaves, telling them to "go, as he had no more use for them nor they for him." "Cumberland today is nearly depopulated, …half-wild horses roam over the …once cultivated fields."

Lucy was fascinated by the description of the island, and she no doubt talked to her husband about it. Cumberland Island, she believed, would be the perfect place to raise their children. The air would be healthy. The children would be free to roam the island, walk on the beach, and swim in the ocean. They could fish in the rivers and lakes, ride horses. The life she imagined was an idyllic one.

General Davis, anxious to leave this place of so much sorrow, contacted Thomas Carnegie. He offered to sell his plantation for $40,000. Carnegie thought the price too high.

Davis wrote a description of his holdings and sent it to Carnegie's representatives. Among its assets were several hundred orange and olive trees, lemon, peach, apricot, pear, quince, fig, and plum trees, grape vines and banana plants, ornamental shrubs, freesia and clematis. "The well is 30 feet deep," he wrote. "In summer the water comes forth at a temperature below 70 degrees. Cattle and horses can be pastured on the island without additional food or shelter. The grass is sweet. There are deer in the forest, wild pigs in the woods, and feral horses that roam the island. The house has four rooms and a new roof. There are several cottages and outbuildings on the property. A carriage house and stable, featuring glass windows, have recently been completed. Though the Dungeness mansion burned during the Union occupation, the walls are sound and can be integrated into any new construction."

The magazine article Lucy had read told the history of the island and of the mansion called Dungeness. English General James Oglethorpe built a hunting lodge on what had been an Indian shell mound in 1736. He called it Dungeness after a headland on the southeastern coast of England. Revolutionary War hero Nathaniel Greene designed the next building but died before construction could begin. His widow, Catherine "Caty" Greene-Miller, built a four-story tabby mansion. Its walls were six feet thick tapering to four as the building rose to its ultimate height of seventy-six feet. The house had thirty rooms, four chimneys, and sixteen fireplaces. It was surrounded by twelve acres of gardens.

Catherine and her new husband, Phineas Miller, were planters, and they prospered. Sea Island cotton commanded premium prices. Its unusual tensile strength made it nearly equal to modern nylon.

The Civil War brought an end to the plantation economy. Union soldiers took possession of Georgia's barrier islands in the spring of 1862 and declared the slaves emancipated. White landowners, fearing an insurrection by the newly freed blacks, fled the island. The Greene family moved away, and Union soldiers moved into the mansion. In 1866 Dungeness caught fire and burned to the ground. Only the tabby walls remained.

Lucy Carnegie wanted Dungeness. Her plan was to turn it into a vacation home and winter retreat for her family.

Thomas Carnegie waited for word from General Davis.

Davis reduced his price to $35,000. Carnegie accepted. He asked that the deed to the property be made to his wife, Mrs. Lucy C. Carnegie.

The Confederate war hero, now a broken old man, requested only that he be allowed to come back once a year to visit the graves of his son and grandson.

But he never did.

4

Charlie's hat, the one with both UVA and UVB protection, has disappeared. He thinks he left it on the ferry, which has pulled away from the dock. I hand him a tube of sunblock, but there's hardly any left. He doesn't ask about insect repellent, so I don't tell him I've forgotten to bring it.

When he saw the sideways crabs in the mud beside the dock, crabs so numerous the beach itself seemed to be moving, he positively shivered with distaste. At any hint of danger, any unusual sound or movement, they dove into their holes. Charlie turned away.

He was equally unhappy when he heard one of the ferry passengers mention the diamondback rattlesnakes that have taken up residence in the ruins of the Carnegie mansion.

The largest predator on the island is the alligator, and Charlie hates alligators. When he saw the posters in the shelter where we docked, posters that showed the varieties of wildlife on the island, he hurried past. I lingered long enough to learn there are alligators in the fresh water ponds, salt marshes, and in the ocean.

Charlie is unhappy. To be at the mercy of ferry timetables, park rangers, protected wildlife that could be dangerous, biting insects, things that crawl and burrow, this is not his idea of a vacation. He'd much prefer a Relais & Chateau in the South of France, a four-star resort in the Swiss Alps, a castle hotel in Ireland.

Those things are nice, and I will be forever grateful to Charlie for taking me to those places. But my roots are in the soil, and I never want to forget that. The truth is, we make a good couple. He knows things I have no knowledge of, and I love that about him. But I think there's value in dragging him to places like Cumberland Island. A creative person, like Charlie, needs to fill up the coffeepot from time to time. You can't keep pouring out, or one day you'll find the pot is empty.

I take his hand and we follow Rhamy down the sandy road that leads to Dungeness. Within minutes we are in deep shade, beneath a forest of live oak trees whose lower limbs stretch out parallel to the earth. The understory is thick with saw palmetto, muscadine vines, and Spanish moss.

Horses have walked here before us; clouds of insects rise up from the piles they've left behind. We reach a four-way intersection. The weathered sign indicates this is Grand Avenue, the road that runs the length of the island. It's rutted and narrow, barely wide enough for a single vehicle. Dungeness is to the right.

Information I'd gleaned from yesterday's brochures might make Charlie feel better, if I shared some of what I'd learned with him. I could tell him that the Carnegies kept a seventeen-foot alligator in a pond by Plum Orchard, and they were fond of him. They built a footbridge over the pond, and the children stood on the bridge and fed him fish they'd caught in the river. When hunters attempted to kill the alligator, the family intervened. The alligator had become something of a family pet.

Maybe alligators aren't as dangerous as Charlie thinks. But it's a childhood thing, I suspect, so I keep quiet.

The beach is eroding on the western side of the island where we docked, and it isn't always a pretty sight. But wait until we get to the ocean side, I might tell him. The white sands stretch from the jetty at the southern tip to the lighthouse at the north. It's clean and wide and deserted, the last undeveloped beach along the entire East Coast.

Diamondback rattlers are not aggressive, I could tell him, and they can only strike about a third of their length. The Carnegie kids, knowing the limitations of the snakes, liked to dangle a live mouse or a bird on a piece of fishing line at the opening of the den. When the snake struck, they would drag him out, his fangs still sunk in his prey.

If I told him these things, if I tried to cajole him into seeing this island as Rhamy and I see it, he would not be impressed.

I could remind him of how Rhamy wanted to go to Chincoteague to see the wild horses when she was a little girl, and we never took her. I could say that though she left home a dozen years ago, we're still her parents. We are at last fulfilling one of her childhood dreams, and I like the feeling that gives me.

Maybe he doesn't remember about Chincoteague. And if he does, I doubt he ever knew how important it was to her. It all seems too complicated to explain, and in this place that is so gloriously beautiful, and unspoiled, I don't want to talk about things from long ago. Better to let them stay in the past.

There's a rustling in the undergrowth to our right. We stop. An armadillo emerges from beneath a thicket of saw palmetto. He crosses in front of us and disappears. We move on, single file now, keeping to the center of the road.

Rhamy is leading the way, moving through dappled sunlight, side-stepping tendrils of low-hanging Spanish moss. Occasionally she reaches out to touch a leaf or a palm frond. She's thrilled to be here. From the moment we drove onto St. Simons Island, I noticed a contentment, a quiet serenity about her I'd rarely seen before. Watching her, seeing how happy she is, I think of a word that perfectly describes her: Islomane. A person who is in love with islands. Someone who feels most at home when they are on an island.

It's a word I first encountered when I was an adolescent, in a book that was forbidden in the household where I grew up. D. H. Lawrence's *Lady Chatterley's Lover* led me to Henry Miller's *Tropic of Cancer* and *Tropic of Capricorn*. I read these books late into the night, flashlight under the covers, hardly believing anyone could write such lascivious things. So this was what sex was all about.

Henry Miller had a friend, I learned. The friend, Lawrence Durrell, was also a novelist.

Born in India of English and Irish parents, Durrell roamed the world but was never able to find a place where he felt at home. For a time he lived on the Greek island of Corfu. He loved it there, and he wrote a novel, *Prospero's Cell*, set on Corfu. I read it, and another Durrell book, *The Alexandria Quartet*. He wrote much as Miller wrote, I discovered. The pages of his books were full of erotic sex scenes. When I finished the Durrell novels, I set the flashlight back on the shelf in the pantry. It would be years before I'd pick up any of those books again. But some of the images stayed with me.

Durrell told of dropping cherries into the lagoon near the house he'd rented on Corfu. They would sink to the bottom, and in that clear water they would remain visible. Durrell's wife would dive for them and bring them to the surface. He told of islanders who measured time and distance by the number of cigarettes they could smoke as they walked from one village to another. If the clocks on the four sides of the church tower were never set at exactly the same time, a wind from the north slowing the delicate hands of the north-facing clock, a breeze from the south hastening the clock on the southern face, what did it matter?

I was perplexed, and curious, when I came across the word in Durrell's *Reflec-tions of a Marine Venus*. A character named Gideon tells of a "rare …affliction of spirit. There are people, Gideon (said) …who find islands… irresistible. The mere knowledge that they are on an island, a little world surrounded by the sea, fills them with an indescribable intoxication." These people, Gideon believed, were islomanes.

I'd never seen the word before. I could not find it in a dictionary. There was no such word, yet there it was in Durrell's book. I had no idea an author could do that, simply make up a word if none existed that quite described what he wanted to describe. Yet that's exactly what Durrell had done.

After the death of his father, Durrell escaped the cold and damp climate of England, which he found absolutely paralyzing, and traveled with his family to sunny Greece. In a fisherman's cottage in northwestern Corfu he lived an idyllic life, writing, fishing, and sailing. It was there, on this tiny speck of land in the Ionian Sea, that Durrell felt most at home.

Then came World War II. The island was bombarded by both Italian and German warplanes. Durrell, his wife, and daughter were forced to flee ahead of the advancing Nazi army.

For the rest of his life he would yearn to live on an island. He was an islomane: a person who comes to an island in search of something he cannot exactly name. Perhaps, as Gideon says, these lost souls are somehow related to the doomed in-habitants of Atlantis. On an island they are content. They want to stay forever. If that is not possible, at least they can visit. They are afflicted with islomania. They are islomanes.

As is Rhamy. It isn't just the horses that draw her here. It's the world they live in, a world separate from other worlds, a world where life is protected. A world where she feels at home.

As do I. I felt it when we crossed the bridge and drove onto St. Simons Island. I felt it when we boarded the ferry at St. Marys, and when we made our way across the intracoastal waterway, and when we stepped onto the dock at Cumberland Island.

But not Charlie. He misses civilization. The comforts of home. His hat.

5

Four months after Thomas and Lucy Carnegie became owners of the plantation on Cumberland Island, workmen razed the burnt-out structure and began construction of a new Dungeness.

Designed as a Scottish castle, it would contain fifty-nine rooms, wraparound verandas, high ceilings, porches, turrets, and a hundred-foot tower. The Carnegie fortune was vast.

Thomas Carnegie died before Dungeness could be completed, but the work went on.

Lucy built a carriage house, golf course, greenhouse, recreation building, laundry, dairy barn, carpentry shop, kennel, living facilities for both black and white employees, dining rooms, bakery, chicken houses, commissary, ice plant, garden shed, and boat dock. She bought every piece of property that came up for sale until she owned all but a small enclave at the north end of the island. To cater to her every whim and those of her children, she employed two hundred servants.

The Gilded Age was a time of great wealth concentrated in the hands of a few families, and the Carnegies were among the richest. But trouble loomed. For the industrialists to build railroads, produce steel, and satisfy the burgeoning need for petroleum, they needed cheap labor.

The influx of immigrants made it possible for them to hire workers at wages so low, a man could barely afford to feed his family. Children as young as three were sent to work in cotton mills and coal mines. If their fingers were torn off by machines, there were other children who could take their places.

A steel worker in a Carnegie plant in 1890 earned an average of $10 a week. He worked twelve-hour shifts, seven days a week. His only holiday was July 4th. He did not bring a mid-day meal; there were no breaks and no time to eat.

Walking along the island road on our way to Dungeness, the heat of the day already upon us, I can only imagine what it must have been like for those workers.

Twelve-hour shifts, nothing to eat, I would have keeled over. Charlie would have been out the door, heading for the nearest restaurant, Rhamy following close behind. The world is a better place now. Times are not quite so hard.

I was a child of eight or nine when I learned of an ancestor who had worked in one of the Carnegie foundries. When my grandfather told the story of what happened to his Uncle Norman, there was no anger in his voice, no fist-raised-to-the-sky gesture. It happened a long time ago.

Uncle Norman, a man who exists only in a family story that has been passed down through generations, was a young man when he left home. He may have wanted to see what lay beyond the Maryland farm where he'd been raised. He had three older brothers, so there were plenty of hands to plant and harvest the crops and care for the animals. Wages of $10 a week would have looked appealing. Forty dollars a month, that's over $500 a year. A few years working in a foundry, he may have thought, and he'd be able to save enough money to buy a piece of property and to marry.

He crossed the Allegheny Mountains and traveled west until he reached Pittsburgh, a distance of nearly two hundred miles. He made his way to one of the Carnegie-owned steel mills and asked for a job.

Once there was a newspaper clipping that told the rest of the story, but it was read and reread and passed around so many times, it finally disintegrated. Nothing of him remains but a story an old man thought worth remembering, and passing down.

My grandfather is always, in my memory, someone who spent his final years reminiscing about the past. Abraham Lincoln tall, his face darkened from years in the sun, he is wreathed in smoke from his ever-present pipe. If I close my eyes today, I can see the room where he spent his days, smell the tobacco, hear the crackle of the fire he kept burning in his potbelly stove. My mother often sent me across the hall to his room to gather up his breakfast dishes, sweep the floor, straighten the doilies his wife had crocheted for the easy chair he kept by the window. If he was in a storytelling mood, I would settle into that chair and listen.

The Carnegie Steel Mill in Homestead, Pennsylvania, my grandfather said, was built on the banks of the Monongahela River. It was a monstrous place of thundering noise, flames, and danger. Efficiency, not safety, was the goal. When

Carnegie's hand-picked manager, Henry Frick, reduced wages, the workers went out on strike. Frick brought in Pinkerton detectives to protect the mill and to drive out the strikers. There followed 143 days of violence and bloodshed. The battle between the armed detectives and the strikers resulted in at least fourteen deaths and an unknown number of injuries. The Amalgamated Association of Iron and Steel Workers, one of the strongest unions in the country, was effectively broken.

"When you're older," my grandfather said, "read a poem called *Dante's Inferno*. Then you'll know what it was like inside those mills."

He told of furnaces glowing like the mouth of hell, air thick with smoke and grime, the terrible stench of the place, the sparks that rose from the burning cauldrons and showered down on the workers, the soot that blackened their faces and clothing, the searing heat. "Accidents were so frequent they were barely noticed," he said. "They usually happened when shifts were about to end: six in the morning or six at night. The men would be tired from working non-stop, dull and sluggish, careless because their minds had begun to drift homeward. Shovel some more coal into the furnace, pull the lever that empties the cauldron, clean up the cooling slag one more time, and their shift would be done."

"Is that what happened to Uncle Norman?" I asked. "He was distracted?"

"There were three of them," Grandfather said. "Three men working under one of the cauldrons when it broke loose. The molten steel poured out on them."

The injured men were carried off to a hospital, he said, and the rest of the men went back to work. There were orders to be filled. The factory was running at full speed, and there was no time to waste. If there was an accident, the foreman would do what had to be done, and the work would go on. When the shift ended, and the men were on their way home, they might talk about what happened, what mistakes had caused the accident, how such a thing could be avoided. But mostly they were too tired for anything except to put one foot in front of the other.

Grandfather sat in his rocking chair, hands folded in his lap, and he was silent for a long time. I thought he might have drifted off. But then he roused himself and pulled his rocker close to the fire, as if the telling of the story had chilled him.

He took out his pipe and filled it with tobacco. In the woodbox beside the stove he found a piece of newspaper. He twisted it, lit it from the fire, applied the flame to the bowl of his pipe, and threw the burning paper into the stove.

He drew on his pipe, sat back in his chair, and stretched out his legs. "You didn't find old men working in the steel mills," he said. "By the time they were fifty, they were all used up. It ruined a man, working under those conditions. It shortened their lives. The same with the coal mines." He sucked deeply on his pipe.

After the Pinkerton affair, he said, the unions lost what power they had. There was no one left to speak for the miners, the steelworkers, the factory men and women. Nothing to protect the workers.

The cauldrons, he went on — they were called crucibles — were held up with chains attached to giant cranes. When the impurities were burned out of the metal, the crane operator would lower the cauldron, and the men on the floor would tip it over, allowing the steel to flow into molds so it could be moved to other parts of the foundry. One of the chains holding the cauldron broke. All that white hot steel came down on them. They were nearly cooked alive.

My grandfather paused, puffed on his pipe, pushed back from the fire. "They said Uncle Norman's burns were not quite as bad as the other two men," he continued, "and for a time there was hope he might survive."

He got out his handkerchief and wiped his eyes before continuing. "He lived for several days. There was time to call a priest to give him the Last Rites."

Grandfather lowered his head until his chin nearly rested on his chest, and he was quiet. After a time I went to him. The fire in his pipe had gone out. I took it out of his hand and set it on the hearth.

His breakfast dishes were sitting on the table, wiped so clean there was hardly a spot of bacon grease, egg yolk, or a crumb of toast left. I gathered them up, carried them to the kitchen, and began to wash them.

Thomas Carnegie was already six years in his grave when the Pinkerton detectives battled strikers at the Homestead Steel Mill. Lucy was little affected. Workers on her Cumberland estate were paid a dollar a day if they were white, fifty cents if they were black. The air was clean, the sun warm, food and clothing provided. Life on Cumberland was pleasant.

The greenhouse provided fresh flowers for the mansion, the gardens fruit and vegetables, the dairy milk, butter, and cheese. There were deer in the forest, crabs, oysters, and seafood all around. Inside the recreation house there was a heated pool, steam room, barber shop, billiard room, squash court, gun room, and doctor's office. Guests could avail themselves of any of these amenities. They could ride horses, play golf, go hunting and fishing.

What battles Lucy fought were mostly local. When Camden County changed the Dungeness property classification from "wild land" to "developed property," doubling her property taxes, she sent lawyers to object. The mansion, recreation house, and forty outbuildings were not "improvements," they argued, since they were not used for commercial purposes. The same when she was assessed road taxes. Why should she have to pay, when she maintained the roads on the island? When an engineer in her power house was called for jury duty, Lucy's manager intervened, arguing that the man could not be spared. His work was essential to the smooth running of the estate.

Dungeness had begun to function as a small principality, and Lucy was its undisputed ruler. The richest of the rich accepted her invitations to come to Dungeness. They spent weeks there, sometimes months, enjoying Lucy's hospitality. Mainlanders watched Carnegie boats make daily runs to St. Marys, Brunswick, and Fernandina Beach to purchase supplies for the mansion. On quiet nights they heard the sounds of music and laughter coming across the waters as wealthy financiers and industrialists partied at the Carnegie mansion.

The people who once hunted and fished on the island could only watch from afar. If they tried to come ashore, Lucy's guards turned them away. Sometimes forcefully.

In the end, the Gilded Age could not last. The social injustices were simply too great to endure. Muckraking journalists wrote of ruthless business practices by the barons of industry, of the appalling conditions of New York tenements, of the abuse of power in politics and government. Social and political reformers became powerful voices for the masses, agitating against poor wages, unsafe working conditions, exploitation of children, and corporate greed.

The 16th Amendment, passed in 1913, gave Congress the right to tax both personal income and corporate profits. Three years later, in order to prevent the concentration of great wealth in the hands of a few, Congress passed the estate tax.

The winds of change were blowing, and they were surely felt on Cumberland Island. An era had ended. All Lucy could do was draw her loved ones around her and try to protect the things she had built. But by then, her health had begun to fail.

When she died in 1916, ownership of Dungeness passed to her children. The great fortune, assailed by taxes, labor and maintenance costs, and disputes among the heirs, began to disintegrate. Income from the Carnegie office building in Pittsburgh, which Lucy had inherited from her husband, plummeted in 1925. In an effort to save money, Carnegie descendants moved out of Dungeness. Four years later, the crash of 1929 further eroded the income stream.

Dungeness stood empty for the next thirty years, until it was destroyed by fire in 1959. The mansion was never rebuilt.

6

If the park ranger who greeted us at the dock were to drive her truck south on Grand Avenue, she would eventually arrive at Dungeness. She would pass between cement columns beneath an arch of decorative iron work, and the forest would open up to reveal what remains of the fifty-nine room Scottish castle. If she continued on in a straight line, she would arrive at the bottom of the grand staircase.

Money buys perfection like that, and there was plenty of money. No matter how much they spent, there was always more. Neither Thomas nor Lucy could have envisioned a time when it might be otherwise. Now, a hundred years after Lucy's death, what's left of the mansion is in ruins. Columns that once supported gables and roofs stand stark against the sky, supporting nothing. The great hundred-foot tower has toppled. Fallen rocks and debris litter the grand staircase. Walls that once soared have been broken off, leaving jagged edges. The grass around the mansion is green and close-cropped. Palm trees dot the landscape.

In the more than half-century that has passed since the fire, nature has reclaimed much of what the Carnegies built. What remains will soon be swallowed up, no longer visible beneath the rampant growth that clings to every surface, emerges from every crevice.

Wax myrtle and palmetto trees have taken root in the courtyard and in the above-ground basement. Resurrection ferns grow out of cracks in the walls. The once-elegant staircase with its curved railing is barely visible beneath the weeds and rubble.

In the St. Marys Visitor Center gift shop, there's a book containing a picture of Lucy Carnegie and her nine children posed on the steps of the mansion. She was a widow by then, her husband having died when Nancy, the baby of the family, was just four years old. Dressed in black, a heavy woman with graying hair piled on top of her head, she leans against a pillar. A rug runner has been brought out of the house to make the seating more comfortable. One of her sons is sprawled on the top of the cement railing. The girls wear lacy dresses. Their hair is styled like their mother's. The boys wear suits, ties, and tall riding boots. One rests his arm lightly on his straw hat. Another holds a similar hat in his lap. Most are looking off toward some distant object, or down, or to the side. None are smiling.

One stands near his mother, almost in her shadow. He's wearing a white shirt, bow tie, and jodhpurs. His arms are folded across his chest, as if he's bored with all this picture-taking business.

Could this be Coleman, Lucy's youngest son, a year older than Nancy and a favorite of their Uncle Andrew Carnegie? Of the six young men posed on the staircase, this one stands out. He's the only one without a jacket. The only one wearing a hat, and it's set at a jaunty angle. The other five are dressed as their mother surely told them to dress. They've found seats on the stairs, jostled themselves about in response to the photographer's orders, but no one has told them what to do with their hands.

Lucy's head is tilted toward the one I believe is Coleman, and there's a look of quiet satisfaction on her face. She loved the island and the home she built there. She devoted much of her life to creating a world where she could keep her children close. The picture attests to the fact that so far, at least, she has succeeded.

Between the years of 1867 and 1881, she bore six sons and three daughters. They're all there, all nine of them, adults now, posed on the steps of Dungeness mansion. Four of the six boys would marry; only Frank and Coleman would not. None of the Carnegie sons would ever hold a job.

There are signs posted at intervals around the mansion: *Do Not Enter. Beware of Snakes. Do Not Climb on Rocks.* Charlie, Rhamy, and I approach, but cautiously. We walk around the mansion, careful where we step, keeping a safe distance from the chain-link fence.

Near what was once the carriage entrance to the mansion is a waterhole, the edges trampled to mud, but the water fresh and clear. Directly behind the ruins, between the house and the salt marsh, is a fountain. Weeds have taken root in the bowl. Farther on, we see two horses resting in the shade of an oak tree. We approach, and they ignore us.

"She's pregnant," Rhamy says, indicating the larger horse. "Look at her belly. The other one is a yearling, probably her colt from last year."

"They're the lawn mowers, I take it."

She nods. "I wish I had an apple."

"Not allowed," I said. "Remember what the ranger said?" But I wonder; might the bed and breakfast have given us apples in our lunches? We move to the edge of the clearing and I begin to search through one of the boxes. I hold up a Gala apple.

Rhamy is thrilled. She takes it from me, looks around for something she can use to break it in half, but finds nothing. She bites into the apple, smacks it against a sharp edge of the fountain. It breaks cleanly.

Holding one half out in front of her, she approaches the horses. They turn to watch her. Ears perked, interested.

"She shouldn't be doing that," Charlie says. "They could be dangerous."

"She's fine," I answer. "She knows horses. I trust her."

The horses move off. She hesitates for a moment, then follows. When she is within fifteen feet, she tosses one of the halves toward them. Gently, so it skips along the ground. Both horses bolt.

I see her shoulders slump. She retrieves the apple, walks to the watering hole, and lays it at the edge.

"What if one of the rangers comes along?" I ask. "They'll see it, out in the open like that."

"These horses have never had apples before," she says. "They don't know what they are." She picks it up, brushes the dirt away.

"We'll try later," I tell her. "Let's have lunch. It's been a long time since breakfast. I'm famished."

We head for the picnic tables at the edge of the terraced area behind the mansion.

The concierge at our hotel was right; the food is delicious. There are layers of turkey and butter lettuce between thick slices of sourdough bread. Three bags of potato chips and three chocolate chip cookies. Lovely Gala apples. The bed and breakfast has even provided a paper tablecloth. We spread out our feast and begin to eat.

To the west are the remnants of Lucy's greenhouse that provided flowers for the mansion. On the level below us, the kitchen garden. By the road that leads to the dunes and the ocean, the recreation building that once housed the pool, game rooms, and several bedrooms. Lucy's bachelor sons stayed there when they were on the island.

Much of the recreation building has collapsed. Only a central, circular section remains.

Directly in front of us is the salt marsh cut through with streams that rise and fall with the tide. Horses are grazing there, moving about the marsh, searching for saw grass. The footing is gray and fluid, the horses sinking up to their fetlocks in mud, some nearly to their knees. When one decides to move, the others follow, and we hear sucking sounds as they pull their legs out of the muck.

"What do you think a diamondback rattlesnake looks like?" Charlie asks.

"They wouldn't be out here in the open," I tell him. "They'd be in a pile of rocks, or maybe under a log."

"Why would they leave that nice habitat in the mansion where there are lots of bugs and mice they can eat?" Rhamy asks. "Out here they're completely exposed. Plus, they could be stepped on by a horse. They do that, you know. If a horse feels threatened, he'll stomp a snake to death."

I open a bottle of water and hand it to him. "I saw one killed on the road one time, when I was a kid. It was brown, the color of dirt, with yellow markings on its back. Shaped like diamonds. It had a big, triangular-shaped head, a thick body. They're pit vipers; they have little indentations, pits, between the eyes and nose. That's how they find their prey. They sense heat, and they go after it."

He turns away from me, toward the marsh, his sandwich forgotten.

Of all the reptiles in the world, alligators are the ones he dislikes the most. Rattlesnakes, I suspect, would be a close second.

I wonder if he'll ever come back to Cumberland again.

7

We finish our lunch and walk down the road toward the ocean. When we come upon Cumberland's automobile graveyard, Charlie is absolutely enthralled. Nothing could have interested him more than this.

There are five antique cars, or is it six? Impossible to tell. They're parked side by side beneath a stand of live oaks, lined up as if waiting for their owners to come and claim them. But the owners never came, and the years went by. The cars are rusting away. Slowly sinking into the ground. Fenders have become detached from bodies. Hoods are askew. Chassis are leaning crookedly, precariously. A windshield resting against a steering wheel mirrors the foliage above.

How did they get here? Who owned them? Why were they parked beneath the trees and left to rot? Standing at the edge of road, trying to take in the stages of decay, I wonder how long until they're completely gone, the materials from which they were created dispersed, reverting to simpler elements.

The charred remains of the Dungeness mansion, bleached by sun and salt air, the recreation building weakened by termites and lashed by the elements, greenhouses and gardens that have reverted to the wild, these are all natural processes. They are to be expected.

But this? Cars ferried across the Cumberland Sound, driven up and down the island roads, then presumably abandoned by their owners? This is totally unexpected.

One looks like an old Model T. Another is similar, but a later model, maybe from the '30s, a car from which you'd expect Chicago gangsters to emerge, carrying Tommy guns, heading for a shootout with the law. The one on the end, fully half of it sunken into the ground, is totally unidentifiable. Is it even a car?

The trees themselves are shaped like vases of flowers. Spanish moss hangs from their limbs and drips down onto the rusted roofs, the fenders and grilles. The ground is covered with dry leaves that have fallen from the live oak trees. Saw palmetto splays its fan-shaped leaves. Vines grow up around the cars, attach themselves to cables, snake up through floorboards.

We stand outside the single strand of rope that surrounds the automobile graveyard, looking in, trying to identify what it is we're seeing. There are headlights, a steering wheel, radiators, doors hanging by hinges, empty window frames, a radiator cap, bits of chrome, hood ornaments.

A white-walled tire, left front, still amazingly white.

"That's an old Studebaker," Charlie says. "Early '50s. Look at that hood ornament." He identifies others: the closest one is a Model A, the one next to it some kind of a coupe, the last one a Model T.

He moves closer to the enclosure, and the dry leaves crackle beneath his feet. "The Studebaker was a convertible," he says. "I can see bits of canvas. Two doors. A Champion convertible is my guess. My uncle had one just like it."

"It's gonna sink into the ground," I tell him. "The hood looks like somebody threw acid on it, and now it's just dissolving away. The ornament is gonna fall off, and it will sink. I'll get it for you, if you want. A souvenir."

"Take nothing from the island except sharks' teeth and seashells," Rhamy murmurs.

"No one would care," I answer.

But Charlie shakes his head. He walks around to the other side of the graveyard. "That's a driveshaft," he says. "And look at those narrow tires, those spoked wheels. They used those on the first cars ever built. There's no telling how old they are."

A rotted seat. Bits of horse hair entwined in the springs. More tires, some looking as if they could still hold air, except they are half sunken into the ground. Even the white-walled tire; half of it is buried. How many years before it all sinks into the ground, I wonder, and horses once more graze here, and rest beneath the trees.

"Why no glass?" I ask. "These old cars, the Model T and the Model A, if that's what they are, there's no glass in any of them. They must have had glass at one point. There's only that windshield on the Studebaker."

"The island is swallowing it all up," Charlie says. "Piece by piece."

"What would a steering wheel be made of, that half of it would rot away, and the other half not?"

"Something fell on it," Rhamy suggests.

A man appears, walking from the direction of the ocean. He carries a satchel. Sunglasses atop his head, blue polo shirt, tan shorts, Adidas and white socks.

"Pretty amazing, isn't it?" he says, indicating the row of cars. He shifts his satchel to the other shoulder, mops his forehead with his handkerchief.

"Do you know anything about them?" I ask. "Who they belonged to? Why they were left here to rust?"

He shakes his head. "I don't. Just that they used to be stored in the carriage house." He points up the road from where we stand. "When the Park Service took over, they pulled them out and parked them here. They wanted to use the building for a maintenance shop. I guess the cars were in the way."

"Did they belong to the Carnegies?"

He shrugs. "Maybe," he says. "Or the grandchildren. I don't know that anybody knows for sure. It was a long time ago. When Lucy Carnegie died, she left everything in trust for her children, but they couldn't sell any part of their inheritance until the death of the last child. That didn't happen until 1962, and in the meantime, the grandchildren had free run of the place. They used to race their cars up and down the beach, it's that smooth. At some point the place got to be too much to keep up, taxes and all, so they turned it over to the Park Service." He smiles, and it's a wry smile. "They didn't just give it to the Park Service, you understand. They sold it, and they got a pretty penny for it."

"The cars were a part of the sale?" Charlie asks.

He shrugs again. "Could be they forgot about the cars. Or maybe they didn't feel like paying to have them brought back to the mainland. There's no bridge, so they'd have had to ferry them across."

He adjusts his satchel again, then continues. "They say some of the grandchildren were pretty upset with the Park Service for doing this." He nods toward the cars. "They thought they should have been preserved. Put in a museum."

"Have you been to the ocean?" Rhamy asks.

"No, just up in the dunes. I'm heading back now to catch the early ferry."

"Did you see any horses?"

"There's a mare and her foal in the marsh, just past the graveyard."

"There's another graveyard?" Charlie asks.

Now his smile is genuine. "This one is a people graveyard. Light Horse Harry Lee is buried there. Robert E. Lee's father. He died here on the island."

He puts on his sunglasses, waves goodbye, and heads up the road toward Dungeness.

8

Madeleine, the youngest of our three daughters, is not in love with horses. Nor is she an islomane. But if her big sister dragged her parents to a place called Cumberland Island a year ago, and if that sister came back to Portland utterly in love with the wild horses and the ruins of a mansion built during the days of the robber barons, and there is also on that island a beach that stretches so far in both directions the ends are lost in the curve of the earth, this is something Madeleine wants to see.

The girls are totally grown and on their own, but they still like to vacation with their parents. And they much prefer to order up separate vacations, if at all possible. Why should they have to share Mom and Dad with their siblings? There'd been plenty of that when they were growing up. Christmas is an exception, of course, and the birth of a baby. But at other times, let's have a little separation, please. Bonding is so much easier. Competition is out the window. Five people (seven if you count husbands, nine if you add in the babies, ten if you include Madeleine's latest boyfriend) in a restaurant is unwieldy. Four is acceptable, but three is best.

So Madeleine books a flight. Like Rhamy the year before, she flies from cool, rainy Portland to hot, humid Atlanta. When she walks out of the terminal and steps to the edge of the Loop Road, I almost don't recognize her.

There are things about Madeleine that never change: she's tall and thin; her clothes are always stylish; she's an animal advocate, a member of PETA, a liberal Democrat. Other things change on a whim. The girl standing on the curb, waving to us, has auburn hair. The wind is blowing, and tendrils have come loose from her ponytail. The new hair color suits her, but so does the jet black of Katy Perry, the honey brown of Jennifer Lawrence, even the white blonde of Cameron Diaz, all of which Madeleine has tried.

She wears bangs, something she's done since high school. An automobile accident left her with a scar on her forehead. When her wounds were healed, we took her to a plastic surgeon. He advised against doing anything about the scar. It was high on her forehead, hardly noticeable. Better to leave it alone, he said.

She never talks about the accident, never mentions the scar. I wonder if we did the right thing by following the surgeon's advice.

When she sees us, her smile is so broad, I almost expect her to jump with joy. I'm out of the car, hugging her, thrilled to see her, loving her new hair color. Charlie stows her bag in the trunk, hugs her, and we're on our way.

Five hours later we drive onto St. Simons Island where, no matter what the temperature, there are those wonderfully cooling ocean breezes.

The King and the Prince hotel is completely booked — June is high season, after all — but Madeleine has found a two-bedroom condo at Harbour Oaks, a development within easy walking distance from the village, the pier, and the ocean. We take a day to acclimate, another to climb to the top of the lighthouse, do the trolley tour, and visit the historical sites on the island. And we plan our trip to Cumberland.

Charlie has no interest in going. He went once, he says, he saw what there was to see, and there's no point in going back. The island is a wilderness.

"Of course it's a wilderness," I agree. "But that's the point. People have lived there for five thousand years, and now they're gone, except for a handful who have retained rights agreements with the Park Service. Soon they'll be gone, too, like the Indians, the Spanish, the English, the plantation owners, and the Carnegies. It's all reverting back to what it was before man ever came to the island."

There's no place in the world like it, I argue. It's the last piece of unspoiled coastal landform on the entire East Coast. It's bigger than Manhattan. Manhattan is one of the most densely populated areas in the world, people stepping all over each other. High-rises and skyscrapers. Cumberland is totally different. It's unspoiled. The only visitors allowed on the island are those who come on the ferry. No cars, a maximum of three hundred people a day.

Madeleine's poor head is swiveling as she looks first at me, then her father, then back at me. How could one parent be so passionate about something, the other so dispassionate, and both of them so determined to have their way?

"We can be three of those visitors," I tell him. "When will you ever again have the chance to go to a place where there are no cars, no Exxon stations, no stores selling worthless trinkets, no developments, no bridges, animals that are free to roam at will, to breed, to struggle to survive."

"I've already been there," he says. "I have no desire to go back."

"Madeleine wants to go," I insist, taking her hand and drawing her close to me. "That's one of the main reasons she flew here, so she could go to Cumberland Island. She wants to see it, and she wants to see it with us. With both of us."

He sighs, but he will not change his mind.

We beg. We plead. We tell him we're helpless females who have no idea how to get to St. Marys. We don't even know in which direction it lies. We can never go without him. He'll be so lonely without us. How will he pass the time while we're gone? We promise to pack his favorite lunch if he comes with us — smoked turkey and provolone on whole wheat bread, sesame honey cashews, pretzels to snack on, spring water.

Nothing works. It's time to change tactics. "We'll have to take the car," I tell him. "There's no other way to get there. If you want to go anywhere on the island while we're gone, you'll have to walk."

He shrugs.

"It's a long way to your favorite breakfast place. Dresner's. Even farther to the fishing pier and the lighthouse. If you try to walk to Fern Village, you'll probably get heatstroke."

He picks up the *USA Today*, scans the front page, then pulls out the Entertainment section.

Normally, when you're on St. Simons, there's a breeze that blows in from the Atlantic. But today, the leaves are barely stirring. "It's going to be ungodly hot," I tell him, and the passion is gone from my voice.

It's all for naught. Our powers of persuasion have failed. But we spent so much time trying to convince him to come, we have no time to pack a lunch. We can try to get something in St. Marys. We'll buy snacks on the ferry, if we have to. Do they sell snacks? I think there are vending machines, but I'm not sure. We have no ferry tickets, but surely we'll be able to buy them at the Visitor Center.

There are three exits to St. Marys, I remember. Exit 1 is the one we want. Get off there, turn east toward the Atlantic, and drive straight to the dock. If we miss the exit, we've crossed the line into Florida. We'll turn around and come back. But it's been a year, and it's all kind of fuzzy. When Charlie drives, I pay little attention to routes and exit numbers. Now I wish I had.

If I'm honest, I'm a little angry with Charlie. How could he leave us in the lurch like this? Why does he have to be so obstinate?

But I have to do it. I have to get in the car and drive to St. Marys. I can't fail. Madeleine is counting on me.

We grab our jackets, hats, purses, and sunblock, walk out of the condo, get in the car, and drive off the island. We climb the bridge over the intracoastal waterway, turn left at the light in Brunswick, and pick up I-95. We're on our way.

Madeleine, sitting in the passenger seat, is quiet. As am I. Charlie should be here with us. It's lonely without him. I still find it hard to believe that he wouldn't, in the end, change his mind and come with us.

I wish he had. He's such a calming influence on me, a voice of reason when things threaten to spin out of control. He likes to plan ahead, would never rush into making a decision that might have unintended consequences. I miss him.

But he didn't come. So what will we do for lunch? We had a scant breakfast in the condo, and if we catch the late ferry back to St. Marys, as we plan, we won't get back to St. Simons until evening. By then we'll be starving.

Madeleine searches the glove compartment for her dad's stash of energy bars but finds none. There's bottled water in the trunk, though, and we can refill them on Cumberland.

The park ranger at the Visitor Center is sympathetic. "Run up to that yellow building on the corner," she says. "It's a curio shop, but the woman who owns it will make a sandwich for you. She does it all the time for people going to Cumberland, people who didn't plan ahead. You have exactly five minutes before the ferry pulls out," she tells us.

"My daughter is vegetarian," I tell the woman in the shop.

"I have eggs I just hard-boiled this morning," she says. "Egg salad sandwich okay?"

"It is. Very much okay. Mustard and mayo, but no pickles, please."

She makes two sandwiches. Wheat bread, iceberg lettuce. She packs them in a heavy, insulated bag, adds a Ziploc filled with carrot sticks. She tops it with a bag of Fritos and two peanut butter cookies. We're set. I reach for the bag.

"You'll need bug repellent," she says. "Cumberland can be bad this time of year."

I'm surprised. "I was there last year," I tell her. "I don't remember there being a problem."

"You weren't there in June, I'll bet."

"It was March."

"You'll need bug repellent." She moves from behind the sandwich counter, takes a bottle of Burt's Bees insect repellent off the shelf and places it by the register. She wraps it in tissue and puts it in a small brown sack.

I pay the bill, we take the two bags, and we race across to the dock where the *Cumberland Queen* is waiting. We're the last to board. They've held the ferry for us.

We find seats on the port side of the boat. "I still can't believe Charlie didn't come with us," I tell Madeleine. "I was so sure he'd change his mind at the last minute."

"We'll have a good time," she says. "I want to go to the beach."

9

The *Cumberland Queen* sails down the St. Marys River, enters the Cumberland Sound, and travels north until it reaches the dock near the Dungeness ruins. If you're deep in conversation, or still so agitated by the divisiveness of the morning, or lulled into a hypnotic trance by the movement of the ship through the water, it would be possible to miss the first stop, the one where we're supposed to get off. It seems unlikely, but possible.

I know something is wrong when the ship engines begin to take on a different sound. They're more guttural now, and there's a vibration I haven't felt before. The ferry is speeding up, heading for open waters. I look back at our wake, then to my right, toward the island. The dock where a year ago Charlie, Rhamy, and I got off the ferry is receding. Getting smaller.

We've missed our stop.

How is it possible that neither Madeleine nor I noticed when passengers around us got up and moved to the starboard side of the ship? How could we have been completely unaware that the ferry was no longer moving through the waters of the Sound, but had tied up at the dock? We leave our seats and go down to the cabin. There are a few passengers still aboard. I approach the captain.

"We seem to have missed our stop," I tell him. "We should have gotten off back there."

"No problem," he says. "Next stop, Sea Camp. Just take the River Trail back up to Dungeness. You'll see signs outside the ranger station."

"How far is it?" I ask. "To the other dock?"

He shrugs. "Half a mile," he says, "maybe more. It follows the river, but it's not well traveled. Most people who get off here go to the campground or straight to the Atlantic. Watch out for varmints along the way."

We don't ask what kind of varmints. Our goal is to find the road made of seashells and sharks' teeth, and to find it as quickly as possible. To erase our mistake, a mistake Charlie would never have made, had he been with us.

The air is thick with mosquitoes. Just moving along the path causes them to swarm. We feel like we're in a tropical rain forest, the air too hot and too heavy to breathe. It is the hottest, wettest, most insect-filled walk I've ever taken. They call it the River Trail. If there's a river, it's hidden somewhere in the jungle. Unless we're actually walking in it, which seems entirely possible. We step over logs, wondering what might be hidden beneath them or on the other side.

We wave our hands in front of our faces to try to keep the mosquitoes away. When we've eaten more than our share of bugs, we walk in silence, heads lowered, mouths tightly closed, grateful that our sunglasses are at least keeping the mosquitoes out of our eyes. Except for those that crawl behind them.

Bless the woman who sold us Burt's Bees insect repellent. When we come to a clearing we stop, dig out the bottle, and apply it to every inch of exposed skin: legs, arms, faces, ears, necks. The smell is overpowering, a deadly combination of eucalyptus, lemongrass, deodorant, and what I imagine is gasoline. It's oily and it burns our skin, especially the areas already red from insect bites, but we slather it on and endure the pain.

Burt's Bees insect repellent doesn't faze them. There's nothing to do but try to clear a path through them and trudge on.

I risk a mouthful of bugs: "I thought mosquitoes were only supposed to come out in the evening."

Madeleine puts her hand over her mouth before she answers: "They're so thrilled to see some warm-blooded creature, it's messed up their internal clocks."

"Garlic," I answer. "There's garlic in this insect repellent."

"It's supposed to be herbal," she says. "Garlic is a natural product. At least there are no chemicals. Like DEET."

"And citronella. I can smell citronella."

She doesn't answer.

"Geraniums. I've always hated the smell of geraniums. They put geranium juice in it."

"I read that if you take Vitamin B for a few days before you're exposed, it changes your scent, and mosquitoes won't bother you," Madeleine says.

I slap one that has landed on my nose. "Austin, Texas, has no mosquitoes," I tell her. "They have bats that nest under one of the bridges, and they fly out at night, down the Colorado River. One bat can eat 20,000 mosquitoes."

She stops suddenly. "I don't think these are mosquitoes, Mom. I think they're no-see-ums."

"Whatever they are, they're sucking our blood," I answer.

Will we never come to the end of the trail? The ship captain must have been wrong about how far it is from Sea Camp to the Dungeness dock.

Ten minutes later the jungle melts away, and we're out of it. The wet, spongy ground, the rampant growth, the overgrown trail gives way to the open pasture by the dock. The air is clear, the sun white hot in a sea of blue.

The area around the dock is deserted, except for three chestnut horses that graze in the meadow by the Ice House Museum. We have to walk past them to get to the water spigot outside the restrooms. Madeleine, never as comfortable around horses as her two sisters, gives them a wide berth.

We wash our hands and arms and faces, but the smell of the mosquito repellent lingers. Madeleine checks inside the bathroom for soap, but the dispenser is empty. We head down the seashell road toward the mansion. Our clothes are damp, but the sun is warm, and we are at last on familiar ground.

Ten minutes later, the ruined mansion looms before us. Nature has made progress in the last year toward her goal of erasing what man has created here. How long, I wonder, before her job is complete?

We walk around the perimeter, happy to keep our distance from the fence that surrounds the mansion. Madeleine knows about the diamondback rattlers that live here; Charlie filled her in last night.

If Burt's Bees is a disappointment, our egg salad sandwiches are not. We sit on the porch of the tabby house, oldest structure on the island, and spread out our lunch. Two horses graze by the pergola, a shaded walkway that trails off to our left. Another drinks from the waterhole by the ruined mansion.

"That's six so far," Madeleine says.

"Six?"

"Horses," she says. "We've seen six horses."

She's keeping track, I realize. She wants to be able to tell Rhamy she saw more horses on the island than Rhamy did.

"You can tell her we were a lot closer to them than the ones we saw last year. She'll be jealous."

Madeleine smiles.

The friendly rivalry between these two girls is delicious. Beneath the competition, the verbal sparring, and the constant quest for "favorite daughter" status, there's a bond that is unshakeable.

We continue down the road, past the mansion, the carriage house, and the car graveyard. There are no more horses, but we have hours to spend on the island before the ferry takes us back to the mainland. Madeleine wants to walk to the ocean. Neither of us has any idea how far it is, but the island, at its widest, is only three miles across. Surely we can make it there and back in time to catch the late ferry.

Beyond the car graveyard are the remnants of buildings erected a hundred years ago by the Carnegie family. Scattered foundation stones are all that is left of the things that Lucy built: stables, chicken houses, dining halls, bakery, living quarters. There was once a kennel and a feed barn. A silo. A commissary. All are gone. The poultry manager had his own house, as did the dairy manager. Gone. Only the building that housed the laundry has been preserved. The Park Service has installed rest rooms in a portion of it.

Carnegie servants once lived in this place. They were gardeners, cooks, dairymen, cobblers, farriers, blacksmiths, horticulturalists, builders, carpenters. Standing on the road, looking out over the rubble that is left, there's a sadness to it. The people who lived here spent their lives providing for the Carnegies and the industrialists who came to visit. They met the guests at the Dungeness dock: Astors, Vanderbilts, Rockefellers, Morgans, Pulitzers, and Hills. They drove them and their mountains of luggage back to the mansion and saw that they were properly ensconced in the rooms to which they had been assigned. They arranged for picnics on the lawn and on the beach, cooked and served meals, cleared the plates, washed the fine china and priceless crystal. They carried golf clubs, saddled horses, arranged vases of flowers in all fifty-nine rooms of the mansion. They washed linens, set up games of croquet, carried fish and crabs back from the streams and lakes.

They were servants to the rich and famous. None among them could ever hope to experience a lifestyle approaching that of the Carnegies and their guests. Except for one, a redhaired, Irish-born, hunk of a man who ran the Dungeness stables. His name was James Hever. Charged with teaching Nancy, the youngest of the Carnegie daughters, to ride horses, he fell in love with her, and she with him. They eloped in May of 1904. Gossips speculated that she was pregnant.

Such talk was anathema to Lucy. She'd known of the marriage, she insisted, and she approved. Andrew Carnegie, Nancy's uncle, gave the couple $20,000 to help them get started. Nancy, the youngest and fairest of his brother's children, had always been his favorite niece. The newlyweds sailed off to Europe where their first child was born.

When they returned to America a year later, they brought with them their baby daughter. During the course of their marriage, Nancy would bear three more children.

Madeleine and I leave the shade of the live oaks that thrive in this ruined community and head toward the ocean. The dunes loom large in front of us, great mountains of sand studded with trunks of dead trees. The sand has smothered every living thing in its path.

It's a landscape that is agonizingly hot, we soon discover.

The Greene-Miller cemetery, a hundred yards off to our right, offers a few minutes of respite. We hike down a shaded path and arrive at the ancient burial ground. It's surrounded by a tabby wall, that mixture of sand, lime, and oyster shells that hardens to near-concrete strength. There's an iron gate, but it's chained shut.

Inside the cemetery we're able to see several above-the-ground vaults, but it's impossible to read the inscriptions from where we stand.

A bronze plaque is attached to the south wall of the cemetery:

In Memory of
Thomas Morrison Carnegie
Born in Dunfermline Scotland
October 2, 1844
Died in Pittsburgh PA.
October 19, 1886

Henry "Light Horse Harry" Lee's stone is upright…

Sacred
to the memory of
Gen. Henry Lee
of Virginia
Obit 25 March…

We'd have to climb over the fence if we wanted to read the rest of it.

"Robert E. Lee had the stone placed here," Madeleine tells me. "He came to visit several times, once with his daughter, to lay flowers on the grave."

"You've done your homework," I answer.

"Rhamy did. She told me not to miss it. She wants to come back next year."

"She loves this island," I answer. "Do you?"

"I want to see the beach," she says.

We climb the first dune and it's like walking through deep snow, sinking up to our ankles, extricating ourselves, only to sink again with the next step. We plod onward until we reach the crest. Ahead of us are a series of dunes that stretch as far as we can see. There are boardwalks, but too short and infrequent. The sun is so blazingly hot it seems to fill the sky. We trudge onward. At some point we begin to hear waves crashing onto the shore. We know we're close.

It's the widest, smoothest, most deserted beach I've ever seen. The tide is out, and it's easy to imagine cars speeding along this super-highway before they were banned by the Park Service. Carnegie guests often came here to swim, to have beach parties, to ride Lucy's polo ponies along the water's edge. Loggerhead turtles came out of the sea in the early summer to lay their eggs. The Carnegie children liked to climb aboard the turtles and ride them into the sea. They threw ropes attached to wagons around the turtles, and let the turtles pull them into the water. They scooped the sand out of the loggerhead nests and carried the eggs back to the kitchens where servants used them in meals served in the mansion.

On this day there are no ponies, no loggerhead turtles, no children, no moneyed guests. There's only the sun, the sea, and the sand. We take off our shoes and wade into the water. The waves crash against us, soaking our shorts and T-shirts. Neither of us thought to bring bathing suits, but it hardly matters. In this heat our clothes will dry long before we're back at Dungeness.

We wade out farther and farther, testing the bottom as we go. The ocean floor is so slightly slanted, it feels as if we could walk halfway to Europe before it drops off into the deep.

The waves come in clusters, gentle surges that escalate into rolling mountains of water, tumbling, foaming, coming upon us so fast we hardly have time to recover from one before we're hit with another. They tower over us, knock us down and drag us under. We come up sputtering, wiping away the water, laughing at this most fun thing we've ever done. We race for the safety of the beach, trying not to look back, not wanting to know how close is the next wall of water rolling up behind us, wanting to bury us beneath all that blue weight.

One catches me, pulls my feet from under me. I'm on the bottom, my knees deep in the sand, turbulent waters above me. Another wave rolls in, tossing me this way and that. I try to stand, but the ocean floor is moving, and I'm knocked down again. The water is moving away from the shore. I'm being pulled into the deep.

I have no idea how much water is above me. Have I been washed out, into the bottomless depths of the ocean? The water is light, filled with bubbles. The sand beneath me is shifting, treacherous. I need air. I need to breathe.

Madeleine is on the beach by now, waiting for me. She has no idea I'm caught in an undertow. I have to free myself, reach the surface and get back to shore. I hold my breath, and I struggle. And all the time I'm thinking of my daughter, Madeleine, looking out across the water, waiting for me to surface.

I can't let this happen. We were having such a good time. She won't know what to do. She can't go for help. There is no help. Help is miles away. When she realizes I'm never coming out of the ocean, she'll wait for me. And wait. And wait. At some point she'll have to walk back to Dungeness, across those dunes, alone. She'll have no choice but to leave me in the water.

I can't do that to her. Somehow, I have to free myself. Swim toward the shore. Reach the surface where there is air to breathe.

Then, just as abruptly and unexpectedly as it happened, I'm out of it. There is sand beneath me, a firm footing that lets me stand. I am safe, but shaken to my very core. I walk out of the ocean and drop onto the beach.

"Are you okay, Mom?"

"Sure. Just a little out of breath."

"You went out too far. Don't do that again."

"I probably did. But I'm fine. The water feels so wonderful. It's so nice being here. With you. Just the two of us."

We lie there together on the beach. When we're rested, we empty our pockets of sand, try to shake it out of our underclothes. After a while the sun begins to feel hot on our skin, and we go back into the water.

But I'm no longer so carefree. Those few moments when I was fighting the current, struggling to get back to shore, I nearly drowned. I underestimated the power of the sea. The pull of the ocean. The unseen power that lurks in those endless waters.

Caught in an undertow, I did exactly what I should not have done. I fought against the current, fought to reach the surface, fought to get back to shore. Back to where Madeleine was waiting.

I panicked. I lost my footing. I almost died.

The water above me was filled with bubbles. The sun and the sky were there, and I struggled to reach them, knowing that if I didn't, if my lungs filled with water, Madeleine would have to make her way back to Dungeness, alone, then on to the ranger station, and tell them her mother had drowned in the ocean.

It's a thought, and an image, that I suspect will never leave me.

An hour later, or maybe several hours later, we begin our walk back to Dungeness, past the *Swim at Your Own Risk* sign that we somehow missed. We're refreshed, salty, and worn out from the sun, the wind, the dunes. We climb up those mountains of sand, through that surreal landscape with its dry bushes and dead trees that is somehow beautiful beyond words. We linger on the last boardwalk before we reach the historic district and look out over the salt marshes.

There's a telescope mounted on a post, but we have no coins to feed it.

"Last year we saw a mare and her foal way out in the marsh," I tell Madeleine. "Rhamy was thrilled. I wish I had a quarter, so I could see if they're still there."

"If you'd brought money, it would probably be in the Atlantic by now," she says.

"Binoculars. I could have brought binoculars."

"They'd be full of sand."

"The foal would be a yearling by now. He might still be with his mother. They could live out there, in the marsh. It's possible."

"I'm sunburned, Mom. Let's get back. We need to find some shade. And some water."

At the end of the boardwalk there's a path that winds around the cemetery and comes out on the seashell road, just below the car graveyard. It's shady and cool, and we decide to take it.

Outside the tabby walls of the cemetery we pause to gaze again through the iron gates.

"Light Horse Harry isn't buried here anymore," Madeleine says. "The Lee family had his body moved to Virginia so he could lie next to his son. They have a crypt at Lee Chapel on the Washington and Lee campus in Lexington."

"But they left the stone here? I wonder why."

She shrugs.

"How come you know all this?"

"Rhamy told me. She looked it up. They have the same birthday, you know. January 29th. Look at the stone."

She's right. In the late afternoon light I can make out the dates that earlier I could not.

She goes on: "He was coming back from the West Indies, on his way to Baltimore, when he got sick. He asked the ship captain to let him off here, on Cumberland Island. It turned out that Louisa Shaw, who lived here at the time, was the daughter of his old friend Nathaniel Greene. Lee and Greene had served together in the Revolutionary War. Louisa took him in. He died a month later."

"March 25th, 1818," I respond. "I can see it on the stone. So he spent his final days at Dungeness. But not the Carnegie Dungeness. An earlier one."

She nods. "The one built by Nathaniel Greene's widow, Catherine. Caty, they called her. Rhamy found a picture of her Dungeness on the internet. It was four stories high, built of tabby. Catherine was remarried by then, to Phineas Miller. They think he's buried here, too, but there's no stone. Louisa is probably in one of those above-the-ground crypts. And her mother."

If there's a stone or a sign to mark the place where Bernard Davis and his son were laid to rest, it is gone. Their graves are lost.

We move on. The path leads into the woods. It's narrow and nearly impene-trable, the undergrowth of vines and palmetto intent on obliterating it. We walk single file, Madeleine leading the way.

Several hundred yards into the woods we hear the sound of horses galloping. They're heading in our direction. The sound gets louder and louder. We stop. I can feel their hoofbeats in the ground beneath my feet.

"They're probably out on that road that goes past the historic district," I tell Madeleine.

"Why are they galloping?"

"Horses do that sometimes," I answer. "Especially in the spring."

Is it true, what I just said? In colder climates, if an animal has been stabled and then let out, it might be. But here, on this semi-tropical island, it seems unlikely.

They're getting closer, the ground vibrating. Madeleine is looking through the trees toward the seashell road.

"Sometimes a horse will nip another horse," I tell her, "and they'll both take off running. One will do something another horse doesn't like, and they'll start fighting. A mare will wander off from the herd, and the stallion will chase after her to try to teach her a lesson. There could be any number of reasons why they're galloping. You don't need to worry. They won't come back along this path. There's no reason why they would. It's too narrow and winding."

But they do. They turn onto the trail, and they're heading straight for us in full gallop.

"Get off the trail, Madeleine." I grab her arm, pull her into the undergrowth, thinking of snakes and alligators and armadillos but mostly of horses. Stallions that have gone mad. Horses that have turned rogue.

Now I can smell them, that unmistakable odor of horseflesh, sweat, and salt. I see them, through the trees. There are three of them, galloping full tilt down the path, thundering toward us.

"Get behind the biggest tree you can find," I tell Madeleine.

She does.

We wait. They burst out of the undergrowth, fly past us, heading for the marsh. The lead horse is a mare.

A minute later, the drumbeat of pounding hooves slows, then stops. They can't have reached the marsh. There hasn't been time. They're still in the woods, and close. Behind our trees we wait, barely breathing.

Three, four, five minutes later, they come back up the path, trotting now. They pass us again, first the two mares, then the stallion. All chestnuts. They look big, and powerful. Sixteen hands, at least.

When we're sure they're gone, we move out from behind our trees, onto the path.

"Do you think they'll be back?" Madeleine asks.

I shake my head. "No," I answer. "I don't think so."

"Why did they come this way, then turn around and go back?"

"Something must have spooked them. They turned onto the path, and maybe they began to feel safe. The danger was over. Or they forgot what it was that scared them."

I motion for her to follow me. Fifty feet back down the trail I see the spot where the horses turned off. Partly hidden among the trees is a boulder, three feet high, four feet in diameter. It shouldn't be here, not in this place of sand and salt. But it is.

The top is shaped like a bowl, deep enough that it can hold a fair amount of water.

"They came here to drink," I tell Madeleine. "They came for a drink of water."

"Yuck," she says, looking into the black depths.

"It's a lot better than salt water," I tell her.

"How do they know not to drink salt water?"

"Instinct, I guess. Or maybe they do drink it, and they find out it makes them thirsty, so they have to go find fresh water. They head for watering holes, like this one, or to one of the freshwater lakes on the island. Why this boulder?" I ask. "Where did it come from? How did it ever get here?"

"The Ice Age?" she suggests. "When ice formed on the northern hemisphere, ocean levels dropped. Maybe this whole island was once part of the mainland, and it broke off. Like people think California is going to drop into the Pacific. When the ice melted, ocean levels came back up, forming Cumberland Sound, turning this into an island."

"And the Okefenokee Swamp," I add. "Or maybe someone loaded this huge boulder onto a ship and brought it here. There's a cottage on St. Simons that was originally built here on Cumberland. When the Park Service took over, the owners sold the house to a family named Bramling. They floated it up the Atlantic and rebuilt it on St. Simons."

I feel guilty, telling the story that way, fudging on some of the details. So I set about to correct them.

"Actually, it wasn't just one house; it was three small cottages. They were dismantled and loaded on a ship, then reassembled into a single house on St. Simons. You can actually rent it."

"I like the story better the way you told it the first time," she says.

"Thanks, Madeleine. That earns you favorite daughter status, at least for today."

I can't see her face, but I know she's pleased.

"If you can put three cottages on a ship," I tell her, "it's possible someone loaded up this rock and brought it here to use as a watering trough for the horses."

She agrees that it could have happened that way.

We head back, exiting the trail just opposite the machine shed. There are no horses along the seashell road nor around Dungeness, but I remember that Madeleine is keeping track.

"That's nine," I tell her. "You can tell Rhamy you saw more horses than she did. And you were a lot closer to three of them than she was."

"A little too close," she says.

From the ruins of the Dungeness mansion it's a short walk to the dock. The ferry won't arrive for another hour, but we're exhausted. We need to rest, drink some water, sit in the shade.

"When we get to St. Marys," I tell her, "I'll call Charlie, ask him to make a reservation at that nice Italian restaurant that just opened. Or the King and the Prince. We need a quiet table, a simple dinner, a glass of wine."

10

Rhamy walks out of Atlanta's North Terminal, and two minutes later I pull to the curb. She's wearing capris and a light blue sweater. It's a glorious, end-of-March day; the sun is shining, there's the trace of a breeze, and the key to our St. Simons rental house is in my purse. We haven't seen her since Thanksgiving. Charlie gets out of the car to hug her and help with her luggage. She needs the hug, but not the help. All she has is a backpack and a carry-on; she gave up checking luggage years ago.

She tosses her backpack into the trunk of our Camry and comes around to take the wheel.

"You've been on a plane for six hours," I tell her. "You need to relax. I've only been driving since Chattanooga."

But she insists, and I give in, knowing Charlie will be happy to ride in back. He's brought several books he wants to read, and he has his new Blackberry to play with. We have five hours of driving ahead of us.

In another time, a meeting like this would be miraculous, but in these days of cell phones and global positioning systems, such coordination is not only possible, but routine. Rhamy's plane left Portland at 6 a.m. Pacific time. She was in the air for two hours before we left Nashville. Charlie programmed the Hartsfield-Jackson Airport into our GPS as soon as we pulled out of our driveway. If her plane arrived on schedule, and she walked directly from her gate to the terminal, we'd be there to meet her.

Atlanta's roads are some of the most congested in America, its interstate system like a ball of hibernating snakes. We've allowed ourselves twenty minutes to spare.

British Emily, the name we've given our dashboard GPS, is the forgiving sort. She calculates arrival time based on posted speed limits. If we hit road construction or a traffic jam, she'll adjust our arrival time accordingly. If we need to make up time by exceeding the speed limit, she doesn't complain. She's happy to subtract the extra minutes in order to get us back on schedule.

We tried out various voices when we first bought her. The American guy sounded too much like a sportscaster. The Australian girl used idioms from down under that we found confusing. We didn't like the Midwesterner's accent — those flat A's grated on our ears. The French guy was a little too sexy, too distracting on long trips. We liked the very sophisticated British accent, and for a time we vacillated between male and female. In the end, we went with the female, and British Emily was born. Her voice was perfect, pleasing and melodic, never harsh nor strident. She became our companion, our angel in the sky who keeps an eye on the roof of our car, making certain we are always on the right road.

Atlanta's Hartsfield-Jackson is a sprawling international airport, the busiest in the world. A maze of roads loops around the terminals and support buildings: Airport Boulevard, Airport Circle Road, Inner Loop Road, Crosswind Drive, South Ramp Road, Terminal Parkway, Cargo Service Road, North Terminal Parkway, Camp Creek Road. British Emily is undaunted. She directs Rhamy away from the airport, out to Riverdale Road, then onto I-85 South.

An hour later Rhamy has filled me in on the important events in her life. Her husband is now the number two real estate producer in Portland. Quest earned blue ribbons at her last two horse shows. A group of her 7th graders have been suspended for visiting websites they should not have visited.

I tell her about the wounded coyote who's been sleeping under the playhouse, the maple tree in the backyard hit by lightning, the story I wrote that has been accepted for publication in the next issue of *Louisiana Literature*.

Charlie is tinkering with his new Blackberry; it's so much better than the flip phone he used to have. When he's explored all the new features, he sets it aside and picks up the book about World War I he's currently reading. Before Rhamy teaches that part of American history, she should call him. He's an expert on the war and its aftermath.

Madeleine, Rhamy tells us, came to her house for dinner night before last. She was upset about the people who bring their dogs to work at the design firm where she's employed. One in particular, a Chihuahua mix, snarls at her whenever she walks past him. But she loves the parties they have, and she loves her co-workers. And yes, Rhamy says, there's one she particularly likes. He always arrives later than she does in the morning, and he parks his car so close to hers she's totally blocked in. If she wants to go somewhere for lunch, she has to ask him to move his car so she can get out.

I tell Rhamy about the book I ordered from Amazon on the history of Cumberland Island. I'm only half way through, but I'm willing to share it with her while we're on St. Simons.

She makes me promise to send it to her when I'm finished so she can read it cover to cover.

We've been talking non-stop, ignoring Charlie. Rhamy glances back at him. "Will you come with us to Cumberland this year?" she asks.

Charlie doesn't answer. He's fallen asleep.

Travelers on their way to Florida stay on I-85 through Macon, but we get off just north of the city. The scenery changes. Instead of houses, gas stations, and strip malls, we begin to see those tall pine trees that grow like weeds in Georgia. The red clay soil and the low, swampy marshland is the perfect habitat for loblolly, longleaf, and slash pine.

"McDonald's hasn't discovered this part of the country yet," I tell Rhamy.

"It's too deserted," she says. "They couldn't make any profit out here."

"It really is time for me to take over," I tell her. "You must be exhausted."

She insists she's fine, and she keeps driving. We're heading due east now, toward the Atlantic. The road has been built up out of the swamp, and there are steep drop-offs on both sides. The trees are tall and spindly, devoid of branches until they've reached a height where they can spread their limbs into the tiny section of sky allotted them.

To catch a flight from Portland to Denver at 6 a.m., she had to have gotten up by 4. She changed planes in Denver, mountain time, caught the flight bound for Atlanta, eastern time. She's crossed three time zones. Yet she won't give up the wheel.

"We have hours to go before we get there," I tell her. "It's three hundred miles from Atlanta to St. Simons. You can't possibly drive the whole way. Let me drive, at least for a few hours."

"Tell me about the book you're reading," she says. "*The History of Cumberland Island.*"

Somewhere along the way, on that four-lane highway heading toward Savannah, the sky ahead of us begins to darken. The red clay of Georgia turns redder. The air smells of the ocean. We begin to see palm trees. There's little traffic on the road, mostly tractor trailers loaded with pine trees, the tree trunks forming a bridge between the cab and the rear wheels.

Charlie is asleep in the back seat. Our GPS, British Emily, is on the dash.

"In one mile, turn right onto Route 301/25."

Rhamy glances at me. "Turn right? Don't we usually stay on Route 16 until we get to I-95?"

"That's what we normally do," I answer.

"In five hundred feet, turn right onto Route 301," British Emily says.

"Maybe it's a shortcut," I suggest.

Rhamy turns right. Our four-lane highway immediately skinnies down to two.

"This is probably just a connector road of some kind," I tell Rhamy.

"She'd never be taking us all the way to St. Simons on two-lane roads. Would she?"

"No. Surely not."

In the next twenty minutes, we pass through one-stoplight towns and settlements with names like Claxton and Jennie, past country lanes called Harmony Church, Hugh Driggers, Slater Durrence, and Wesley Deloach. The road never widens.

"Where are we?" Charlie asks. He's awake.

"On our way to St. Simons. We'll be there at 8:03 p.m."

"But this isn't Route 16. How did we get off 16?"

I glance at the display on the dashboard. "It's State Route 301," I tell him. "British Emily told us to turn. We think it's a shortcut."

"You should have stayed on 16," he says, and I know from the tone of his voice that he's irritated. He never trusts my driving, never trusts me to find my way. Once, coming home from Knoxville, I missed a turn. When he awoke from his nap, we were on the outskirts of Chattanooga, when we should have been in Nashville. He never lets me forget it.

"I think she's saving us time," I tell him. "Before we turned, she had our arrival time at 8:23 p.m. That's twenty minutes she'll have saved us."

The road twists and turns, past towns that are no more than crossroads, gas stations that have been swallowed up with weeds, abandoned shops, and ramshackle houses. British Emily is with us every step of the way, clearly happy to have brought us here.

"In one mile, turn right on State Route 57," she says.

"In five hundred feet, turn right on State Route 57."

From the back seat, a female voice: "Turn around at your first opportunity."

It shakes us, Rhamy and me, to hear this strange voice. I look around, but there's just Charlie. "Where did that come from?" I ask. "Who said that?"

"Daddy? Who's talking?"

The voice repeats: "Turn around at your first opportunity."

"Daddy, what's going on? Where is that coming from?"

"It's my Blackberry," he says.

I grab my phone, hit the "on" button, and scroll through the icons. When I see the globe icon, I realize what's happening. Embedded in the innards of our new cell phones are global positioning systems. Like British Emily, but not like British Emily.

We have dueling GPS women. Whenever we come to an intersection, no matter how insignificant, the woman in the back tells us to "turn around at your first opportunity."

"We've come too far to turn around," Rhamy says, and there's a touch of irritation in her voice.

"I trust British Emily," I tell Charlie. "She doesn't always get it right, but mostly she does. What I think she's doing is cutting off the corner. If we'd stayed on Route 16, we'd have been going due east. Then when we hit I-95, we'd turn south. The way she's taking us, we're going southeast. I say we trust her. She knows what she's doing."

The Blackberry woman in the back seat is having none of it. "Turn around at your first opportunity," she says, for the third time.

The voice is disembodied. Dictatorial. She gives us no choice. Do what I tell you or you'll be hopelessly lost in this godforsaken country where few strangers have ever ventured before.

British Emily would tell us she is recalculating. We love that about British Emily. To recalculate means she's subservient. If we've made a wrong turn, she's there to help us, not berate us. She understands that we may have made a mistake. We might have been distracted. She would never dictate to us what we should do. Her job is to suggest an alternate route.

The Blackberry woman will not give up her haranguing. At every intersection she issues forth her command: "Turn around at your first opportunity."

"Call Connor," Rhamy says. "He'll be able to tell us if we're going the right way or not. Use my phone. He's on speed dial."

Rhamy's husband is on my speed dial too, right after Charlie, Rhamy, Kate, and Madeleine. The girls are in the order of their birth, so they're easy to remember. Connor has been married to Rhamy longer than Matt has been married to Kate, so Connor's number comes before Matt's.

It's embarrassing, to have to call all the way across the country, to ask my son-in-law if we're on the right road. But there's no help for it.

He picks up on the third ring. I tell him our situation.

"You don't have a map?" he asks.

"We have British Emily," I answer.

"You should never travel without a map. You never know when you might need one."

"Ask him to look on his computer," Rhamy says. "See if Route 301 will take us to I-95."

"We used to have a map," I tell Connor. "It was in the trunk of the car. It was there when Madeleine and I drove to Portland. I remember seeing it."

There's silence on the other end of the line. Is he trying to find a map, or searching for a website that will tell him what we need to know? He could be rolling his eyes, appalled that his wife and mother-in-law have been so foolish as to get themselves lost in some backwoods part of Georgia.

"You're heading south," Connor says. "It looks like Route 301 runs parallel to I-95."

"Does it ever intersect with I-95?"

"If you stay on 301, you'll end up in central Florida. Gainesville is the next large city."

"We don't want to go to Gainesville," I tell him.

We're approaching an intersection. The Blackberry woman tells us once again to turn around. We ignore her.

"It looks like you can turn at a place called Ludowici," Connor says. "Route 57. That'll take you over to I-95. From there it's a straight shot down to Brunswick."

"Thanks, Connor. You're the best. That's exactly what British Emily is telling us to do."

"You might have been better off to stay on 16," he adds.

Rhamy rolls her eyes. Charlie says not a word.

Ten minutes later, we make the turn onto Route 57. British Emily is happy. I-95 is just twenty miles away, she tells us.

The Blackberry woman, who has been unusually quiet, has changed her tune. She tells us to drive for twenty miles, then turn right on I-95.

"Enough of that woman," Rhamy says. "She's irritating. Turn her off, Daddy."

A few minutes later she relents: "If she's going to ride with us, she has to have a name. British Emily has a name. She needs one, too."

We begin to brainstorm. Between the two of us we come up with a dozen possibilities. But nothing fits, until Charlie joins in. "Black Betty," he says. "Let's call her Black Betty."

It has a nice ring to it, we decide. Black Betty. We like the alliteration. And the rhythm, the harshness of the first word balanced by the gentleness of the second. Anglo Saxon men with helmets and swords followed by a soft, Latin-sounding word that suggests swishing skirts and dancing feet. Black Betty. Paired with British Emily, it sounds good.

"No, we can't call her that," Charlie says. "It's racist. We have to come up with something else."

"You suggested it," Rhamy reminds him.

"I've changed my mind."

"What's racist about it?" I ask.

"We'd be identifying her by the color of her skin."

We take a few minutes to consider while the countryside rolls by. A barn covered with license plates. A tombstone by the side of the road marking the spot where a child, killed by a hit-and-run driver, was buried. Roadkill, visible only when the half-dozen scavenger birds rise up and fly to a nearby tree to wait for us to pass.

We've seen no cell towers, but if Charlie is able to get decent reception, I should, too. I turn on my Blackberry.

Wikipedia has different ideas about the name we're considering. "Black Betty" was once a nineteenth century work song, I read. Men sang it to pass the time while they chopped cotton, cut corn, or scythed hay. She was a musket with a black-painted stock; men in battle kept her close. She was the wagon used to transport criminals to the penitentiary. She was the whip used to keep prisoners in line. She was a bottle of whiskey that brought solace to the lonely. In a song recorded by Leadbelly, Ram Jam, and Tom Jones, she was at once a prostitute, an unwed mother who birthed a blind child, and a drug dealer.

"It's settled," I announce. "Her name is Black Betty."

"I'm almost out of juice," Charlie says. "She's eating it up."

"Good," I answer. "We've had enough of her. Let her be quiet for a while."

"There's a charger in the glove compartment. I can recharge."

"No you can't. British Emily is using the outlet."

"You can unplug her," he says. "She'll run on battery for a while."

"We're still out in the middle of nowhere," I tell him. "We can't take the chance."

But even as I say it, it's no longer true. Rhamy turns onto I-95, and we head south, toward St. Simons. We've visited the hinterlands of Georgia and survived. British Emily has indeed cut off the corner. Despite the turns, stoplights, and two-lane highways, she's saved us twenty minutes.

Black Betty is either out of juice, or chagrined that she was so wrong. I have to admit, though, now that we've given her a name, I don't feel quite so antagonistic toward her. She has her ways of doing things, and I can get used to them. I'll be able to live with her for the next two years, which is the term of our new cell phone contracts.

It's dark when we turn onto the Torros Causeway. There's only a sliver moon, but it casts a sheen on the water like floating plates of silver scattered across the wetlands. Spartina and cord grass stretch to the horizon on our left, to the St. Simons Sound on the right. Tidal creeks, five of them, wind their way through the marsh, twisting and turning back on themselves, as if never completely certain which way they want to go. Twice a day all but the tallest of the grasses sink beneath the tidewaters. When the moon is full, it pulls at the earth, and it raises the tides to new heights. The water floods the marshes. When it recedes, it washes marine life out to sea: crabs, fish, shrimp, mussels, and oysters.

Near the end of the causeway, the road climbs high above the Frederica River where, in 1742, dozens of Spanish ships sailed up the waterway to do battle with the entrenched British. Their intent was to claim for Spain the "debatable lands" between Florida and South Carolina. Rebuffed at the Battle of the Bloody Marsh, the Spaniards scuttled back to St. Augustine.

Rhamy drives down off the bridge, leaving the causeway behind, and we are on the island. She slows to read the familiar sign: *Welcome to St. Simons Island, Georgia.*

The island has been calling to us, and we have heard her. We've come back.

If it was quiet when we were on the causeway, four miles across that wide, intracoastal waterway, now the silence is deeper, more profound. We've crossed over to a place where civilization has clung for thousands of years, where rice and cotton plantations once thrived, where in the early nineteenth century a group of

Ebo slaves from Nigeria, chained together by their captors, walked in unison into Dunbar Creek and drowned. Union soldiers during the Civil War took possession of St. Simons Christ Church, smashed the stained-glass windows, burned pews, dragged the altar out under the trees and used it as a butcher's table.

The church has been restored, windows replaced, a new altar constructed using some of the wood from the old one. St. Simons values her history.

"How many times have you and Daddy been here?" Rhamy asks.

"Four times, I think. Charlie?"

"Four or five," he says. "The first year we came twice, remember? Once in the spring and then again that summer."

"I love it here," Rhamy says. "I'd like to come for a month. A year. I'd like to buy a house and live here for the rest of my life."

I think of that peculiar, made-up word: Islomane. Where did her love of islands come from? Why do I have it, too, and Charlie doesn't?

We bear right onto Kings Way, and the live oak trees close arms over us. The sliver moon disappears. The road narrows. It's all so familiar.

We've left the mainland. The sense of separation we feel is palpable. The rules and regulations that govern the United States of America seem not to apply here. The reach of all things material is tenuous. We've crossed to a place that is built of sand, a land deeply affected by wind and tide, a barrier island that protects the mainland and is in turn protected by the Gulf Stream that swirls from the tip of Florida up along the coastline before heading out over the Atlantic.

Hurricanes rarely hit these islands, yet when they do, they can be vicious. Geologists believe it was a hurricane that lopped off the northern part of St. Simons, making into two what had been one, causing the formation of a new island called Little St. Simons. Above that, Egg Island and Little Egg Island, Wolf Island, Cow Island, Queens Island, Sapelo and Little Sapelo, hundreds of islands constantly being created, augmented, eroded, moved from one place to another. Are there some that have sunk beneath the water? Like Atlantis?

Cumberland Island long ago became Cumberland and Little Cumberland. Both islands are now slowly moving to the south, migrating toward Florida. Will they one day join Amelia Island?

Yet the land beneath us is as solid as we need it to be. And it feels peaceful in a way that the mainland does not.

The house we've rented is on a cul-de-sac at the end of Fish Fever Lane. Rhamy claims one of the upstairs bedrooms. She has to chase a gecko out of her bathroom, but she takes it in stride. We're relaxing in the living room, wine glasses in hand, when she mentions my mother.

"I'm sorry I wasn't there for the funeral," she says.

"It's okay. She wouldn't have minded. It was a nice service. You live so far away. She would have understood."

"I loved the eulogy you wrote. Thanks for sending it."

I twist the stem of the wineglass in my fingers.

We'd all known she was dying. I'd begun writing the eulogy when she was admitted to Hospice, three months earlier. During those terrible weeks and months I'd written and rewritten, added and taken away, edited and edited again. I was never satisfied. A week after I came home from the funeral, I took out the eulogy and edited it one last time. That version, slightly different from the one I read at my mother's service, was the one I emailed to Rhamy and her sisters.

"And Aunt Jeanne," Rhamy says, "just a week later. I didn't make it to her service, either."

My glass is nearly empty. "It's okay," I tell her. "Really, it's okay."

"Where is Coop buried?" she asks, and I marvel at how easily our conversation has skittered off into a new direction.

"Near the stream below the house," I answer. "Where we've buried all the animals we've had since you three were kids."

And then I wonder; is it really a new direction? My mother saved Coop from certain death when she found him, an abandoned kitten in the chicken house, eyes still pasted shut, starving. She carried him into the kitchen and we fed him with an eyedropper. I brought him back to Nashville with me where he lived for the next fifteen years.

I finish my wine, and a thin trickle slides down the inside of the glass. "I bought a stone to mark his grave," I tell Rhamy. "You can see it next time you come home."

I get up from the couch and turn out the porch light, thinking how much easier it is to talk about a grave for a cat than it is to talk about my mother. And Charlie's Aunt Jeanne, whom I loved almost as much as I loved my mother.

"I have a picture of you holding Coop when he was a kitten," I tell Rhamy. "He was a good cat."

"All those deaths," she says. "All in the same month."

Rhamy's words surprise me. I have to stop and think. Did all these things happen in the month of March? How is that possible? And why did that not occur to me?

But of course, she's right. My mother died on March 1st. Jeanne, seven days later. And Coop; we buried him in our pet cemetery just a week ago. There are still a few days left before the month is over.

The streetlight in the cul-de-sac goes dark, and the single lamp burning on the table beside the fireplace glows brighter. I refill my glass and return to my chair. Rhamy is looking at me, waiting for me to talk about that month, wanting to hear whatever I have to say about it.

"When we got home from my mother's funeral," I tell her, "Jeanne was in the hospital. We'd driven the whole way that day, all seven hundred miles, but we got in early enough there was time to visit her. She asked about my mother. They were the same age, both 78. I think as long as my mother was okay, Jeanne thought she would be, too.

"'She's fine,' I told her. 'My mother's doing just fine.' What else could I say?" Jeanne just kind of nodded.

"You know," I continue, "they never met — my mother and Aunt Jeanne. Odd, isn't it, that Jeanne would care about my mother, and they'd never actually met."

"Maybe it was you she cared about," Rhamy says.

I sip my wine, thinking of Jeanne in that darkened room in the Hospice facility, and of my mother, cared for by Hospice nurses in the bedroom she once shared with my father. "I think they would have liked each other, my mother and Aunt Jeanne. They might have become friends. But they lived so far apart, Jeanne in Wisconsin, my mother in Pennsylvania. Then after Jeanne moved to Nashville, my mother was no longer able to travel."

Charlie joins us. "There's a gecko in our shower," he announces.

"I chased him out of my bathtub," Rhamy says. "We need a cat."

"Is that why you insisted on driving?" I ask. "Because of my mother, and Jeanne, and Coop? Losing all three in the same month?"

She shrugs. "I thought you could use a break," she says. "I felt bad about not coming for the funeral. She was my grandmother. I should have been there. All those summers we spent on the farm when we were growing up. I should have been there. She was always so good to us."

"I'm not taking a shower if there's a gecko in the bathroom," Charlie says.

"He won't hurt you," I tell him. "Just shoo him out. Or pick him up and take him outside."

"Can you hear the surf?" Rhamy asks.

It's late at night, and the traffic on the island roads has dwindled to an occasional vehicle. Most of the lights in the houses and bungalows have been turned off. There is no wind to stir the trees. We sit in the living room of our rental house on Fish Fever Lane, and we hear the Atlantic washing up against the shore, and retreating, and coming back, again and again and again.

"Let's go for a walk by the ocean," Charlie says. "Maybe the gecko will be gone by the time we get back."

It seems a good idea.

We leave the door unlocked. This is St. Simons Island. Nothing bad can happen here. It's a place of healing.

11

Charlie has planned for himself a perfect day. Much like he did last year, he'll walk to the gas station at the corner of Ocean Boulevard and Mallery Street. He'll buy this morning's *USA Today* and *Wall Street Journal*, then head down to Dresner's. He'll sit at one of their round tables by the window, read his newspapers, and enjoy the most wonderful breakfast available on the island, maybe in all of Georgia. He'll have to choose between blueberry pancakes with oats and nuts, ham biscuits and grits, huevos rancheros with fresh island fruit, or a western omelet. It'll be a tough decision, but I think he'll be able to handle it. When he's finished, he'll stroll down to the fishing pier to see what's happening.

People on the pier are always happy to talk to you. They like to open their coolers and show you the fish they caught. If their coolers are empty, they'll tell you why the fish aren't biting, what bait they should have used, and where the best fishing spots are. The weather, the tides, the ships that come through the Sound heading to Savannah or Shanghai, these are things of supreme importance when you're out on the fishing pier. Never mind if the stock market is plunging, the Middle East imploding, or gun violence is spiraling out of control. None of that matters.

Rhamy is reluctant to leave him here by himself. But I think he enjoys having a day when he can be completely alone and able to do exactly what he wants to do. I might like a day like that. Except I'd worry about what adventures I might be missing. That's my mother talking: "Which will you remember," she used to say, "that you went on a trip to someplace you've never been, or you stayed home and swept the kitchen floor?" It's also Edna St. Vincent Millay: "…there isn't a train I wouldn't take,/ No matter where it's going." I keep that bit of poetry pinned to the bulletin board above my writing desk.

This morning, the train is going to Cumberland Island, and I'm buying a ticket. It's been almost a year since I was there with Madeleine. Things will have changed on the island. Foals will have been born, mares will have died.

While Rhamy and I rush around gathering the things we'll need for the day, Charlie heads for the front porch. Through the window I see him strumming his guitar, trying out different chords and progressions. When he lifts his head and gazes out toward the cul-de-sac, I imagine he's seeing the lyric he's trying to fit to the melody.

"He'll be fine," I tell Rhamy . "There are times when he likes to be alone. He has his guitar, his computer, camera, credit cards. We'll come back this evening and he'll have had a wonderful day."

When we're ready to leave, he props his guitar against the railing and walks with us to the car. I kiss him goodbye and Rhamy hugs him. We drive away, heading for St. Marys, confident we're well-prepared. We have our lunch, bottled water, a Ziploc with Off mosquito repellent, sunblock, first aid cream, and Benadryl. We have a bag of apples for the horses. We know how long it takes to drive to St. Marys, and we've allowed ourselves plenty of time. Last night we filled the car with gas, and Rhamy got directions from our rental agent. We'll be on the boat dock ready to board the *Cumberland Queen* with time to spare.

The directions are different from what they were in previous years. "It's a much better way," the agent told Rhamy. "You'll cut off at least five miles. Get off at Exit 3 and go left on East King Avenue. It'll turn into Osborne Road. Take that straight into St. Marys. It's so easy, you won't even need your GPS."

The agent is wrong. East King Avenue never turns into Osborne Road. We end up outside a naval submarine base we never knew existed. Signs posted by the main entrance identify it as *Kings Bay Naval Submarine Base*. In the massive field in front of the complex is the equally massive *USS George Bancroft* ballistic missile submarine. Stripped of her nuclear capabilities and decommissioned, she was brought here in 1993 as a monument to the sailors and support staff of the Ballistic Missile Submarine Fleet. From the road, the submarine looks like a giant whale rising up out of the ground.

Somehow, I've made a wrong turn. And I continue to make them. No matter which way I turn, I end up at yet another base entry, gated and policed by soldiers in guard houses. The facility is huge, reaching all the way to the intracoastal waterway, and impossible to avoid.

"Let's ask one of the guards how to get to St. Marys," Rhamy says.

"They have guns," I tell her.

"We don't want to call Connor again," she says. "Or Daddy."

"No. We don't want to do that."

Driving up to the guardhouse, feeling the coldness and austerity of the place, I consider changing my mind. But the soldier who approaches is baby-faced, guileless, and welcoming. He's happy to give us directions.

He's never been to Cumberland Island, he tells us, and someday he'd like to go. "Take the Charles Smith Sr. Highway south, turn left on Osborne Road, go about ten blocks, and you'll be at the dock."

It isn't quite as easy as he makes it out to be. First we have a navigate a maze of one-lane streets through a poverty-stricken neighborhood. Following the direction indicator in the rearview mirror, we keep heading south, and when we finally reach the highway, I breathe a sigh of relief.

"Next year we'll get off at Exit 1," I tell Rhamy.

"And let's not use that rental agent ever again," she says.

12

Madeleine with her nine horses, the most any of us have ever seen on the island, is soon toppled from her throne. Grazing in the new spring grass around the mansion are so many horses Rhamy and I can't count them.

There are horses drinking from the artesian well dug by the Carnegies when the mansion was built. It's been a wet spring; fresh water is bubbling up out of the ground. Judging from the tracks around the pool, horses from all over the island come here to drink.

A pregnant mare rests in the shade of a palm tree near the tabby house where the Greene family once lived. Two more horses, a pinto and a dun, graze in front of the pergola. Another group crops grass from around the ruined recreation building. More horses move about the distant salt marshes.

We set our lunches on the weathered picnic table behind the mansion, but neither of us is ready to eat. We just want to sit and absorb what's going on around us. When will we ever again have the chance to picnic among so many wild horses?

A foal is sleeping near the watering hole, his mother close by. He's stretched flat out in the grass, eyes closed, soaking up the sun. His hooves are shiny black and curled toward his body, so perfectly formed and so clean they look as if they've never touched the ground.

"Did you ever get that watercolor framed?" I ask Rhamy. "The one you bought at the King and Prince the year we stayed there?"

"I did," she answers, but she's distracted. The pregnant mare is moving toward us. Rhamy opens the mesh bag that holds the apples and takes one out. With the plastic knife she put in our lunch bag early this morning she cuts the apple in half. She puts one half in her pocket. Holding the other half in her hand, she moves toward the mare, walking slowly, one careful step at a time. The mare turns to look at her, ears tipped forward in an attitude of curiosity but also vigilance.

Rhamy inches closer. When she's within ten feet, the mare lowers her head, grabs a bite of grass, and moves away.

Rhamy comes back to the table. "I think she's about to give birth. Her belly is huge. I could see the baby moving."

We watch the mare disappear into the woodland behind the tabby house.

A group of horses graze by the fountain, three mares and a yearling. Near the barrier that surrounds the mansion is a stallion, a dark bay with one white stocking, thick through the neck, heavy and muscular. On the fringes of the herd is another stallion, this one old, sway-backed, and painfully thin. His coat is dull. There are patches of bare skin on his flank and neck.

"He's lost his harem," Rhamy says. "These mares and that stallion, they're a family group. They're letting this old guy stay with the herd, as long as he obeys the rules."

"Stays away from the mares, you mean."

She nods. "Normally, a stallion that loses out to another stallion is banished. For whatever reason, they've decided it's okay for him to hang around."

"He looks awful."

"He's lucky, in a way," Rhamy says. "Horses are such social animals. They don't like to be by themselves. Plus, when you're part of a herd, you're under the protection of the group. It's a complicated system that protects them from predators. Notice how the foal stays in the middle of the herd? That's the safest place. And the stallion, the bay with the white stocking? He stays on the edges. He's kind of a sentry. If he senses a predator nearby, he'll alert the group, and the boss mare will take off running. She'll choose which way to go, and the others will follow. He'll bring up the rear, make sure there are no stragglers."

"What about him?" I ask, indicating the old stallion. "What happens to him if a pack of coyotes attacks?"

"He'll try to stay with the herd, if he can."

I remember seeing pictures of coyotes on one of the posters at the dock. And foxes. It's not nirvana, being on an island. It's not without danger.

We watch the old stallion graze at the edge of the herd. When another horse approaches, he moves away, as if he's saying, *you can have this patch of grass; I'll find another.*

"He's probably full of worms," Rhamy says. "That's one reason he's so thin."

"We could bring a tube of Ivermectin next year. Figure out a way to give it to him."

"He may not be here next year," she says. She takes the apple meant for the pregnant mare and walks toward him. He lifts his head, watches her approach, ears forward. He shows no sign of fear.

She holds out her hand, the half-apple in her open palm. He takes a step toward her, nostrils flared, a little nervous, but curious.

That thing in her hand, what is it? Have I smelled it before, tasted it?

Lucy Carnegie willed that upon her death, all her horses — polo ponies, Arabians, Thoroughbreds, and Appaloosas — all were to be set free where they could wander wild on the island. Does this old stallion have some dim memory of ancestors who carried Carnegie children and their guests on his back, ate sugar cubes from their hands, participated in games and hunting expeditions in golden years of long ago?

The Carnegies raised vegetables, kept poultry and livestock. They planted fruit trees, as did the Greenes before them. Were there apple trees among them? I have no way of knowing. Nothing I've read provides the answer.

The stallion takes another, hesitating step toward Rhamy. She moves, almost imperceptibly, closer to him, the apple in her outstretched hand. Like Eve, she is tempting him. Like Adam, he is considering.

There could be danger.

For Rhamy, as well. He's a stallion. Stallions are unpredictable. He could rear up, bring his hooves down on her. But Rhamy knows horses. I have faith in her.

He stretches out his neck and takes the apple from her hand. And lets it drop onto the ground. One ear back now. As if a part of him is suddenly fearful. He lowers his head and nuzzles the apple. Then he picks it up and begins to chew.

Adam has succumbed to temptation. He has tasted of the apple. And I'm able to breathe again.

Rhamy takes the other half from her pocket, but she only stands there, the apple hidden in the hand that hangs by her side. The old stallion retreats from her, and it's almost as if he wants to get a better look at this creature who has brought him this delicious thing. He can only do that if there's some distance between them.

He finishes the apple. Drops a piece, finds it, takes it into his mouth. When it's gone, he looks at Rhamy, expectantly, and takes a step toward her. He's under the spell of this woman. He wants more of what she has brought him.

She holds out the second half, and he takes it, wrapping his lips around it, careful of her outstretched hand, and he chews until this one, too, is gone.

She's talking to him. I can hear her voice but not the words. She shows him her empty hands. *All gone*, she's telling him.

She turns her head slightly, and the breeze carries her words to me: "Bring another," she says, her voice only slightly louder. "Cut it in half. Come slowly. Don't do anything to scare him."

I do as she asks, and as I'm walking toward them, I see her reach out and stroke the side of his face. He tosses his head, *no one has ever done that to me before*, but he settles, and he allows her to touch him, stroke his neck, his withers.

He eats the second apple, and I wonder if he might want to join us at our picnic table. But then he looks across the clearing, and he sees that the herd is moving away. The boss mare is heading into the woods where Nancy Carnegie once had her playhouse. The old stallion trots after them.

We don't see him again for the rest of our time on the island.

13

The following spring, it's okay that Charlie doesn't want to come with us to Cumberland. This is the year Rhamy and I will visit the island not once, but twice. Three months from now, in June, our whole family will gather on St. Simons. When we've all recovered from our journeys, car trips and plane rides, and when our watches and cell phones are comfortably set on island time, we'll go to Cumberland.

Fish Fever Lane will be too small for all nine of us, so I plan to book two condos in the Ocean View complex; a three-bedroom for Charlie and me, Madeleine, Rhamy and Connor, and a two-bedroom for Katie, Matt, and the kids. For the first time in their young lives, Riley and Lucas will take a ferry ride down the Cumberland River and up the intracoastal waterway. They'll see wild horses that are so used to visitors they're almost tame. Their biologist dad can point out wildlife they've never seen before and explain how the various plants and animals affect the different ecosystems on the island. Their veterinarian mom can study the horses, tell us if they're thriving, how their lives are different from those of domesticated horses. If we're lucky, she'll cast a practiced eye on Rhamy's old stallion, give us her professional opinion of his condition, estimate how long he might live and what his ultimate fate might be. If there's anything we can do for him, maybe she'll tell us.

Connor will love seeing the buildings on the island in their various states of decay. He'll be especially interested in the facilities at Sea Camp Campgrounds. We aren't there yet, but the day may come when we decide to camp out for two or three days on the island. When we do, we'll stay at the campgrounds. And Connor, outdoorsman extraordinaire, will be our camp leader.

Charlie hasn't committed to coming with us in June, but how could he refuse when his three daughters will be going, his two sons-in-law, and his grandchildren. Not to mention his wife.

To ask him to come with us now, and then again in June, would be too much. Rhamy and I are happy to go by ourselves.

It's been a harsh winter, but spring is already well advanced in southern Georgia. The temperature in St. Marys is expected to be in the high 70s. We dress accordingly, both of us wearing shorts, tank tops, and sandals. My sandals are Crocs. The company took its name from the "multi-environment, amphibious nature of crocodiles," so my choice of footwear seems appropriate.

No one should own as many pairs of Crocs as I do. I like my Slides best, but I have others: Patricia wedges and Mary Janes, Cleo sandals and Retro clogs. Patricias come in beige and brown. I own both. I even have a pair of clogs that are especially made for bad weather. They have thick tread on the bottom, in case I'm walking through mud or puddles of water.

I read about a man in New York City, a chef, who is so in love with Crocs he owns fifty pairs. He likes them because they are blissfully comfortable, they come in lovely colors, and they are nearly indestructible. When they get dirty, he throws them in the washing machine. No matter if they are bubblegum pink, ocean blue, or tomato red, they come out looking brand new. You can even put them in the dishwasher, the famous chef told the reporter. Top or bottom rack. Take them out, let them cool a bit, put them on and they mold themselves to your feet.

George Bush was once seen wearing gray Crocs with white anklets. Michelle Obama has been spotted strolling across the White House lawn in her Mulberry Alice flats. She owns at least one other pair, turquoise Malindi flats that perfectly match a Gap outfit she once wore.

I'm wearing black Crocs. I actually like my fuchsia ones better, and they'd look nice with my beige shorts and navy top, but they might be a bit showy for traipsing around the island. Not as bad as that New York chef who was photographed wearing orange Crocs with green socks and short pants, of course, but fuchsia is a bright color, and it might scare the horses.

There are no horses around the Carnegie mansion this year, which is unusual. None by the recreation building where the grass is long and lush. Nor in the clearing behind the auto graveyard. Could this be the year we see no horses? Could poachers have come onto the island, captured them and taken them away? Food became so scarce in the fall and winter the herd was reduced to a few stragglers who are hidden away in the forest, trying to survive on leaves and tree bark?

We walk down the narrow path through the woodland, past the Greene-Miller cemetery, out onto the boardwalk. Beneath us, mud snails and fiddler crabs scurry about the tidal flats in search of food. The tide is out, the spartina tall and green, and there's the smell of the ocean in the air. In the marsh pools and creeks, schools of fish swim beneath the oily surface. Far out in the marsh, silhouetted against a stand of live oak trees, we see a single horse.

I've come prepared. I reach into my pocket, bring our four quarters, and hold them out to Rhamy.

"You brought money?"

"There's a telescope a bit farther on. I saw it when I was here with Madeleine. It looks out over the marsh. If there are horses out there, we should be able to see them."

She's thrilled. We head down the boardwalk, toward the ocean. Within five minutes we're there: the telescope sits at the edge of a platform built out over the marsh. I feed a quarter into the slot.

"I see him," Rhamy says. "And there are others, back in the trees. A chestnut and a gray."

"They're on solid ground, not in the marsh?"

"I think so," she says, and she adjusts the knob to bring them into sharper focus.

"Look off to the right," I tell her. "There are more."

She moves the telescope. "It's a band," she says. "Four or five, at least."

"Is the old stallion among them? The one that ate the apples?"

"They're too far away. I can't tell."

A quarter buys you a minute on the telescope. When my coins are gone, we linger there on the platform. The chestnut and the gray disappear into the woods. The band moves farther into the marsh until they are no more than splotches of brown and black. We can no longer be certain they are horses at all.

Rhamy is disappointed. "Next year we're bringing binoculars," she says.

"This summer, remember? We're coming back in June."

"Is it really gonna happen?" she asks. "Can we really get the whole family to come to Cumberland?"

"Absolutely," I assure her. "Connor will come, won't he? It's just Madeleine who hasn't decided yet. We'll have to wait and see if she can get off work, but Kate is coming, with Matt and the kids. And if we all come to Cumberland, surely Charlie will, too. He won't want to be left behind, and it'll just be his second time."

"But if there are no horses, everyone will be disappointed."

"There'll be horses," I tell her. "And other things: burned-out mansions and falling-down recreation buildings, old cars sinking into the ground, and the ocean. We'll bring our bathing suits, and we'll take the kids swimming. We'll picnic on the beach, just like the Carnegies used to do. It'll be wonderful."

"We won't have servants," Rhamy says.

"That was the Gilded Age," I answer, "and look what happened. In just a few generations, it all slipped away. The children and then the grandchildren spent all the money, until it reached a point where they couldn't afford the upkeep on the mansion, or the taxes."

They were loafers, I tell Rhamy. Raised to a life of leisure, it never occurred to them that someone would have to do something to earn money. And if it did, they had no idea how to go about it. So they raced their cars up and down the beach and drank and fished, and then one day it was over. The ground beneath them had shifted.

"At least one of them married a commoner," Rhamy says. "Let's see if we can find Nancy Carnegie's playhouse. Kate's kids would love to see that."

We have a map, so we know the general location: across from the mansion and the recreation building.

Twenty minutes later we're standing at the edge of the clearing, looking into the forest opposite the mansion. The undergrowth is thick with tangled vines, saw palmetto, cedar trees. Neither of us is brave enough to try to break a path into it to look for the playhouse.

We sit at the picnic table behind the mansion eating our egg salad sandwiches, gazing out over what was once the Carnegie gardens. The Cumberland Island book I bought on Amazon had sketches of what the gardens once looked like. Nature has taken it all back. What is left is an innocent field, content in its transition from careful cultivation back to wild abandon. Tall marsh grasses, brown and yellow, stretch to the horizon, and there's a mist rising from the land as the sun bakes the salty moisture out of it.

Lucy Carnegie's goal was to make her plantation self-sufficient. To that end, she hired landscape architects to design a Garden of Eden. They sketched out plans to turn the marsh into a vast cornucopia of fruit trees, flowering shrubs, and vegetable plots. They would build dikes to hold back the tides, terrace the land, and turn the marsh into fertile acreage. They would amend the soil by adding necessary nutrients. In the plots closest to the mansion they would plant fruit trees and ornamentals. When evening settled over the land, Lucy and her guests could stroll among the trees in the upper garden, and when the fruit was in season, they could reach up and pluck it from low-hanging branches: cherries, peaches, and pears. They would plant citrus, apricot, and nectarines trees. There would be olive, pecan, almond, and filbert trees. For color and variety they would add dogwood, oleander, crepe myrtle, and flowering plum trees.

The lower garden, farther from the mansion, would contain plots for growing vegetables that would be prepared in the Carnegie kitchen and served in the Carnegie dining room: lettuce, tomatoes, radishes, peppers, carrots, pumpkins, beans, cucumbers, corn, and potatoes. There would be strawberry beds, blackberry patches, and grape arbors.

The garden would provide every delicacy the island could offer up. When the work was done, it would rival Eden in its bountifulness, its richness, its abundance and variety.

The landscape architects presented their plans to Lucy, and she approved.

In the golden days and years that followed, industrial and technological advances would bring unparalleled growth to the nation. The industrial and financial giants — Mellons, Morgans, Vanderbilts, Astors, Rockefellers, and Carnegies — made more money than they could possibly ever spend. Lucy invited many of them to her island home, and she entertained lavishly. They stayed for weeks and sometimes months at a time, enjoying Lucy's hospitality and all the things the island had to offer. In the midst of all that wealth and luxury and abundance, the nine Carnegie children grew to adulthood.

Now, the fruit trees are gone. The terracing so meticulously built and maintained is eroding. The dikes have been breached and the ones that remain are crumbling.

A group of horses have been moving closer and closer to where we sit, but the distance is still too great to tell if this is the band from last year. Rhamy and I pack up what's left of our lunch and head down the road, past the ruined greenhouses, toward Cumberland Sound. If we get close enough to the herd, we might be able to see if Adam, the old horse who ate the apple, is among them.

And we'll be able to take pictures. Rhamy has promised to send some back to her equestrian friends in Portland. As soon as we have internet access, I'd like to send a few to Charlie, just so he can see what he missed. Blackberries have other functions besides being phones and GPSs. They are also cameras.

14

The marsh is like quicksand. You take a step, and you think you're on solid ground, but you aren't. You sink deep into the muck, and it's squishy, and it pulls you down. It's hard not to panic, because you have no idea how deep you're going to go, and what if you find you're unable to pull yourself out?

But there are the horses, and they're having no trouble. They're grazing in the marsh, eating the tough, spartina blades, moving easily from place to place. They don't seem to mind if they sink up to their fetlocks or on occasion to their knees. They simply pull themselves out, one foot at a time, and they go on.

Rhamy and I try to stay on high ground, but the tidal creeks are so labyrinthine in their meanderings, we're forced to either wade through them, jump across, or backtrack. We try to avoid the mudflats covered with snails, hundreds of them, eating whatever is in the film on top of the mud, so many the very surface looks like a moving carpet.

It smells of decay: decomposing plant matter, bacteria, rotting animal carcasses. Yet the marsh is also a place of rampant growth. The spartina grass is tall, the leaves vividly green. There are pools of briny water where crabs, clams, mussels, oysters, fiddler crabs, and shrimp proliferate.

A cluster of spartina collapses under my foot and the muck oozes over the top of my sandal. I wash it off in a tidal pool; the footbed is slippery, my legs stinging from the salt. My steps now are less certain. When we get back to the dock, I'll wash my legs and my Crocs under the faucet outside the restrooms.

Rhamy, who is wearing Nikes, stays close to the edge to the stream. Somehow she's managed to keep her shoes relatively clean, mostly by profiting from my mistakes.

The secret, I've learned, is to carefully test the footing before you fully commit to taking the step. And be prepared to reverse course. The consistency of the muck is different on the surface from what it is down under. Nothing is to be trusted.

The farther into the marsh we go, the less I care. We are edging ever closer to the horses, close enough that we can hear the sucking sounds as they extricate their hooves from the mud. I step onto a patch of what I think is dry land and my foot goes deep into the marsh. It happens so fast, there's no time to stop it. I try to pull it out, but the mud has closed around my leg, and it holds like a vacuum.

I cry out to Rhamy for help. The horses look up, their ears perked. One lowers his head and snorts, two long, low exhalations. I wonder if he's communicating fear or simple wariness.

Unable to go backwards, I have no choice but to step farther into the muck. It works. My foot comes out of the marsh, blackened and smelling foul. But my shoe is gone. I look down into the hole, hardly believing what has happened. Almost immediately, the indentation fills with thick, gray water.

Somewhere down in that stew of slop is the black Croc I slipped into this morning. I have to retrieve it. I can't walk all the way back to the dock with just one shoe. There's nothing to do but reach down into the muck, this mess of putrefaction, with my bare hand.

I'm up to my elbow in muck, fishing around in this watery mess, trying to find my shoe, and Rhamy is laughing. She thinks it's funny. She raises her phone and snaps a picture.

I reach down into that muddy soup and pull up something I can't identify. Black, but not my shoe. I wish I'd worn my fuchsia ones. They might be easier to spot.

I toss whatever I've pulled out of the hole away. I reach down again. Grab hold something that is softer, more pliable. The mud does not want to give it up, but I wrestle with it, and I win. My Croc comes up out of the marsh. Dripping.

Rhamy snaps another picture. I scowl at her.

I look around, searching for the most solid way out of the marsh. It's all the same: muddy, watery, untrustworthy. There's nothing to do but take off the other shoe and wade through it until I'm back on solid ground.

The horses have been watching, but now they begin to move away. If the old stallion is among them, I don't see him. Nor do I see the bay with the white stocking.

On dry land, back on the oyster shell road, Rhamy shows me the pictures she took.

"Delete them," I tell her, knowing she won't.

15

We're walking down Grand Avenue toward the Dungeness dock when one of the park rangers falls in step with us. She's wearing olive green pants, a gray shirt, gold name tag above one pocket, badge above the other.

She looks us over, scrutinizing our clothes, our shoes. "Are you calling it a day?" she asks. "Planning to catch the early ferry?"

"We've been in the marsh," I tell her. "Nearly up to our knees."

She laughs. "You should have gone to the beach. There's always a breeze over there, and the ocean is just lovely. It's a nice day for a swim. No rip tides, just gentle waves. Not a cloud on the horizon. And completely deserted."

She's a tall woman, and a fast walker. Already she's four feet ahead of us. We hurry to catch up, keep pace with her.

"We got a report of a dead sea turtle washed up on the beach, and I went out to investigate," she says.

"Did you find it?" I ask.

She nods. "It was a loggerhead, and a big one. I'd estimate over two hundred and fifty pounds. Looked like it'd been hit by a boat propeller." She stops suddenly, takes out a handkerchief and mops her face, gazes into a thicket of palmetto bushes. "Armadillo," she says. "Do you see him?"

We hear a rustling sound, and he waddles out from beneath the thicket into a patch of sunlight. His armor plates move with the movement of his body. In this place that has reverted to wilderness he seems a throwback to prehistoric times. We watch him until he disappears.

"They're not native," the ranger says. "They shouldn't be here."

She sets off again, and we struggle to keep up. "That loggerhead over on the beach, that's the tenth one so far this year. We're seeing more and more strandings like that. We're not sure why. Maybe there are more of them, so more of a chance they'll get caught in a shrimp net or hit by a passing boat. Last year we had over two thousand nests on Georgia beaches, nearly three hundred here on Cumberland. For a threatened species, they're recovering pretty well."

"You like your job, don't you?" I ask.

She looks surprised, and for a moment she doesn't answer. When she does, her voice is softer, her words less hurried. "I love this island," she says. "I love everything about it. It's a miracle the Park Service was able to keep the developers away, so it could go back to being what it was meant to be."

We continue down the road, crushing oyster shells and dry leaves under our feet, and there's no other sound but the echo of her words and the sentiment they have engendered.

"If we come back in June," Rhamy says, "might we see a loggerhead?"

"They mostly come ashore at night," she answers. "They dig nests up in the dunes, above the tide line, deposit their eggs, cover them up, and head back to the water."

"I read where the Carnegie children used to climb on top of them and hitch a ride into the ocean."

She nods. "The turtles are generally exhausted by the time they finish laying their eggs. A nest might contain 140 or 150 eggs. So it's a struggle for them to get back to the ocean. And yes, that was great sport for the Carnegie kids. The water is pretty shallow for quite a ways out."

"What did you do with the dead loggerhead?" Rhamy asks.

"We'll let nature take care of it. A day or two and it'll be gone. It's our policy to not interfere. Same with the horses. We don't manage the herds and we don't provide any kind of veterinary care. There's a concern about the ecological damage the horses are doing, and we try to be sensitive to that. When they graze the sea oats, which they do all the time, it causes the dunes to erode. The same with the marshes; eating the grasses causes the marsh areas to shrink. But in the end, we just let them be horses."

Rhamy draws in a breath. "You'd put a horse down, wouldn't you, if it needed to be done? If he were suffering…" She's thinking of the old stallion we called Adam, I'm certain.

"Like I said, we don't interfere."

The road narrows, and she moves ahead again. But I notice that she's let her hand drop to her side, and her fingers brush against the revolver she carries on her hip. That tiny movement tells me she's skirting the truth, that there have been occasions when she has intervened.

Rhamy hurries along the road until she's beside the ranger. I hear her ask about the old stallion from last summer.

The ranger remembers the bay with the white stocking and his harem. "They spent a lot of time around the mansion," she says. "I don't recall an old stallion. He probably didn't make it through the winter. Food can get pretty scarce, and a lot of the old ones don't survive."

"He didn't look like he was in very good shape," Rhamy says.

"Horses in captivity can live twenty or thirty years," the ranger says. "Here, eight or ten is pretty much the limit. The mares, less than that. They drop foals every year, and it takes a toll. Have you noticed how skinny they are? This old stallion, you think he's been forced out of a band, and this group let him join theirs?"

Rhamy nods. "Either that, or it was his band, and when he lost it, the new stallion let him hang around."

"As long as he stayed on the periphery. It's possible."

"He seemed almost tame," Rhamy says.

We're walking three abreast now, the road having widened out I glance at my daughter, worried she's about to mention the apple she fed him. Or worse still, our plan to have Kate come with us when we visit the island in June. "We don't provide any kind of veterinary care," the ranger had said. Kate has been a practicing veterinarian for five years. What would this park official say if she learned we wanted to dose the old horse with Ivermectin, get rid of his parasites, and maybe buy him a few more years? It's time to change the subject.

"Do you know where Nancy Carnegie's playhouse is?" I ask. "I read that she had one, somewhere across from the mansion. We'd love to see it."

"I'm certain it's gone by now. Rotted away. I think I know where it was, though. I remember seeing some timbers in the woods…" she points off to her right "…when I first started working here. That was twelve years ago. I doubt there's anything left by now. Termites are bad on the island. Unless a building is taken care of, it goes back to the earth. The recreation house is a perfect example."

"You'd think there'd be foundation stones scattered around."

"*Scattered* is the right word. Things change on the island. We have feral pigs that are doing an enormous amount of damage, uprooting trees, digging holes. If the horses are bad for the environment, the pigs are a whole lot worse."

We're walking beneath deep canopy, the sun almost completely blocked, and I think how much I'd like to go into the area the ranger indicated, the spot where she first saw the timbers. I'd like to search the ground for some remnant of that time when Nancy was a little girl, the prettiest of the Carnegie daughters, the favorite of her Uncle Andrew, the one who would likely inherit the bulk of his money. The one who ultimately disgraced the family.

I wonder if someday an archeologist from the University of Georgia will come here with a group of students, and he'll discover the ruins of a child's playhouse. He could set up a grid and start excavating. A hundred years from now, if he unearths a piece of porcelain in these woods, what will he think? I imagine he'll turn it over in his hands, and at some point he will determine that the fragment is not from a dish as it first appeared, but is instead from the head of a doll. The cloth body will have long ago disintegrated. This archeologist might learn that the doll was made of unglazed porcelain brought back from Europe where porcelain dolls were first manufactured. He might wonder if it was a gift from the infamous Andrew Carnegie to his brother's youngest child.

My mother once had a doll like that. When she retrieved it from the ruins of her mother's house, which had been destroyed by a tornado, all that was left was the head. The painted eyebrows, the rosy cheeks, and crimson lips were faded, but she picked it out of the rubble and brought it home. She cleaned the soot and grime away, and she put it in a drawer. I remember the day she showed it to me, and that I wondered, at the time, how a child could ever play with such a thing. But I sensed that it had once been important to her.

In the bedroom of my mother's house, standing in front of the dresser beside my mother, the mirror tilted so it reflected truncated parts of both of us, there were things in the room that demanded nothing of me but my silence. The doll was one of them.

Now here I am, on Cumberland Island, thinking of her, and wanting to hold her doll in my hands. And if that's not possible, and of course it isn't, I would at least like to see the playhouse that was built here for a little girl who is gone and for a way of life that seemed so beautiful and perfect until it all came tumbling down.

Might this archeological team find metal toys and buttons from doll clothing, broken bits of china from a child's tea set, toy trains, metal horses, and carts?

The ranger breaks into my reverie: "Nancy Carnegie and her second husband lived at Plum Orchard for a while," she says. "I take groups of tourists through the mansion every second and fourth Sunday." She pauses, looking into the woods at an animal trail. It's narrow and barely discernible. Twenty feet from where we stand it curves to the right. Where it goes from that point is impossible to tell.

The ranger glances at her watch, then at the two of us. "Let's go take a look," she says. "I have some time, and I think I can at least show you where the playhouse used to be."

We follow her into the forest, single file, pushing our way through the thick undergrowth, careful of each footfall. The path is so overgrown it seems to disappear at times, then reappear. Our guide keeps up a running chatter as we make our way deeper into the tangled jungle. I wonder if she's trying to scare away unwanted critters who might be lying in wait for an unsuspecting victim.

Both the Carnegie and the Coleman families were from Pittsburgh, she tells us. Lucy Coleman, Nancy's mother, had her heart set on her youngest daughter marrying royalty. It was all the rage back then for young heiresses to marry British royalty. Nancy had been a bridesmaid when her cousin Alice Thaw married the Earl of Yarmouth. That turned out to be a disaster. A scandalous affair. It seems the earl was not only penniless, but he'd run up debts back in London. His creditors managed to have his accounts transferred to a group of Pittsburgh attorneys.

She stops, looks over her shoulder at us, then goes on; "According to newspaper accounts," she says, "the earl was 'being dressed for the wedding' when the authorities grabbed him. He was served with a writ that demanded $1500. On the spot. He didn't have it, of course. The guests were all waiting at the church, Nancy among them, while the earl tried to come up with the money. That was in 1903.

"The bridesmaids were dressed in white chiffon," she adds. "White straw hats trimmed with ostrich feathers. They carried bouquets of white and purple lilacs."

We walk on. The path splits, and the ranger hesitates. Decision made, she takes the more-traveled one that branches off to our right.

"A year later, Nancy eloped with her riding teacher."

I stop. Rhamy, behind me, stops. "But what happened with the wedding?" I ask. "You're skipping the best part. Did the earl leave her at the altar?"

She laughs, turns her head to the side so the answer comes back to us through the humid air. "The church was filled with the wealthiest, most aristocratic families in America. They sat there waiting for something like forty-five minutes. When the earl finally showed up, he had a contract in his pocket that guaranteed him an income from the Thaw family for the rest of his life."

"So the family paid off his debts? And they bribed him to go through with the ceremony?"

"It would seem so," she says.

We've reached a clearing in the woods, green all around us, blue above. It doesn't seem possible this is where the playhouse once stood. Surely nature would have filled it in by now.

The ranger walks slowly over the ground, searching, scraping away mounds of dry oak leaves with her shoe, moving on to other locations within the clearing. She stops and looks off to the west, toward the chimneys of Dungeness. Above the tree line to the south we can see the ruined wooden tower of the recreation building.

"I think this is where it was," she says. "Nancy's playhouse."

"But wouldn't it be all grown up by now? It's been over a hundred years."

"One thing the horses do is eat the saplings," she says. "If the Carnegies cleared the land to build the playhouse, it's possible the horses kept it that way. And other grazers, of course. Deer, for one."

She unearths a chunk of tabby, the concrete-like material used for most buildings on the island. She stoops to examine it, then goes on: "It would have been close enough to the house that the kids could come running if something was wrong, but far enough away they felt like they had some privacy. Lucy often had tea on the veranda in the afternoon, so she would have been able to hear, maybe even see them. Lucy and her guests, I should say. She had house guests nearly all the time when she was here. Many of the people at the Thaw wedding had visited Cumberland at one time or another. They would stay with the Carnegies for weeks at a time, formal dinners every night, fishing, skeet shooting, playing golf, riding horses, hunting wild boar and turkey in the daytime. These families were very close. And they wanted it that way. They wanted their children to marry their own kind. George Carnegie, Nancy's older brother, was married to Alice Thaw's sister Margaret. But the families were competitive, too. When Alice snagged herself an earl, Lucy Carnegie just had to have one for her daughter. Nancy had evidently caught the attention of an English duke who was one of Alice's wedding guests. He was the perfect candidate, except that Nancy was in love with someone else."

She presses the chunk of tabby back into the soil. "Several years earlier," she continues, "Lucy had hired an Irishman, James Hever, to take care of her horses. Nancy began taking riding lessons from him, and they fell in love. At some point Hever approached Lucy and told her he wanted to marry her daughter."

The ranger picks up a heavy stick and begins to clear the leaves and brush from a mound of earth. "It's storybook, isn't it? The stable boy wanting to marry the daughter of the rich people who live in the mansion? No one knows exactly what Lucy said to him, but he was out of a job shortly after that meeting. The romance continued, only now, it was forbidden. Which probably made things worse."

"And definitely sweeter," I offer.

"Yes," she says. "It came out later that Nancy went to her uncle, Andrew Carnegie, and asked for his help. He gave the couple $20,000 and sent them off to Europe."

The ranger sighs, as if sympathizing with the intensity of young love, or the mother's shattered dreams, or the tragedy of Nancy's young life.

"They managed to keep the whole thing quiet," she continues, "until Nancy came back a year later with her husband and baby. They had another child with them, a daughter Hever had put in an orphanage when he came to America. There was no mention of Hever's other children. It's possible they never existed.

"The newspapers had a field day, as you can imagine. A family like that, brought down by scandal. There were headlines about Nancy having been secretly married for a year. And that when she came back from Europe, Lucy refused to meet the boat. The papers called her 'an unforgiving mother.'

"Andrew Carnegie, though, was totally supportive. He told reporters he'd much rather his niece marry 'an honest, sober, good man, without wealth, than a worthless duke.' Reporters speculated he was referring to the Duke of Manchester, a man with whom he'd had business dealings.

"The marriage had taken place a year ago, Carnegie said, and no one in the family had the slightest objection to the union. He himself had been abroad when the couple married, and none of the family were in town for the event."

The ranger uncovers another chunk of tabby, this one larger and flattened on both sides. She prods it with her stick.

"Among the more than two hundred servants who were employed by the Carnegies," she says, "some would have had the skills to build a playhouse for a little girl." She turns her face to the sky, as if she's not sure she wants to tell the end of the love story. We wait for her to continue.

"Hever turned out to be a drunk," she says. "And he was evidently abusive to Nancy. They say when she came back to Cumberland, she was a pathetic sight. But she must have loved him. After they separated, when he was dying of cancer, alone and dead broke, she went to New York to care for him. She stayed there, with him, in his tiny apartment, until he died."

The chimneys of Dungeness are silent. We in the clearing are silent. If there are artifacts from a little girl's playhouse buried in the soil beneath our feet, they will remain there.

16

A pregnant mare and her yearling are grazing by the side of the seashell road when we emerge from the forest. The ranger stops to look at them.

"If you see horses on the island with conformations like this," she says, indicating the mare, "it might be because of Nancy's second husband, Marius Johnston. He was a physician. Lucy brought him to the island to take care of her family. But being a doctor was more of a second calling. He'd grown up in Kentucky, and he loved horses, maybe as much as Nancy did. He had this idea of trying to improve the genetics of the herd, so he had one of his Thoroughbred stallions shipped down from his estate in Kentucky. They used him to breed some of the wild mares."

"The bay stallion we saw last year." Rhamy says, and there's excitement in her voice. "That would explain it. He was at least sixteen hands, maybe more. Tall shoulders, well-proportioned, chiseled hind quarters, he looked so intelligent, and confident. Not like some of the other horses we've seen."

The ranger steps around a pile of fresh horse droppings. "Others tried to introduce some genetic variety into the herd before Marius. Thomas Carnegie supposedly brought in some Paso Finos and Tennessee Walkers. Then when Lucy died, they opened the barn doors. All her horses were set free: Appaloosas, polo ponies, Thoroughbreds. So what you see here is quite a mix."

"How many horses are there?" Rhamy asks. "All together?"

"There are three herds on the island," she answers. "One up north around Lake Whitney, another that hangs around Dungeness, and a third group, the largest, in the center of the island. As far as how many, we haven't done our annual count yet, but the population has been pretty steady for the last five or six years. Somewhere between 130 and 150. I expect that's about what it'll be this year. There have been years when we had as many as 220. Other times as low as 100."

"Would you count her as one, or two?" Rhamy asks, pointing to the mare.

"By the time next weekend rolls around — that's when we're scheduled to do the count — I'd say that will be two. If the little one survives."

We walk down the rutted path toward the intersection with the road to the Dungeness dock. The ranger stops suddenly, leans over, and picks something up.

"Hold out your hand," she says to Rhamy. Rhamy does, and the ranger drops something into it.

"Shark's tooth," she says.

It's small, triangular in shape, less than an inch long.

"Lemon shark," the ranger says. "A souvenir from your visit. Or it could be from a sand shark. If you find a big one, that'll be from a Great White. Sometimes you'll see them washed up on the beach."

Rhamy closes her fingers around the tooth and we continue on our way, looking for more sharks' teeth.

"They're hard to spot," the ranger says, "unless you know what you're looking for."

We reach the crossroads, Sea Camp directly ahead, Dungeness dock to our left.

"Come on the Plum Orchard tour next Sunday," the ranger says. "We take a boat from Sea Camp. It's about ten miles up the coast. There's no playhouse, but Nancy loved to spend time there. She liked to garden, especially flowers. She won prizes for her hollyhocks and delphiniums. The family lived in Kentucky for most of the year, on the Johnston estate, but they came back to Plum Orchard every year at Christmastime and again in the summer. Nancy always wanted to come back to Cumberland. It's like she drew strength from being here."

"I know what you mean," Rhamy says. "This is my third visit. I can't imagine not coming back. If for some reason we couldn't make it, at least once a year, I'd feel like something was missing from my life. I feel alive when I'm on the island, like this is where I was meant to be."

"Maybe we can join your tour this summer," I tell the ranger. "We're coming back in June, this time with the whole family."

We part then, the ranger heading off to Sea Camp, Rhamy and I to the water faucet where we can wash the muck and the salt off our legs and I can clean my Crocs.

We're on the starboard side of the ferry as we travel down the Cumberland Sound, and somehow, our Blackberries are able to access a cell tower on the mainland. Both Rhamy and I have four bars.

We could send a message to Charlie, but if we did, he might respond, and our visit to Cumberland would be over. We'd be back on the mainland. We'd rather stay on the island a bit longer, pore over the lives of those who lived here and whose names come up when rangers tell the stories of how they changed the island, and how the island is now erasing those changes.

Rhamy Googles the Earl of Yarmouth. "His name was George Francis Alexander Seymour," she announces. "He was heir to the estate of Hertford, though the 'estate' part had been lost to creditors. When he arrived in New York, he was penniless. He found work as a bartender, actor, writer, dancer, and transvestite."

"Where are you getting that?" I ask.

"Newspaper articles," she says. "*Impecunious Bridegroom Arrested on His Wedding Day.*"

"Impecunious?"

"Broke," she says, and she scrolls down to read the article.

Alice Thaw was not the first woman he courted, we learn, but she was the richest and the most willing. Financial arrangements between the two families were agreed upon. Papers were signed. Then came that fateful day and the terrible indignities to which he was subjected.

"...Yarmouth, in his glad wedding garments, came out of the elevator and was seized..."

Adversity can lead to opportunity. The perfumed and powdered actor, scion of English nobility, saw a chance to turn the affair to his advantage. With the guests waiting at the church, and the constable determined to carry him off to jail if he did not come up with the money owed his London creditors, the earl announced that, unless the Thaws were prepared to double the annual amount he was to receive, he would refuse to go through with the wedding. Instead of $5,000 a year, now he wanted $10,000. Furthermore, if Alice were to die without issue, her entire fortune would go to the Hertford estate.

Harry Thaw, Alice's older brother, the person who had introduced the earl to his sister, wanted to chuck the whole thing. Send the guests home, and see the earl imprisoned.

But there was Alice, waiting at Calvary Episcopal Church with her wedding party, Nancy Carnegie among them in her white chiffon dress and straw hat decorated with ostrich feathers. Guests from the richest and most aristocratic families on the East Coast filled the church. The wedding march was played over and over again.

The Thaws caved. Their lawyers hastily drew up new documents and laid them before the parties. Harry wrote a check and handed it to the constable.

Alice, wearing a magnificent gown of ivory satin, stood at the altar beside this painted scalawag, and the marriage was solemnized. Afterwards, the bride gave each of her attendants a bracelet made of diamonds and amethysts.

Rhamy looks up. "*New York Times*, April 30th, 1903," she says.

"You added some details."

She shrugs. "I just filled in some of the blank spots. They spelled the word jail 'g-a-o-l.' I wonder if that's a typo."

"They didn't use the word *scalawag*, did they?"

"No, but it fits."

"*Scoundrel* would have been better."

"*Blackguard* would be nice."

"That's pretty old-fashioned. How about *villain?*"

"Yep. I like that. *Villain*. But I'm gonna stick with *scalawag*. I think that's the best description of the Earl of Yarmouth."

We sit on the bench that curves around the side of the ship, watching the birds that follow in our wake, the marker buoys that keep us in navigable waters, the uninhabited islands that glide by.

"Five years later," Rhamy says, again reading from her Blackberry, "Alice asked the London courts to grant her an annulment on the grounds that the marriage had never been consummated. The earl did not refute the charge, and the annulment was granted."

Several passengers are crowding around us, leaning close to where we sit. This is salacious material.

Rhamy scrolls until she finds more articles: "The earl was a guest at Plum Orchard when Alice's mother announced their engagement.

"On the morning he was to be married, he neglected to pay the customary fee of fifty cents for the marriage license. When reminded, he peeled off a bill and told the clerk to keep the change."

Another article tells of a lawsuit lodged against him by a valet alleging nonpayment of wages. Still another tells of a rumor that the earl had previously proposed to Alice Thaw's niece but had been turned down.

Enough about the earl. We search for other stories. We learn that Marius Johnston once owned the famous racehorse Saracen, but sold him when he was a yearling. The four children Nancy bore her first husband changed their names from Hever to Johnston. When the children swam in the ocean, Marius often accompanied them, and he brought his gun with him. Sharks had been known to venture into the shallow waters near the beach.

Our fellow passengers begin to lose interest, but Rhamy and I are insatiable.

I look for a copy of Lucy's will: did she really have her lawyers include a provision that all her horses were to be set free when she died? That they would wander the island and breed with the wild ponies? If such a document exists, either it's not on the internet, or I haven't used the right words in my Google search.

I wonder if Marius Johnston's experiment with his Thoroughbred stallion had given Lucy the idea of freeing her horses. Or did she love them so much she wanted them to live out their lives on the island, as she planned to do, and as she hoped her children might.

Did she lie in her bed at night, and hear the wild stallions from the different bands whinnying to her pampered pets, and they answering back?

Another Google item: Lucy Carnegie, having lost her husband, wanted to keep her children close. She promised to build houses for them when they married. Plum Orchard was the home she built for her son George, who married Margaret

Thaw, older sister of Alice Thaw, who married the Earl of Yarmouth, whose real name....

We talk of these things, Rhamy and I, as the island recedes and we approach the mainland.

Always our conversation drifts back to the horses, free to roam the island, the high mortality rate of the foals, the lack of good pasture, parasites and mites, skin diseases, the shortened life span. Just as the horses must pay a price for their freedom, so must the people. If Nancy who married the stable boy was a disappointment to her mother, at some point they reconciled; it was Nancy who was by her mother's side when Lucy's favorite child, Coleman, died.

In the end, we decide, in the final analysis, life on Cumberland is worth it.

"A bracelet of diamonds and amethysts," Rhamy says, and she leans back, head against the side of the ferry, eyes closed, a half-smile on her face.

The town of St. Marys with its white picket fences, wide streets, and ancient trees dripping with Spanish moss is within sight.

"What color is amethyst?" Rhamy asks. We're in the car, heading west on Osborne Road, on our way to the interstate.

"Purple," I answer. "The color of wisteria." I point to a vine that has climbed the side of a stone church, obscuring an entire corner of the building. Clusters of lavender flowers hang suspended from branches that cling to shutters, rain spouts, and gutters. The grass beneath the vine is covered with spent blooms.

"Wow," Rhamy says. "How could one plant produce so many flowers? Let's turn around and go back. I'd like to see what they smell like."

But the sun is nearing the horizon, and we have an hour's drive ahead of us. Charlie will be anxious about us, not to mention ready to go to dinner.

"Call Daddy and tell him to pick out a restaurant," I tell her.

But she has other things on her mind. "The ranger said the bridesmaids carried bouquets of white and purple lilacs," she says. "That's the reason for the amethyst bracelets. Alice's wedding colors were white and purple. She would have had the bracelets specially made for her attendants. I wonder what happened to the one she gave Nancy? Did Nancy have daughters she might have given it to?"

I have no answer, but it occurs to me she might have sold it to support her first husband.

"Alice Shaw's wedding took place in April, 1903," Rhamy muses. "Nancy Carnegie came back from overseas with her baby two years later, 1905, so she'd have been married in 1904. When Andrew Carnegie told reporters he'd rather his niece marry a poor, deserving young man than a worthless duke, he'd have known about the earl and how he treated poor Alice."

"It puts his comments about the 'worthless duke' in a different light, doesn't it?"

The road has narrowed from four lanes separated by a tree-lined center area to two lanes. The stately homes of St. Marys have been replaced with strip malls, gas stations, and fast-food franchises.

"A scandal like that," I continue, "poor Alice left at the altar, her family in effect blackmailed, it makes sense that America's aristocrats were becoming disillusioned with British royalty. But doesn't it make you wonder how many other young girls living in the Gilded Age were encouraged by their mothers to try to attract these impoverished earls and dukes? It can't have started with Alice Thaw. And what was the motivation: did having a countess or baroness in their midst give these families a profile they might otherwise not have had? Why the fascination with royalty?"

Rhamy doesn't answer, and I look over at her. She's reading something on her Blackberry.

"Nancy Carnegie Hever Johnston had five children," she says. "Two girls and three boys. The girls were named Margaret and Lucy." She sighs. "It doesn't say which one got the bracelet."

"You didn't really expect to find that on the internet, did you?"

"You can buy them on Amazon," she says. "Diamond and amethyst bracelets. Want to see a picture?" She holds the cell phone toward me, and I glance at the screen.

"They're priced anywhere from $25.00 to... here's one for just over $6,000."

"Shall I tell Connor that's what you want for Christmas?"

"I really like this one," she says.

The road ahead of me is clear, and I glance again at the picture. It's a thin bracelet of white gold, the jewels spaced around the chain, each one small and delicate and lovely.

"It's you," I tell her. "Put it in my cart."

"No," she says. "It's too much money."

"How much?"

But she's clicked away from the website and is on to other things.

We know we're nearing St. Simons when we see the silver cables of the Sidney Lanier Bridge. From I-25 the pylons rising out of the Brunswick River look like giant H's, cradling the concrete slabs that form the bed of the bridge. The cables run in perfect symmetry from the columns to the sides of the structure. When you are in their midst, you feel safe.

The causeway leading up to the bridge curves as it rises, and it holds you captive. Once you're on it, you can't change your mind. You have no choice but to go to the top.

Several years ago three pedestrians out for a morning jog had to run for their lives when a tow-truck driver lost control of his vehicle, smashed into the center barrier, veered to the opposite side and dumped his load into the river. Locals who walk across the bridge are fewer now, and they're a bit more watchful.

When you reach the top, it's a thrill to see the watery landscape spread out before you. There's the salt marsh, great stretches of it, and dozens of streams that cut through it. Beyond that, the intracoastal waterway.

The bridge is a marvel of engineering. The view from the top is our reward, though it means we've left Cumberland Island behind.

Later tonight, when we're at dinner, we'll explain to Charlie how it is that Lucy Carnegie was related to the Thaws through her Coleman cousins, and how CNN's Anderson Cooper is related to the Carnegies through his Vanderbilt mother. We'll tell him how Thomas Carnegie wanted to buy land on Jekyll Island, but there were plans afoot for a group of wealthy businessmen to establish a hunting club there. It would be the richest and the most inaccessible club in the world. Membership would be limited and exclusive.

If members wanted to build vacation "cottages," they could do so, but these "cottages" were to be modest and unpretentious. It wouldn't do for someone to build a mansion when the point of the Jekyll Island development was to build small vacation homes and winter retreats. There were many millionaires with families whose blood ran blue. The Carnegie money was newly earned. Thomas and Andrew Carnegie were foreign born; they'd been brought to the United States as children.

Rebuffed by the developers, Thomas and Lucy bought Dungeness with its 4,000 acres, and they cast a net for other land on Cumberland. In time, the Carnegies came to own all but the very northern tip of the island. Lucy, a widow by then, was satisfied. The slight, if there had been one, was avenged. Let the hundred or so paid members of the Jekyll Island Club build their modest homes where they could spend their winters. Lucy had her own island, it was a mere stepping stone away from theirs, and she could build what she wanted.

We'll explain to Charlie how the Carnegies demolished the Dungeness mansion built by Caty Greene and smoothed out the several hundred years' accumulation of oyster shells. When the new foundation was laid, the base of the building was nineteen feet above sea level. From there it rose a hundred feet into the air. When Lucy Carnegie climbed to the tower, she had a panoramic view of the salt marshes and the ocean beyond. The house became a landmark for sailors far out at sea.

I think Charlie will be impressed. Come June, he'll be able to tell Connor and Matt all about the history of the island. Rhamy and I can listen in. If he gets something wrong, we won't correct him.

17

Madeleine decides, at the last minute, she can't come to St. Simons. She's too busy at work. She can't afford to be away for a whole week. If it were later in the summer, she might have been able to make it.

It's not later in the summer, and if it were, Rhamy and Connor couldn't make it, or Kate and Matt and the kids. Or Charlie and I would have a conflict.

"I'll come next year," she says. "I promise."

"But we've been planning this for months," I argue. "Who knows what could happen by next year? When will we ever be able to get all of us together again?"

"I'm not sure I want to go back to Cumberland Island," she says. "I was already there once."

This is heresy. How could she not want to go? Didn't we have a great time, just the two of us? But I think I understand. The family is too big, too diverse, too scattered. When we're all together, we pull at each other. Her sisters treat her like the baby of the family, which of course she is. But she's been out in the world, on her own, for five years. She bounced from job to job until she found one she loves. She's survived. She resents it when her sisters give her advice, or they tease her, or they ask questions she does not want to answer.

I try to keep peace, and mostly I'm successful, but on occasion, someone says something hurtful, feelings are bruised, one of the girls needs time away from the others. I understand. Still I yearn for connection, for the way things used to be.

"Remember when we climbed the dunes, Madeleine, and we walked all the way to the ocean? We had no idea how far it was, and what would we do if got lost, and we missed the ferry back to the mainland? We can do that again, walk across the island. We'll bring our bathing suits this time. We can rent bicycles at Sea Camp, ride all the way to the north end of the island, see the Settlement, those chimneys that are all that's left of the slave quarters from before the Civil War. With all of us there, it'll be wonderful."

But all of us there is exactly what she does not want. Her mind is made up. She will not be persuaded.

The two condos we've rented are a disappointment. They're supposed to be next door to one another, and they are, but they're back to back. To get from one to the other, you have to go out onto the landing, down a flight of stairs, past both buildings, and up another flight. The complex itself is old. Everything is in need of fresh paint, new carpeting, modern appliances. The gate to the swimming pool is chained and padlocked. The workout facility has just two treadmills and a stationary bike. Our neighbors on the bedroom side of our condo keep their TV at max volume late into the night, and the walls are thin.

We've only been on the island for two days when the news breaks that Michael Jackson is dead. We rush back from the fishing pier to our condo and turn on the TV. They're showing footage of the hospital where he was taken. They're playing his music, over and over again: "Thriller," "Beat It," and "Billie Jean." Fans are crying. His personal physician is being questioned.

It takes us back to the world we left. Reporters churn up all those old rumors about Jackson's obsession with little boys, his Neverland Ranch, his comeback tour, his debts. None of this belongs on our island. It is an intrusion.

Outside, it's raining, and there's rain in the forecast for the next several days. If we're to go to Cumberland, there's only a short window. Kate and Matt have to be back in Auburn by Monday.

We'll go tomorrow, I decide. But in the morning, it's pouring rain. Cumberland is impossible.

The Grand Dining Room at the Jekyll Island Club closed at 2 p.m., but the host will be happy to seat us in the sun room. With a fluid movement of his hands he indicates the way. I wonder if we're being shuffled off to a room less elegant, more suitable for tourists. Counting Kate's two kids, we're a party of eight, though Lucas is only nine months old. We're all dripping wet. We've been to the Georgia Sea Turtle Center, and when we exited the rehab section of the facility, we had to run through pouring rain to get to our cars.

The host follows us into the room, pulls out a chair from a round table. "High chair for the little girl?" he asks, his gaze shifting from me to Kate.

Riley, four years old, frowns. She thinks she's too old for a high chair.

"Booster," Kate says.

"And the baby?"

"He'll be fine in his infant seat," Matt answers.

The room is circular, windows all around, with a view of manicured grounds, salt marsh, and river beyond. A sailing ship is making its way toward St. Simons Sound. If this is a room meant for tourists with kids, I can't object.

Once, when the Jekyll Island Club admitted only club members and their guests, there were three dining rooms: one for men, one for adults of both sexes, and a third for families with children. If guests had been hunting, fishing, crabbing, or gathering oysters during the day, they surrendered their catch to the chefs, and it would appear on the menu that evening or the next day.

After the crash of '29, the club fell into decline. Yachts that once sailed from ports in Boston, New York, and Philadelphia now made the trip less frequently. Special trains from Chicago had fewer cars than before. The Club held on through the '30s, though its financial situation became more and more precarious.

Soup kitchens and bread lines appeared in churches, missions, and fire stations across the nation. A drought of biblical proportions hit the West, and the monster winds that accompanied it picked up tons of topsoil. The skies turned black, and the dust fell on New York and Washington, and on ships at sea. Thousands of banks closed their doors, wiping out the savings of millions of Americans. The nation was in utter despair.

The Depression affected even the very wealthy. Membership in an exclusive island club began to be seen as an extravagance, an indelicate if not indecent display of wealth and privilege. Between 1929 and 1931, half the members of the Jekyll Island Club left. Many simply quit coming, preferring to spend the winter months in the cold climates of the North. Some declined to pay their dues, and their names were removed from the membership list. Some could not pay. The Club fell into disrepair. Membership dropped from a high of 150 in its heyday to fewer than a dozen.

In April of 1942, a German submarine torpedoed two unarmed oil tankers off the coast of St. Simons. The explosions shattered windows in Brunswick. Twenty-three crewmen were lost. Debris from the sunken tankers washed ashore on Jekyll. Thick, black oil fouled the beaches. The Club shut down for good.

Five years later the state of Georgia purchased the entire island and everything on it for $675,000. The people of Georgia now owned the remains of the old plantation homes, the dilapidated Club House, and the cottages built by the likes of Joseph Pulitzer, Richard Crane, and Frank Henry Goodyear.

Even in those hard times, the state was able to raise the money to build a six-mile causeway over the marshes and a vertical-lift bridge across the Brunswick River. Once the island was accessible only by boat; now visitors could drive from the mainland directly onto Jekyll.

That's what we did a few hours ago. After stopping at the Visitor Center to pay the access fee, we drove to the north end of the island and walked along Driftwood Beach. Photographers from all over the world come there to take pictures of the ever-changing configurations of driftwood. Across the waters we could see the St. Simons Lighthouse, the King and Prince hotel, and the fishing pier.

On your way back to Jekyll's historic district, we stopped at the William Horton plantation house, a tabby structure built in the 1740s. Its former inhabitants are at rest in the nearby cemetery.

The Jekyll Island complex was designated a historic landmark in 1978. Several years later a group of investors leased the club from the state of Georgia. They spent millions to restore it to something approaching its original grandeur.

Chefs from Delmonico's are no longer cooking the game that club members shot, hooked, seined, or trapped, but the hotel is proud of its offerings. Our host hands menus all around and indicates items we can still order: island crab cakes, poached pear salad, sea scallops, rotisserie chicken salad, Jekyll shrimp and grits, Rockefeller club, veggie croissant.

Riley wants chicken fingers and French fries. The waiter arches his eyebrows, then nods his head. Surely the kitchen can accommodate. He moves around the table. He has no pad, no pencil. A second waiter brings water goblets filled to the brim and topped with lemon circles.

Riley, who caught a glimpse of the swimming pool when we drove up, wants to see it. Kate brought bathing suits for both kids, but swimming at the condo on St. Simons seems doubtful. If the management ever removes the chain from the pool gate, Kate will want to be certain the water is properly chlorinated, safe for the kids to swim. She's a careful mother. A germaphobe, Riley calls her, a word she learned from her father.

No such worries here. The hotel is thriving since it reopened as a resort hotel in 1986. The pool will be meticulously clean, life guards on duty, stacks of hotel towels available for anyone who needs them. I haven't the heart to tell Riley the pool is reserved for guests only. But we can at least visit. I glance at Kate, wanting permission to take her daughter on a tour of the building. She nods. Charlie wants to come, too. He gets up from his chair and follows us out of the room.

We head toward the grand dining room, Riley between us. *Grand* is the right word to describe it, with its ionic columns, twelve-foot ceilings, oak wainscoting, fireplaces with marble surrounds and intricately carved mantle pieces. The hotel is a labyrinth of hallways, shops, cozy reading nooks. The original barbershop, smoking room for the gentlemen, and parlor for the ladies have been replaced with modern shops that sell newspapers and magazines, bathing attire, sunblock, snacks, and personal items. We find our way to the pool, careful to stay under the awning. There's a Poolside Grill, closed now because of the rain.

"Can we come back tomorrow and go swimming?" Riley asks.

"Maybe," I tell her, and I look at Charlie. Can we just sit by the pool and have a drink? Surely no one would mind.

He shrugs, which I take to mean he's willing, if the weather cooperates.

We visit the pub located on the lower floor of the hotel. You can have a beer, cocktails, and snacks while you're watching the sporting event of your choice on the big-screen TVs. In the long hallway there are dozens of stuffed animal heads, trophies bagged by Club members long ago. I hold tight to Riley's hand and we hurry past. She'd like to stop and look at the pictures: there are photos of kids on bicycles, riders on horseback, ladies picnicking on the beach. Interspersed among them are photographs of slaughtered deer hanging from hooks, men standing over dead boars, one very happy hunter smiling broadly at the camera while holding up two dead turkeys.

The original club members liked to hunt. They liked it so much the Club employed a gamekeeper to manage the wildlife on the island. He corralled and sold off the long-horned cattle that roamed the island, sent the feral horses to Thomas Carnegie at Cumberland, and stocked the island with pheasants, turkeys, quail, and deer.

The three of us climb the stairs and head toward the sun room. Passing through the hotel lobby, Charlie hesitates. He looks at me, and I know what he's thinking. He wants to ask how much it costs to spend the night.

It's something he often does: if we're staying at a Hampton Inn and there's a four-star hotel nearby, like the Grove Park Inn in Asheville or the Peabody Hotel in Memphis, he'll go up to the desk and ask their rates. I used to be embarrassed when he did it; wasn't it J.P. Morgan, a member of this Club, who, when asked about the cost of operating his yacht, responded with the infamous quotation: "If you have to ask, you can't afford it." I never want to give a clerk the chance to make a judgment like that about me.

But with Charlie, something else is at play. It all goes back to when he was a teenager, and he caddied for golfers at the Shaker Heights Country Club. *Cosmopolitan* had named Shaker Heights, the Cleveland suburb where he grew up, the wealthiest community in the country.

Charlie hated every minute of his caddying job. It seemed so silly to him, grown men and women trying to knock a ball into a hole. But what he found deeply offensive was having to cater to the whims of these executives and scions of wealth. He hated it that he was a faceless nothing to them, someone who would do their bidding for the few dollar bills they would hand him when they'd finished their game.

Shortly after we married, we were invited to a dinner at that same country club. Charlie drove past the valets waiting to park our car. The Cadillacs were lined up in the front row of the parking lot, their grilles all facing out. Any car not a Cadillac was parked in the back row. Charlie was driving the Chevy Nova we'd bought a few months before. He drove past the valets, between the two rows of cars, then pulled into a spot in the front row. He touched my arm to tell me to stay put, got out of the car, and walked around to open my door.

We walked up to the club entrance, my arm in his, and when we passed the valets he nodded to them.

"You cheated them out of a tip," I told him as we stepped inside the club. "And, you messed up their system. All those Cadillacs, lined up in a row, and one, lonely Chevrolet."

He took my jacket and handed it to the coat check girl. "They needed a little diversity," he said. "Besides, there were cars in that back row worth a lot more than those Cadillacs. I saw at least two Mercedes."

The day would come when he would buy a Mercedes, and he drove it for several years. When Rhamy was in high school, he gave it to her and bought himself a new one. Then he switched to Camrys, and he's just as happy.

I for one am glad we never bought a Cadillac. If I had one, I wouldn't know where to park it. They're such boats. The women who drive them are too often draped in furs and dripping with jewels. That's not me. I grew up on a farm. I milked cows before I went to school in the morning.

Besides, Camrys are awfully good cars.

Riley and I walk down the main hallway, admiring the bathing suits, beach wraps, and sun hats displayed in shop windows. We stop to gaze at pictures taken a hundred years ago: an elderly woman in a short skirt aiming a rifle. A man and a woman posing with their tennis racquets. Four men in a gasoline-powered dune buggy racing along the beach. A lady dressed for a party, riding sidesaddle. Ships unloading supplies at the wharf, horses and carts waiting to haul them away. Frolicking dogs. A man holding a cat. An elderly couple seated in wicker chairs by a window, reading. A portrait of four young girls, all wearing long, white dresses, all with their hair pinned up. Golfers. Skeet shooters. Yachts at anchor. Five men gathered around a table, one speaking into a telephone. The caption tells us the first transcontinental phone call was made from Jekyll Island on January 25, 1915.

Charlie catches up with us outside the lobby bar. "We can rent the presidential suite for just under $500 a night," he says. "They have rooms available in the Crane and the Cherokee Cottages."

"How much?"

"The one in the Cherokee is a king suite," he says. "Same price as the presidential suite."

"Sounds like a bargain," I tell him. "But we'll need at least three rooms. Did they offer a discount?"

"I'll go ask," he says. But of course he's joking. I turn to Riley, who is fingering a beaded headband. "Try it on," I tell her.

She does, and she turns her head this way and that in front of the mirror, and the headband sparkles against her blonde hair.

"I like it," she says, looking up at me. "Will you ask my mom if she'll buy it for me?"

"I think she'd want you to have it. Why don't I just pay for it now, and you can surprise her when we get back to the table?"

Charlie has gone off to look for a book on the history of the island. And to buy a new hat, preferably one that is waterproof. He wants to visit some of the cottages in Jekyll's historic district. Surely we'll be able to walk on the beach and go for a swim in the ocean at some point. It can't rain all four days we're here.

Just outside the sun room, I catch a glimpse of a picture I hadn't noticed before. A group of men are gathered around a banquet table. The centerpiece is a forest of flowers, candles, and greenery. Strands of ivy cascade from the chandelier to the table and trail between the place settings to the floor.

To the left of each charger plate is a fish fork, dinner fork, and salad fork. To the right a dinner knife, fish knife, fruit spoon, and oyster fork. At the tip of the dinner knife a water goblet, red wine glass, white wine glass, and champagne flute. Butter plate with knife above the forks.

There are at least sixteen men seated or standing around the table.

And one woman.

The caption beneath the picture says the dinner was given in honor of Andrew Carnegie, and that it was probably taken in 1903. Lucy Carnegie, owner of Cumberland Island, had likely accompanied her brother-in-law to Jekyll for the occasion, it states. Carnegie is seated fourth from the left, next to Joseph Pulitzer.

Riley has no interest. She runs ahead, into the sun room, to join her family and to show off her new headband.

The picture is grainy. I step closer to get a better look. I love old pictures. I love what you can see if you really examine them, love the things you discover if you truly look at the subjects and try to think why they're doing the things they're doing. It is clearly posed. Four chairs directly in front of the photographer are empty. The men standing behind the other diners were likely asked to give up their seats, and to move around the room so everyone would fit into the picture. One man has a walrus mustache. He looks angry, as if he'd like to get on with dinner. Another is nearly hidden behind a Tiffany lamp. None are smiling. Only one man is wearing a vest beneath his dinner jacket: Andrew Carnegie.

The woman is so unobtrusive, I almost miss her. But once I see her, her presence becomes a mystery that tantalizes me. The neckline of her dress reveals more than a woman would normally reveal in the early 1900s. The fabric looks heavy. Velvet, perhaps. Young women usually wore lacy dresses with high necklines. This woman is not young. Nor is she old.

Carnegie has a full beard, neatly trimmed. He's looking directly into the camera, his head slightly upturned. There's an air of confidence about him. A fearlessness. Directness. This is how he would have looked when he told the reporter he'd rather his niece marry an honest, hard-working man than a worthless duke. Wanting there to be no doubt about his words, he'd repeated them. "A worthless duke," he said to the reporter. "Make sure you get that in there. A worthless duke." After Thomas Carnegie died, Andrew often visited Dungeness, sailing his yacht past Jekyll south to Cumberland to visit the family his brother had left behind. Always careful with his money, he often chided Lucy for her spendthrift ways, her constant building projects, her lavish entertaining, her yachts.

Did Andrew feel a sense of responsibility for his dead brother's wife, or did he come to Dungeness because of his love for her and her children? What of the rumor that he once proposed to Lucy Ackerman Coleman, and she turned him down to marry his younger, more handsome brother? When Thomas was in his grave, and Lucy was alone, he reportedly asked again. Again she rejected him.

The woman seated across the table from Andrew Carnegie can't be Lucy Coleman Carnegie. Despite the caption beneath the picture, the graininess of the photo, the sepia tone, the poor lighting, it can't be Lucy. Her hair is too dark, her nose too straight. That décolletage.

I remember the Lucy Coleman Carnegie who stood on the veranda at Dungeness, surrounded by her nine children. This is not the same woman.

I hear footsteps behind me. I turn. It's the man who showed us to our table.

"That's Andrew Carnegie," he says, looking at the picture. "The dinner was held in his honor. He was never actually a member of the Club, but he visited here rather frequently."

He rocks back on his heels and goes on: "The Carnegies owned Cumberland Island, you know. The younger brother bought it in the early 1880s. It's just five miles from here. Andrew Carnegie used to visit there several times a year. When he was at Dungeness—that's what they called the mansion—he would often bring the whole family up to the Club for dinner. There were a bunch of them, nine children. They'd all climb aboard his yacht and sail up the Atlantic."

"Who's the woman? It's not Lucy, is it?"

"The caption would suggest…"

"It says Lucy likely accompanied Andrew…"

He leans forward and studies the picture carefully. "I always assumed it was Lucy. But maybe not. It could be Frances Emma Baker," he says. "Wife of Frederic Baker. They owned Soltera, one of the cottages here. That's where the dinner was held. Or, it might be Andrew's wife, Louise Whitfield. They were engaged, off and on, for something like ten years, but his mother didn't approve. After Mrs. Carnegie died, they married. Andrew was fairly old by then, over fifty. Louise was quite a bit younger."

"Children?"

"One daughter, Margaret, born ten years later." He pauses, studying the picture, then goes on: "Andrew was quite a yachtsman, you know. So was his sister-in-law, Lucy. Sometimes they'd come on his yacht, sometimes on hers. There are pictures of *Skibo* — that's what he called his yacht — in several of the history books we sell in our bookstore."

"And Lucy's yacht? What was it called?"

"*Dungeness*," he says. "Back then there was no access to the island except by boat. So it made sense to own your own, if you could afford it."

"And they could," I answer.

The distance this head waiter has kept between us, his careful demeanor, his deliberate choice of words, has dissolved. Before all this opulence of a world that once existed here, we are equals, two people standing at a point in history, looking into the past. Then he lifts his head and straightens his back.

"Your lunch is ready to be served," he says. "We've been holding it in the kitchen."

There is, in his voice, a hint of disapproval. We've kept the staff waiting. We've created disorder in a place that values order, and timeliness, and deep respect for tradition.

Sometime around midnight there's a downpour, and then it's over. By morning, the skies are clear. Dawn breaks gloriously over the island, the sun slanting through the blinds into the kitchen, spilling onto the countertops. I make coffee, pour a cup, carry it out to the landing, down the stairs, past the building, stopping a moment to smell the clean washed air and to feel the warmth of the sun before climbing the stairs to Kate and Matt's condo.

Kate answers the door. Lucas is sitting on the floor by the couch, holding his blanket, crying. "He's caught a cold," Kate says, "and he's miserable. I was up with him half the night. I think I'm gonna call his pediatrician."

I set my coffee on the end table and pick him up. We walk to the window. He's warm and he smells of urine and fabric softener, though Kate never uses fabric softener. Who knows what chemicals might be in it, and what harm it might do to her children.

I point to the outdoor pool and tell Lucas things that are not true. "There's a kiddie pool for babies just like you," I tell him, "and tonight after dinner we'll take you down there and you'll love splashing in the water. We'll bring your rubber duckie and a float and a swimming tube."

He stops crying, interested in my voice and in the view of the pool.

"Your mom brought a special bathing suit that is just perfect for a little boy who's still in diapers, and it'll be so much fun."

Kate is in the kitchen. Even from that distance, I hear her sigh.

Always, with this baby, my daughter goes back to those first weeks of his life, his constant crying, his balled-up fists, the fever that would not break. Though he was just over a week old, hardly home from the hospital, he seemed consumed with pain or anger, no way to tell which. Kate could do nothing to comfort him. He only slept when he had exhausted himself with crying.

Back to the hospital, a spinal tap, a diagnosis of viral meningitis. All she could do was try to soothe him and trust in the medical expertise of the doctors. But there was that odd smell of frying bacon. Why on earth would a hospital smell like that? How could kitchen smells waft all the way out into the parking lot and onto the street? What was it about that hospital? I'd noticed it when I first arrived. Not clean, I thought. Something was wrong.

So it was easy to blame the hospital for what this baby was going through, might never recover from. But where else could Kate and Matt turn for help? They had no option but to trust the hospital that smelled of bacon. And in the end, baby Lucas was fine, but the family had been traumatized, and in ways that can never be determined with any certitude, changed.

He's a sturdy little boy now, just beginning to walk, no ill effects, but he came so close. For Kate, it's always there in the back of her mind. He might have died. Lots of babies diagnosed with meningitis die. Lucas lived, and now she can take no chances.

I understand. Cumberland Island fades. She will not come with us. If the old stallion, the one we called Adam, is still alive, she won't ever look at him with that critical eye of one trained in animal care, won't give us her assessment of the herd, won't point out things Rhamy and I would never notice.

In truth, I can't explain why I want that from her. I only know that if we all go to Cumberland Island, see the wild horses together, it would add a new dimension to the stories we as a family share. It would restore a link that has tarnished with the passage of time, mend a cord that has frayed.

"What about Riley?" I ask, putting Lucas down on the floor. "Can we take her? Rhamy's told her so much about the wild horses, the foals, the ferry ride from St. Marys. I think she'd love to go."

But Kate is worried her daughter will never be able to walk all the way to the beach.

"Is it really three miles across the island?" she asks. "She'll never make it. One of you would have to carry her."

"We can do that. We can take turns."

She wavers; "If we all went, Matt could carry Lucas in his backpack carrier. But it's almost July, the heat will be awful, humidity, bugs, it just doesn't seem like a good idea. The second ferry leaves when? 11:45? Is there even time to pack lunches and drive all the way to St. Marys?"

"We'll go swimming in the ocean," I tell her. "Riley will love that. Has she ever seen the ocean? There's nothing like the Cumberland beach. And the live oaks on the island, they're just amazing. The limbs are absolutely parallel to the earth, and they're just begging for a kid to climb, to sit on the branches."

"The dunes, how high are they? What's it like walking across them? You said there was a boardwalk part of the way, but you have to climb dunes that are huge? It sounds like too much."

At some point, she'd like to take the kids back to the Georgia Sea Turtle Museum on Jekyll. They'd loved the skeleton of the prehistoric sea turtle suspended from the ceiling of the gift shop. We were so pressed for time, had gone through the museum so quickly, they'd missed much of it. There were games for the kids that teach them about sea turtles. And a section where injured turtles are brought to be treated and released back into the ocean. We'd barely had time to see it.

Matt, always the sensible one, always one to stand back and survey the situation, says there's a front moving in later this afternoon. Rain is forecast for the entire Florida peninsula.

He shows Kate the radar weather pattern on his computer. "I'd hate to be caught on an island with no shelter," he says.

"What would we do if we were there, and Lucas started running a fever?" Kate asks. "Why don't we just take the kids to the swimming pool down by the pier? Neptune Park?"

I carry my empty coffee cup back to our condo.

Our new plan is for Rhamy and me to take Connor on a grand tour of the island. We'll lead him through the live oak forest to the ruined mansion, past the collapsing recreation building to the carriage house, on to the cars that are sinking into the ground, to the graveyard where Bernard Davis and his son rest and where Light Horse Harry Lee was once buried. Then on to the Atlantic. Along the way we'll show him horses that roam free on the island, foals born in the spring, bachelor groups watching for a chance to snag a mare and start a band of their own. We'll tell him everything we know about Cumberland and its history, and surely he'll fall in love with the island as much as we have.

The seashell road is full of horse droppings. A fairly large band has passed through recently. We pick our way past steaming piles of manure.

Connor knows more about building and home construction than anyone I know. He can do a walk-through on a house and tell you how long before you'll have to replace the HVAC system, the roof, the hot-water heater. A few minutes in the basement and he'll know if termites have eaten away at the timbers, if there is moisture, and if the electrical system is up to code.

A realtor, Connor sells everything from bungalows that date from the early 1900s to million-dollar homes built as "infills" on tiny city lots. Portland is a city more European than American with its sidewalks, close-in housing, mom-and-pop shops with living quarters above, and family-owned restaurants. It's a city that preserves its past, would never think of tearing down in order to build something bigger, glitzier, more modern.

The Dungeness mansion is unlike anything he's ever seen before. This is Gilded Age opulence, dismantled by taxes, changing mores, family feuds, and fortunes frittered away. Ultimately, it is the inexorable pull of nature that will bring it all down. Given enough time, nature will put things right on the island.

Connor moves out from beneath the canopy of live oaks into the clearing. We follow. The three of us stand on short-cropped grass beneath a blue sky, in awe.

For Rhamy and me, it's always this way. The mansion and the life it represents never lose the power to inspire, to remind us that others have sought the things we seek on this island. It is the place where we come so we might be refreshed.

"They designed it as a Scottish castle," I tell Connor. "Thomas and Lucy Carnegie. It took years to build. Everything had to be shipped from the mainland or from Europe. Fifty-nine rooms. Notice how high the first level is."

"They were thinking of hurricanes," he says. "And storm surges."

"Hurricanes almost never hit these islands," I tell him. "Because of the way the coastline curves inward — they call it the Georgia kink — the winds tend to push storms away from the coast toward the northeast. They're more likely to hit Savannah or Hilton Head or somewhere in New England."

"This was the third Dungeness built on this spot," Rhamy says.

"Named for Dungeness crabs?" he asks. "Like we have in Oregon?"

"No," she answers. "For a fishing village in southern England. Dungeness was the name of James Oglethorpe's county seat, back when he was a member of Parliament. He built a hunting lodge here in 1736. Before that it was a shell midden, left by the Indians."

Connor, clearly, has no idea of the history of the island.

I intervene. "James Oglethorpe was a bit of a reformer. He thought Georgia might be a good place to send people who'd been released from debtors' prisons. They tended to congregate in cities, London especially, and when they couldn't find work, many of them fell back into a life of crime. Oglethorpe thought there might be a better way. He talked Parliament into giving him a charter for a new colony. He brought the first group of settlers to America in 1732 and established the colony of Georgia."

Rhamy picks up the story: "Everyone was welcome — Puritans, Lutherans, Quakers — everyone except Roman Catholics. Not surprising, in light of the religious wars a century earlier. Remember Henry VIII, Defender of the Faith, the one who split from Rome and established the Church of England?"

"Always the Anglophile," Connor says, and he's looking at her with a fondness that tells me he approves. They have a good marriage, I think.

"Next summer I want to go to England again," she says, and I can see the yearning in her eyes. They'd spent six months in the British Isles when they were in college, Rhamy attending Oxford, Connor at Trinity in Dublin.

"Maybe," he says.

"The Spanish down in Florida were all Catholics," I continue, "and they were seen as a bloodthirsty lot. Sure enough, they brought an army north to try to capture this new colony. Oglethorpe led the British forces against them."

"Guess who won?" Rhamy asks.

"Oglethorpe," Connor responds.

"Right. Oglethorpe. Battle of Bloody Marsh, St. Simons Island. The marsh ran red with Spanish blood, they say. Can you imagine a more descriptive name for a battle? Bloody Marsh?" The three of us move closer to the mansion.

"The second Dungeness," Rhamy says, "was built by Catherine Greene, widow of Nathaniel Greene, Revolutionary War hero. It was four stories high. Their daughter Louisa was living in the house when Robert E. Lee's father came here to die. He was on a ship, coming back from the West Indies, and he asked to be put ashore here.

"We'll show you where he was buried," she adds. "It's on the way to the beach."

I go on with the story: "Union soldiers occupied the island during the Civil War, and they lived in the mansion. It burned down in 1866. The locals blamed it on their drunken parties, but they might have been prejudiced. They probably weren't too fond of Union occupiers."

"General William Davis bought the property in 1880..."

"He was a relative of Jefferson Davis," I interject.

"...and he sold it to the Carnegies a year later. Lucy and Thomas Carnegie planned to spend winters here. They knocked down what was left of the Greene house..."

"...the walls were six feet thick at the base..."

"...when Davis sold the property to Thomas Carnegie, he said the foundation was solid, and that he could easily incorporate them into the construction of a new building..."

"...but that's not what happened. They brought in bulldozers..."

Connor looks at me, and he's frowning.

I offer a different version: "they knocked down the foundation walls and started from scratch."

"...Thomas had retired from the business by then..."

"...early retirement; he would have been only 43 or so..."

"...he died in 1886, just five years after he bought the property, long before the mansion was completed."

We walk out into the open, carefully avoiding the piles of fresh horse manure.

"He was supposedly a heavy drinker," I continue, "so maybe cirrhosis of the liver. Some accounts say he died of pneumonia. Others say typhoid, that his mother and brother had both contracted it, and only Andrew survived. No one knows for certain, though."

Rhamy stops to gaze at a band of horses resting in the shade near the recreation building. "The reason you almost always see horses around the mansion," she says, "is that before the Civil War most of the southern part of the island was cleared for cotton. Sea Island cotton. So there's more open land here, more opportunity for grazing."

"Wouldn't you love to walk up those steps?" I ask. "Stand on that veranda?"

Rhamy takes Connor's hand. "Let's not get too close," she says. "Remember what the ranger said, that it's full of rattlesnakes. Diamondback rattlesnakes."

"Is that why Charlie won't come?" Connor asks.

"We've never seen one," I answer. "And the fence might be to keep people from climbing on the rocks. The Park Service could be liable, if someone got hurt."

We stroll around the mansion, and I tell him the rest of the story: that Lucy Carnegie died in 1916 and is buried on the island beside her son Coleman. By 1925 the mansion was vacant. It burned in 1959. Supposedly a poacher came onto the island, and a caretaker shot him in the leg. A few nights later, the mansion went up in flames. They say it lit up the sky, and that you could see the flames all the way to Brunswick.

"They had a yacht anchored down by the dock," I continue. "It was found listing in the water, partially burned."

"What happened to it?" Connor asks. "Did it sink?"

"It's frustrating, the lack of a historical record. No one knows. Someone must, or someone knew at some point, but they're gone, and the memory is gone."

We walk toward the ocean, stopping to gaze at the horses who roam the open fields or rest in shady areas, the car graveyard, the Greene-Miller cemetery by the marsh. Sand dunes studded with blackened tree trunks loom before us.

The tide is out when we reach the Atlantic, the beach so wide and empty, we might be the last people on earth. No one has been here since the ocean rolled up into the dunes during the night, then retreated, taking with it all signs of trespass, leaving behind only its own regurgitations: driftwood, bits of marine life, seashells, the occasional shark's tooth.

The sand has been swept clean, and it is ours. All ours, and ours alone. Civilization has retreated to other parts of the island or other islands or to the mainland. Except for the distant towns on the mainland, there are no signs of life. Even the horses that come to the beach for the cooling sprays are absent.

Yet other forms of life are teeming. Sea gulls congregate on the beach, bickering among themselves. Piping plovers and least terns skitter along in their never-ending search for food. American oystercatchers rush in to grab some tasty morsel and then rush out. A pelican flies overhead, circles, and returns to his perch somewhere in the dunes.

The ocean is calm, the waters lapping tentatively at the shore. It calls to me. Rhamy and I are both wearing bathing suits under our clothes. I kick off my sandals, step out of my shorts, and run toward the ocean. Rhamy is close behind me. Only Connor hangs back.

No wonder. He's wearing hiking boots, shorts, a long-sleeved shirt, and a wide-brimmed hat. In his backpack are our sandwiches, water bottles, granola bars, apples, extra socks, and tablets for purifying water. Connor never goes anywhere without being prepared.

"Come on, Connor," I call to him. "Take off your shoes and come on in. The water feels wonderful. It must be 80 degrees."

He shakes his head. Rhamy, who's wearing a new bikini, begs him to join us, to no avail. He promises instead to keep an eye on our clothing. I tell him how Marius Johnston, Nancy Carnegie's second husband, would bring their children to this same beach, and while the kids frolicked in the ocean he stayed on shore, watching for sharks.

"Do that for us, Connor," I tell him. "Keep an eye out for sharks. Warn us if you see anything, so we can get out of the water."

There is no record of a shark attack anywhere on the island, but he promises to keep watch.

"You could look for loggerhead turtle nests," Rhamy calls to her husband. "Just above the tide line. That's where they lay their eggs."

"We might see some," I tell her, "if we walk down the beach. When they come out of the water, they leave trails in the sand. It's the right time of year. Let's do that. Let's head south, toward Fernandina Beach and Amelia Island."

It's a plan. In the meantime, there's the question of how far out I can go before I reach the point where the ocean drops off, the water so deep it would swallow me if I took one more step. I walk as far as I can, taking careful steps, remembering. I stand on my tiptoes, my head tilted back so I can breathe, and still I don't find it.

Rhamy and I leave the ocean, and the three of us begin walking down the beach. We splash through pools of water, stop to pick up shells, veer into the ocean when the heat overcomes us, return to hard sand when we are cool. The smoke stacks rising from the pulp mills on Amelia Island are visible, but barely. A cloud hangs over that distant island, as if the air has absorbed all the pollutants it can stand, and now has itself become a pollutant. On Cumberland, though, the sun is shining and the air is sweet. When our bathing suits are dry, Rhamy and I pull on our shorts and shirts and resume our trek down the beach. We have hours ahead of us, there's a lovely breeze off the ocean, and I'm with my daughter and her husband. We're happy beyond measure to be in this place. Best of all, Connor seems to understand what it is Rhamy and I love about this place.

"Next year," Rhamy suggests, "let's plan on camping here. We'll bring Daddy. We'll reserve a spot in the campground at Sea Camp. We can stay for two nights or maybe even three. Connor knows everything there is to know about camping. He'll set up the tents and fix gourmet meals and even arrange for hot solar showers. We'll rent bicycles and bike to parts of the island we've never seen before."

I'm skeptical we'll ever get Charlie to go camping, but sometimes he surprises me.

An hour of walking on the beach, the smokestacks on Amelia coming closer and closer, I begin to wonder if it's possible to walk around the southern tip of the island.

"Let's see if we can circumnavigate the island," I suggest. "Let's just keep walking until we come to the trail that leads back to Dungeness."

Connor is skeptical.

"How far can it be?" I ask him. "The Dungeness dock is on the southern part of the island. It's the first stop on the ferry from St. Marys. We've already walked more than a mile, haven't we? We must be getting close. Wouldn't it be wonderful to stand at that most southern point and think of the things that happened there, and of what might be buried beneath the waters?"

Connor does not respond.

We walk on, and I tell him of the battle that took place between those hated Catholics down in Florida and the very proper English general who saved Georgia for the British king.

To defend his new colony against the Spaniards, General Oglethorpe built Fort William on the southernmost tip of Cumberland in 1740. Constructed of tabby and logs from live oak trees, the fort overlooked the inlet that allowed ships to enter the inland waterway. It was a strategic location.

Two years after Fort William was completed, a Spanish fleet consisting of fifty men-o'-war, plus schooners, sloops, and galleys left St. Augustine bound for the Georgian islands. They sailed past Cumberland and Jekyll into the St. Simons Sound and dropped anchor. The troops went ashore, captured Fort St. Simons, then headed north toward the British stronghold at Fort Frederica.

By then it was late in the day, and the Spanish soldiers decided to overnight near Gould's Inlet, just north of Demere Road. They put their weapons aside, unpacked their cooking pots, and were preparing dinner when the English attacked.

Taken by surprise and low on ammunition, the Spaniards retreated down Military Road toward the safety of their ships. Completely routed, they sailed for home, leaving behind the bodies of their dead. That's the Battle of Bloody Marsh.

By the time they got to Cumberland, their courage had returned. They still had an armada of nearly fifty ships and two thousand soldiers. Why not attack Fort William? If they could capture this southernmost fortress, they might be able to work their way north again, occupy Fort St. Andrews at the north end of Cumberland, jump across to Jekyll, then back to St. Simons for a second assault.

Fort William was manned by only fifty or sixty British soldiers, but they had two eighteen-pound cannons mounted on moving platforms. It was enough. The Spaniards attacked, and again they were defeated. Georgia was safe. She would forevermore be a colony of England.

Today, nothing remains of Fort William. Archeological digs have been unable to locate any remnants of either the fort or the village that once surrounded it.

20

The sky ahead of us is darkening. What we thought was pollution is actually a storm cloud. Connor has been watching it, and he's worried. He thinks we should turn back. He reminds us of Matt's forecast of rain for the entire Florida peninsula.

But on Cumberland, the sun is shining. "This is Georgia," I argue, "not Florida. The storm, if that's what it is, won't come north. It'll go out to sea. Like the hurricanes do."

"Weather systems generally don't have much respect for state boundaries," Connor says. "It's a huge system, and it's moving this way."

I look at the clouds, and they're darker than before.

"They're rain clouds," he says. "There's gonna be a downpour. We should turn back."

"Why not try to make it around the tip of the island and take that trail across to Dungeness?"

"Because we don't know how far it is," he says, "or what we might encounter."

"We've been walking for a long time," Rhamy says. "To go back the way we came will take forever."

"If we keep going," Connor says, "who knows what we might find. There might be a marsh we can't cross, a body of water we don't know about. We could be in real trouble."

I've seen Google Earth pictures of a jetty built out into the Atlantic. What changes to the shoreline might it have caused, I wonder. And what of the St. Marys River that empties into the Cumberland Sound? Rivers gather sediment as they pass through the land — gravel, sand, debris — and they drop it when they enter a larger body of water. Sometimes they carve new channels in their rush to the sea. Could there be geological features we know nothing about?

Lightning splits the sky. Thunder crashes as the two sides reunite. Trying to make it around the tip of the island no longer seems such a good idea.

Reluctantly, we turn back. I'm disappointed. I'd wanted to stand on the beach at the southernmost point of Cumberland Island and look out over the waterway, to picture fifty Spanish naval vessels sailing toward that tiny fort which was all that stood between the Golden Isles and the Georgia mainland. If the tide were out, we might see chunks of tabby that were once part of the village that surrounded the fort. Unless it has all sunk into the sea.

Eighty years after the battle, Lucy Coleman, not yet Lucy Carnegie, attended boarding school in Fernandina Beach. A slender girl with dark hair and brown eyes, she might have stood on the opposite shore and gazed across the waterway. Fort William could still have existed then. Her teachers might have told stories of gallant British soldiers, booming cannons, bullets piercing the logs of the fort and cannon balls tearing through the hulls of the Spanish ships.

She could not have imagined she would one day own all but the very northern part of the island. That she would spend winters there, and row a flat-bottomed boat up and down Little Creek. That she would ride horses, and play golf, and hunt with her sons. And when she got too heavy to walk, she would drive an electric car around the island. She would bury a beloved son. And one day she would be laid to rest in the Carnegie graveyard near Dungeness.

The rain, when it begins, is gentle. A few drops, falling softly. The sun still shines, but the clouds are moving northward. White caps have begun to appear on the water. We quicken our pace.

The war between the Spanish and the English had its roots in an earlier incident I'd read about in my Cumberland Island book. The Spaniards, ensconced in Florida and the Caribbean, sent their Coast Guard out to harass a British merchant ship, the *Rebecca*, commanded by Captain Robert Jenkins. Spanish officials boarded the ship and accused Jenkins of smuggling. As punishment for his misdeeds, they sliced off Jenkins's ear. Seven years later that severed body part, pickled by its owner, made its way to London where it was displayed in Parliament's House of Commons. This was a stain on the honor of a nation. It could not be ignored. *The War of Jenkins's Ear* was joined.

Though it would rage for another ten years, what happened at Fort William in 1742 marked a turning point in the hostilities. The defeat of the Spanish at that tiny fort effectively brought to an end hostilities between the Spanish and the English. Jenkins's ear was avenged.

The rain is steady now, and it's worrisome. We begin to look in earnest for the signpost that marks the path back to Dungeness.

Connor takes a Ziploc out of his backpack. "Better give me your cell phones," he says.

I'd forgotten. Rhamy had forgotten. Cell phone companies have ways of discovering if you leave your phone out in the rain, or you drop it in a glass of water, or forget it's in your pocket when you walk into the ocean. None of which we did.

We hand Connor our phones. He slips them, and his, into the Ziploc, seals it, and puts it in an inside pocket of his raincoat. It's a Columbia jacket, waterproof, hooded, pockets inside and out.

The sky above us has turned from blue to an angry shade of purple. Lightning flashes, thunder booms. I turn to look behind us. Sheets of rain are falling. I can see a clear line of demarcation on the sand between what is wet and what is dry. The rain is moving toward us, pursuing us up the beach. And it is coming heavier now.

All we can do is keep walking. The rain soaks our hair, our clothing. Rhamy's and mine. Not Connor's. He has that raincoat. At least our phones are safe.

Then the downpour hits, rain coming so hard and fast we can barely see ten feet ahead of us. There is no place to shelter. To our right, sand dunes, to our left, an angry ocean tumbling over itself in its reach for the shore.

We have no choice but to keep walking.

Connor halts, takes off his rain jacket, offers to shelter us until the worst is over. The three of us huddle beneath his coat, waiting for the rain to let up. Surely this is just a squall, and it'll end soon.

But it doesn't. It goes on and on, the rain pooling above us until it threatens to bring the coat down on our heads. At the count of three we lift up, and the water pours down in a cascade all around us.

A slanting rain attacks whatever part is exposed. The coat provides little shelter. We are three adults. This is one jacket. We can't stay under here forever. We cast it off and resume walking, not caring anymore how much it rains. It's chilly, but not cold. This is the end of June. Summertime.

There's a uniqueness to our situation, a singularity to it that is oddly appealing. For the three of us to be alone on this deserted beach, walking in the rain, having given up all hope of staying dry, opening our arms to whatever the heavens can pour down on us, this is something we could never have planned. It could never happen again. We will carry this memory with us forever.

Trudging up the beach, rain washing over us, the sand still hard-packed, safe on our island beneath a leaden sky, it occurs to me I can't possibly get any wetter. Why not go back into the water? It can't be colder than it was earlier. Maybe, just maybe, it'll be warmer.

I break away and walk into the ocean, and a wave rolls over me, knocking me down, and I remember being here with Madeleine just two short years ago. What a wonderful time we had, the two of us being knocked down by the waves, getting up, walking out again, farther out, until another wave hit and tossed us back toward the shore.

Rhamy follows me into the water, and she's beside me, laughing, brushing her hair back from her face, spitting out salt water. We watch for the biggest waves, and when they are nearly upon us we jump, trying to overtop them but not caring if we make it. The ocean is at once tumultuous and gentle, full of danger and delight. The sky bursts open with scrambled veins of lightning, and I call to Rhamy to duck under the water. Thunder rattles across the heavens, closing up the lightning streaks, putting things right again.

Connor calls for us to get out of the water. "It's not safe to be swimming when there's lightning," he yells. But the waves are crashing, the ocean roaring, and how could we possibly hear what he's saying? And what fun would it be if we never took chances, never did things we hadn't done before, never jumped into water until we knew it was exactly the right temperature?

He walks up the beach, leaving us in the water, but before he's gone thirty feet he turns and comes back. He cups his hands around his mouth and calls to us: "If you get struck by lightning, there'll be nothing I can do. There's no way I could help you. I can't call anybody; we're out in the middle of nowhere. Come on, Rhamy, get out of the water. Get your mom out of the water."

Another wave is forming, one so tall a champion surfer would shiver in antic-
ipation. But there stands Connor, alone on the beach, our cell phones safe in the
inside pocket of his jacket, caring about us and what might happen to us. How
can we not take pity on him.

The wave breaks as it approaches the shore. It churns with foam and sand, and
it gathers both Rhamy and me into its roll, and then deposits us in water no more
than two or three feet deep. We get to our feet and walk to where Connor is waiting for us.

"Lightning was touching down all around you," Connor says. "You could have
been killed."

"We weren't wearing any metal," I tell him. "Isn't it metal that attracts lightning?"

"Lightning rods are made out of metal," Rhamy says. "What about the snaps
on your raincoat? Could that have attracted lightning? You might have been in
more danger than we were."

Connor picks up his backpack and starts up the beach. We follow.

"And what about your zipper," I ask. "Remember the scene from *All the Pretty
Horses* where the kid takes off all his clothes because he's afraid he'll be struck by
lightning? What a wonderful scene."

"I remember," Rhamy says, and she runs ahead, then turns to face us, breath-
less and excited. "Jimmy Blevins was his name." she says. "He tells about all the
people in his family who were struck. Lightning went down a mine shaft to kill his
grandfather. Some other relative got blown out of an oil rig. And there was a cousin
who was walking across his yard and he got hit. It melted the fillings in his teeth
so he couldn't open his jaw. The family thought he'd had a stroke because he
couldn't talk."

"Fiction," Connor says. "It couldn't happen. And it isn't necessarily metal that
attracts lightning. Trees get hit all the time. Think of the forest fires that are caused
by lightning strikes."

Rhamy links her arm through Connor's. "Then you were in more danger than
we were," she says, "because you were on the beach. That made you more of a
target. Carrying an umbrella puts you at risk because it makes you taller. We were
in the water, so we were safe."

"I don't have an umbrella," Connor says.

"But you were higher up, and you have lots of things that are metal in your backpack. Buckles and water bottles. Plus the frame. Lots of metal."

She continues: "The kid in *All the Pretty Horses* took off his jeans because of the brads, and his shirt because of the brass buttons, and his boots because of the nails, and his belt, because of the buckle. He got down in a ravine. When the two guys he was traveling with found him the next day, all he had on was a pair of shorts."

"Fiction," Connor says again.

"Fiction is based on reality," I tell him. "There are people who claim they're human lightning rods. I remember a guy on some TV show who claimed he'd been hit seven times. He was a park ranger, and he made it into the *Guinness Book of World Records*. Maybe it runs in families. There might be a lightning gene that gets passed down from father to son."

I glance at Connor, and he's looking straight ahead, and I'm sorry we're joking about it. "People do get struck by lightning," I tell him, "but I always look at the odds. If one person in 100,000 gets hit every year, I'm gonna assume I'll be among the 99,999."

I stop to pick up a sand dollar. "I remember a neighbor boy who was working for my dad. He went out in the pasture to find a calf during a storm, and he swore he got hit. My dad didn't believe him, but I remember the boy crying when he came into the house. His face was all cut up, and he'd lost his eyebrows. They were gone, completely singed off his face."

The rain is steady now, no longer the heavy downpour that sent us into the water. A half mile farther on, I see the sign that marks the trail back to Dungeness. The wooden post, half hidden by blowing sand, has been blackened by the rain. In front of it, between the dunes, is the trail.

The path looks different from when we were here earlier in the day. The sand is dark with moisture. The dune grasses lean under the weight of the water. The boardwalk has turned from a weathered gray to a soggy black.

We splash through pools of standing water at the start of the trail. We climb dunes and the sand clings to our feet and legs. We walk along the boardwalk, dodging the low-hanging branches that overarch the wooden walkway. The rain never lets up. The walk back to Dungeness takes longer than it's ever taken before.

We find shelter in an open shed at the edge of the historic district. Inside is a tractor, a jumble of rusty farm implements, half-rotted burlap sacks, fertilizer bags brittle with age, rusted gasoline cans, rubber hoses, ropes of sisal and hemp, newer ones of nylon. Dusty saddles, bridles, halters, girths, bits. The floor is oil-stained dirt. We stand at the edge of all these relics from earlier times, remnants of antiquity that have been stored here and forgotten, and there's barely room for the three of us. We scan the sky, hoping for some change in the solid gray. We are disappointed.

Rhamy, interested in the tack, threads her way through the farm equipment until she reaches the back corner of the building. She gazes at an English saddle that sits atop a wooden sawhorse. She picks up a riding crop from the ledge, examines it, puts it back. A pair of stirrups. A set of spurs. She runs her fingers over a bundle of leather straps suspended from a roofing timber. She touches a pair of chaps that hangs from a nail. The leather, all the bits and pieces of it, is so old, so brittle, so dry, it is but a few steps from disintegration.

When we have rested, we leave the shed and walk up the winding trail toward Dungeness. The temperature has fallen. The rain is cold. Our clothes are full of sand, our skin rough with salt. Rhamy and I are miserable, Connor in his raincoat is not quite as drenched, but close.

"There are restrooms at the dock," I remind them. "We can wash off, rinse the sand out of our clothes, try to dry them under the hand dryers. If we have time. There's that sheltered area on the dock. We can wait for the ferry there."

If it hasn't already gone, I add mentally, wondering what time it is. We walked farther than ever before. What if we've missed the last ferry? What if we have to stay overnight, without food, without dry clothes, without a place to sleep? Rangers live on the island. Might one of them take us in? Could we walk to Greyfield, the Carnegie home turned bed and breakfast, and beg to spend the night? Offer to wash dishes in exchange for a night's lodging?

"_All the Pretty Horses_," Rhamy says. "Do you realize we've hardly seen any horses on this trip? Just those few by the recreation building."

"They're hiding out somewhere," I tell her. "Because of the rain. I'm gonna read that book again. It's one of my all-time favorites."

"Connor's first trip to the island," she says, "and I promised him there'd be lots of horses. The foals would be born and the herd would be bigger than it's ever been. And we've hardly seen any."

"They're in the woods somewhere, Rhamy, sheltering under trees. Horses don't like rain any better than we do."

She takes Connor's hand and looks up at him. "Will you come back with me next year? Spring break?"

"Of course I will," he says. And ten steps later, "but maybe we can pay more attention to the weather forecast?"

The water that spews from the faucets in the women's bathroom is cold. But the idea of sitting in wet clothes that are full of sand during the 45-minute ferry ride and then the hour's ride back to St. Simons is more than we can bear.

Rhamy and I take turns at the sink, rinsing out our shorts and tops, regretting now that we'd gone into the water wearing our clothes instead of changing back into our bathing suits.

The dryer works for five minutes, then dies. We wring out our clothing by hand.

"Maybe there's one in the men's room," Rhamy says.

"We could ask Connor to go check."

"He's already down at the dock."

"There's no one out under the trees? Sitting at the picnic tables?"

She shakes her head.

I pull on my shorts and blouse, open the door, step across the hallway to the men's room. Rhamy follows close behind.

There are two dryers. One for each of us. I look for a stone outside the building, select the biggest one I can find, carry it into the men's room and prop it against the door.

We spend the next ten minutes attempting to dry our clothes. We are marginally successful. Until we put them back on.

"The heat of our bodies will dry them," I tell Rhamy.

"Sure, Mom. In about an hour. Assuming we can stay out of the rain. Which we can't. We have to walk over to the dock. And it's still raining."

21

In phone calls, emails, and text messages over the following winter, Rhamy and I discuss such important matters as who came to Cumberland which years.

"When you come to St. Simons in March, will it be your fourth visit, or your fifth?" I ask.

"Is there a chance," she wonders, "we might be able to get the whole family together again this summer?"

"We can try," I answer.

"When you and Madeleine went to Cumberland, did you really see more horses than we did? I think she made that up, just to make me jealous. How many did you actually see?"

Connor doesn't think he'll be able to join us this year. Like Madeleine last summer, he's too busy. He's hired an assistant, and he can't leave him on his own.

"But I need Cumberland more than ever," Rhamy says. "And St. Simons. And the ocean, no matter how it's acting up."

"Is that why Connor won't come? Because we dragged him to the beach, and we got caught in that awful storm?"

"No, he loved it. He thinks he might be able to make it next year."

"Tell him we'll rent a house, just for him. Fish Fever Lane, if it's available. Or we'll look for a five bedroom, and talk Kate into coming. Maybe we can find something on Amelia Island. Charlie and I stopped there once when we were on our way to Orlando. We had lunch in the historic district, but we didn't have time to do anything else. There's a beach in the center of the island where black people used to go to swim. Before Civil Rights. And a nightclub where Ray Charles and Louis Armstrong performed. It was a part of something called the Chitlin' Circuit."

"I'll bet Daddy would love it, if we took him there. We'll do it. It'll be a way to make up for all the times we left him alone on St. Simons while we went to

Cumberland. What did you call it, the Chitlin' Circuit? I'll see if I can find a book about it."

"I doubt you'll find much. But anything about the history of music, he'd love. Rock & roll, jazz, the blues, he'd be thrilled."

A pause in the conversation. Then Rhamy tells me she's thinking of quitting her job. Twelve years is long enough. The new principal is driving her crazy.

"We've accepted two new students; you'll have thirty-one in your classroom in September instead of twenty-nine." "Would you mind editing our new school handbook? In your spare time?" "Is that a jean skirt you're wearing? Jeans are not allowed, you know. The same for athletic shoes. They just don't look very professional."

Rhamy's next door neighbor who lives in a hot-pink house thinks Rhamy should have her house repainted. Beige is such a blah color, the woman says. The neighbor on the other side has put up a fence designed to keep Rhamy's cat from coming into her yard.

She needs a break. She needs four days on St. Simons, and at least a day on Cumberland. St. Simons has restaurants, a fishing pier, and artists in love with the beach, the marsh, the sunsets over the water. Cumberland is a nearly deserted island with no amenities, but it is a place that will give her some perspective on her life. On that wide beach she can begin to unloose the strings that have entangled her.

Most islands can never return to the pristine state they once enjoyed. They are too large, too populated, too easily accessible, too tied to the mainland. But Cumberland is none of these things. Four thousand years ago, the Timucoa Indians came there to fish her waters, collect her shellfish, harvest her edible plants. Like those tall, dark-skinned people of long ago, we come for sustenance, and we leave satisfied.

Spring has finally arrived. Rhamy and I are on the ferry, just pulling away from St. Marys, when we decide we won't get off at the Dungeness dock. Instead, we'll go on to Sea Camp. The year Madeleine and I missed our stop, we were both so panicked, neither of us knowing where we were or how to get to where we wanted to go, we paid little attention to our surroundings. This will be different. We're old hands now. We've studied maps. We know about the First African Baptist

Church at the north end of the island where John F. Kennedy, Jr., and Carolyn Bessette were married. We know about Stafford House and the chimneys that are all that remain of the slave quarters. We know about Plum Orchard and the Grey-field Inn. We know the shape, length, and breadth of the island, and the general location of historical landmarks. We've walked on Grand Avenue, the backbone of the island. If not for the storm last summer, we might have made it around the southern tip of the island. When we stood on the Dungeness dock waiting for the ferry, wet and cold and bedraggled, and we watched the *Cumberland Queen* leave the dock at Sea Camp and head toward where we waited, we realized the two docks are not that far apart.

From the Sea Camp Ranger Station we'll walk through the campgrounds, across the island, to the Atlantic. If a rental house on Amelia Island won't lure Connor back this summer, when we tell him about the campgrounds where you can stay for three nights, and how you can watch the sun set over the marshes, and that you can sleep under the Cumberland sky, he won't be able to resist. Rhamy and I know nothing about camping, but Connor is an expert. He'll take charge, Rhamy says. It'll be a wonderful experience.

The path to the ocean meanders beneath a canopy of live oaks, their branches spreading, twisting, jutting, some so heavy they rest against the earth. It's like a scene from a Hitchcock movie — gnarled limbs reaching out to grasp one another, to compete for a patch of sunlight, to fill the sky.

The trees are mature, but this is not virgin forest. Most have sprouted from the roots of trees harvested during the Revolutionary War. Wood from the island was used to build the *USS Constitution*. During the War of 1812, British cannon shot bounced off her sides, earning her the nickname *"Old Ironsides."*

The campsites, cut into the undergrowth along the path, come complete with fire rings, picnic tables, grills, and food cages. If Charles Fraser, developer of Sea Pines Plantation on Hilton Head Island, had had his way, these campsites would have been replaced with luxury homes.

With the death of the last of Lucy Carnegie's children in 1962, the heirs were free to dispose of their inheritances as they saw fit. By then the Carnegie trust was nearly exhausted. Upkeep of the Cumberland property was costly. Property taxes were high. The empire Andrew and Thomas Carnegie had built could no longer support the spendthrift ways of Lucy Carnegie and of succeeding generations.

Andrew Carnegie III and Thomas Carnegie IV needed money. Fraser offered $1.55 million for their combined properties, just over three thousand acres, one fifth of the island. They accepted Fraser's offer. Other members of the family, those who still lived on the island and those who loved it, were shocked. Some were angry.

Fraser sailed his ninety-foot yacht from Hilton Head to Cumberland. He built his island headquarters at a place he named Sea Camp, and he began a campaign to convince the rest of the island landowners to sell him their land. His intent, he wrote to the owners, was to develop the island in a way that would be ecologically sensitive, much as he had on Hilton Head. He would build golf courses, roads, marinas, vacation villas, hotels, and gas stations. He spoke glowingly of what his plan would do for the island, but he warned that anyone who owned at least sixty acres and refused to come to an agreement with him would jeopardize the entire project.

A short, heavyset man, Fraser was aggressive, brash, and bold. Calling himself "the golden boy of the Golden Isles," he roamed the island with rolled-up land plats under his arm. He would dredge Lake Whitney and push the dunes away from the water. There would be playgrounds, fishing piers, swings hung from oak trees.

Nothing was sacred, island landowners began to realize.

In the midst of all this, love bloomed. A Carnegie descendant, Nancy Johnston of Lexington, met Landon Butler, an executive who worked for Fraser. They married at Plum Orchard. In the midst of the reception Fraser brought out a series of maps, spread them on an antique mahogany table, and began to lay out his plans for the island. He spoke of conservation easements and restrictions that would prevent landowners from developing their land in ways that did not comply with his plans. When some of the wedding guests questioned these restrictions, he called them idiots. He left the reception shortly afterward.

He pushed efforts in the Georgia legislature to create a Camden County Recreational Authority that would be empowered to acquire land on Cumberland Island by condemnation. He supported a bill that sought to extend the power of eminent domain to the entire state of Georgia. Island families fought back. Native son Jimmy Carter, then a state legislator and Cumberland Island aficionado, led the movement to defeat the two bills.

During those turbulent months, Fraser met with various members of the Carnegie family. They were skeptical of his plans. Fraser's "Cumberland Oaks" was a profit-making scheme, they believed, and it would destroy the very nature of the island. They hated the idea of a causeway and a bridge connecting their island to the mainland. A car-ferry with parking facilities on Cumberland would be nearly as bad. They despised Fraser's plan to construct a series of towers and cables that would carry people to and from the island on arial gondolas. They envisioned paved roads, strip malls, hot-dog stands, billboards, and souvenir shops. They were appalled.

Fraser was determined. Invited to Greyfield Inn for dinner one evening, he was met at the door by Lucy Ferguson, granddaughter of Lucy and Thomas Carnegie. Mistaking his hostess for a maid, he laid his coat over her outstretched arm and swept into the room. When dinner was done, he spread a twelve-foot map on the living room floor. Tiffany lamps lit the room, sending a rainbow of color over the velvet sofa, antique chairs, and Oriental rug. Fraser walked around the edges of the map, drink in hand. He hovered over it, sketching with words and gestures his vision for the island.

The whitened skulls of long-dead island ponies and loggerhead turtles sat silent on deep windowsills. Carnegie portraits looked down from the walls, and the fire in the fireplace burned brightly.

He would build airstrips, medical facilities, a helicopter pad, shopping malls, athletic and amusement facilities, apartments. The beach would feature tiki bars and hot tubs. Vendors would sell cold watermelon in summer, roasted oysters in winter. The arial gondolas—some called them sky vans, arial trams, or flying boxcars—would bring in food and supplies.

The more the Carnegies heard, the more they hated everything about this man and his schemes. Their island was sacred. It had been their home for eighty years. They had been good stewards. They showed Fraser to the door, and they began negotiating with the National Park Service.

Unfazed, Fraser sent bulldozers onto the island to begin clearing for an airport. The 5000-foot runway he planned would be big enough for corporate jets to land and take off.

Negotiations between the landowners and the federal government went on for years. Owners fought for compensation and for retained rights for themselves and their descendants. Some took the Park Service to court. If an agreement used the word *issue* as opposed to *children*, did that word apply to all lineal descendants including grandchildren, great-grandchildren, and beyond? Why was this person granted an extension of his "reserved property," and that person was not? Why did one agreement specify twenty-five years, others forty years, still others to remain in effect until the death of the last surviving grandchild? Some owners built houses in order to increase the value of their properties. Developers swooped in, bought up land, and subdivided it. Prices skyrocketed. It was a messy business.

And what of the holdouts? Lucy Ferguson, owner of the Greyfield Inn, was one of them. Her position had hardened; she refused to negotiate, refused to even talk to the government men.

The Park Service was patient. They fought the battles that arrived on their doorsteps, and they waited. In time, they will succeed. In their back pocket is a wild card; they have the power of condemnation.

The cedar-sided building Fraser built and used as his headquarters is today the Cumberland Island Welcome Center: Sea Camp Ranger Station. Campers go there to find their assigned campsites, bikers to rent bicycles, hikers to pick up maps, islomanes to learn about the island and its history.

Charles Fraser, an embittered man, sold most of his holdings to the National Park Foundation for just under $800,000. He moved on to the next barrier island in the chain, Amelia Island, off the Florida coast.

22

The dunes are invading the campgrounds. Inch by inch, they're moving westward, toward Cumberland Sound. If Charles Fraser were still here, and if he still owned twenty percent of the island, he would not allow this to happen. He would bring in giant earthmoving equipment — Caterpillars, backhoes, and shovels — and he would push them back toward the ocean.

Left alone, the dunes will smother everything in their path, he would argue. They would jeopardize his Cumberland Oaks development. They would wrest control of the island from its rightful owners and ruin all the improvements he'd made.

Fraser would do battle with these meandering mountains of sand. He would push them back again and again.

Other things might happen. Dunes come and go. They rise and fall. A tree might grow in such a way as to change the course of a moving dune. A hurricane could sweep across the island, decapitating the tallest dunes, sending tons of sand back into the ocean, or to the inlet south of the island, or north to Jekyll.

Nature is patient. Her plan is more long-term than Charles Fraser's. It may take her a millennium or two to have her way, but in the end, she will.

The path leading from the eastern edge of the campground to the ocean is steep and treacherous. Rhamy and I have to grab onto half-buried trees and tree branches to pull ourselves up. When we reach the top, we look out over a succession of dunes. No longer shielded by the live oaks in the campground, we swelter beneath a sun that is searing hot. The wind across the dunes is like a blowtorch.

We step onto the boardwalk and walk until we reach a high point over a valley of sand. It is deep and littered with driftwood, marsh grasses, sea oats, a cluster of yucca plants. An empty water bottle. A discarded T-shirt. A piece of black plastic pipe, grayed by the elements.

Ripples in the sand, created by some combination of wind and rain, look like water flowing over gravel. There are tracks left by tiny shore birds and great birds of prey. Hoofprints. Farther on, horse manure. A vulture sitting on a high branch of a dead tree. More dunes. They surround us, sandy hills and valleys, ridges and chasms, the boardwalk following some geological feature no longer discernible.

The beach, when we finally reach it, is wide, empty, and cool. We splash into the water, and it refreshes us. When we emerge, the sun is welcome. We head toward Dungeness, meandering down the beach, moving from ocean to dune back to ocean. Once we stop to gaze at the shell of a horseshoe crab. We go on.

It's different from last summer. Then, there were three of us. We knew there was rain in the forecast, but none of us expected what we will forever call "the storm from hell." It washed away our footprints, sent our words reverberating out to some far-off galaxy, and somehow, somehow, drew us closer than we'd ever been before.

Now it's just Rhamy and me. An hour or two of splashing along the water's edge — we've lost all sense of time — and we're hungry. There are no picnic tables, no trees, no shade, but there's warm sand, a salty breeze, and ocean. In Rhamy's backpack are the egg salad sandwiches we brought from St. Simons, water bottles still iced from overnighting in the freezer at Fish Fever Lane, granola bars, and apples.

When we've finished eating, we throw our apple cores to the seagulls. We watch them scramble for this unexpected treat. We wash our hands in the ocean and dry them on our still-damp clothes.

Rhamy takes a clean Ziploc from her backpack and begins to fill it with sand. She's careful to select only the driest, the purest, the whitest.

"I need it for my Zen garden," she says.

I nod, understanding. Several years ago Madeleine bought her a tabletop Zen garden for her birthday. Measuring no more than eight by ten inches, it came complete with sand, a packet of polished stones, a rake, and a brush. She keeps it on the mantel above her fireplace.

Your Zen Garden will bring serenity, the brochure said. *The sand represents water, the stones represent the mountains. In times of stress, spend a few minutes with your Zen garden. Raking, brushing, smoothing the sand calms the mind, rids it of the chaos that surrounds us. Create a swirl around a mountain. Rake the sand into a pattern that suggests rippling water. Move your garden to a windowsill and note how the shadows deepen as the sun arcs across the sky.*

Rhamy holds up the Ziploc. "Somehow," she says, "the sand in my Zen garden manages to disappear, and I have to replenish it. I don't like the sand from the Oregon coast; it's too coarse. Not white like this."

"It's like sugar."

"Sugar sand," she says, savoring the words. She combs the area around her with her fingers, checking for dampness, bits of shell, living things.

"A few years ago," she says, "I took some sand back from St. Simons, but this is more special because it's Cumberland sand." She picks up a tiny, angel wing seashell, white on the outside, pink inside, utterly perfect, but fragile. She holds it in the palm of her hand, studies it for a moment, then lets it slide into the bag.

"The garden Madeleine gave me came with rocks and a few marbles," she says. "After a while, I decided to collect my own. They have more meaning. The same with the sand. This will be special. It'll be like taking a piece of the island home with me."

She lets the sand sift through her fingers, and the sun beats down on us, and the ocean slides toward us. "I have a rock that Madeleine gave me," she says. "It's about the size of a nickel, chestnut-colored, and it looks like a horse's head in profile. It reminds me of Taylor. That's actually why she gave it to me. She found it on Brighton Beach in England. I have a few from the Oregon coast. Some are just stones I found that I like. One is from the farm where Taylor used to live. Where I scattered his ashes."

Her bag nearly full, she sits on the sand, pulls her legs up and wraps her arms around them. "The therapeutic part of it," she continues, "is that you arrange the rocks and the sand in a pattern that shows you how to get out of whatever painful situation you're in. It's like a prayer. It brings tranquility. Like when Quest had that abscess in her foot last year, I arranged the rocks to look like a horse with feathers on her feet. I raked the sand in a kind of a wavy, light pattern."

She sighs. "It might seem silly, but it had meaning for me. And it helped. I kept thinking I might have to put her down, like I did Taylor. Foot problems in a horse are what I dread most."

"Coffin bone," I murmur, but so softly, I doubt that she hears me.

I think about my flight to Portland to be with her at that awful time, and before that, when it was happening, Taylor's laminitis going from bad to worse. There were days, even weeks, when he seemed to improve. Other times he would lift his feet, one after another, in an effort to relieve the pain. He'd look down at them, then at Rhamy, as if he wanted her to do something to help him. His front feet were the worst.

The vet would stop at the farm and go into Taylor's stall, unwrap the bandages, replace them with new ones. He would consult with the farrier: if we cut the hoof just so, try to take the pressure off, might that help? In the end, it did not. Nothing could stop the trajectory we were on.

I needed to understand what was happening to this horse my daughter had owned for more than ten years. Kate would know. I would ask her.

We were at a restaurant in Auburn. She took a napkin from the holder and drew a picture of a horse's foot. She labeled the different parts, and when she was done, she slid the napkin across the table to me.

"His coffin bone is sinking," she said. "Sometimes they can go clear through to the ground. You have no choice but to put the horse down. It's the only humane thing to do."

"Coffin bone," I repeated. I asked her if there wasn't a more technical name for it.

She shrugged. "Pedal bone," she said. "Distal phalanx. In vet school we just called it the coffin bone."

"Awful name for it," I said. I took the napkin with the drawing, folded it, and slipped it into my purse. Not to show Rhamy. She didn't need to understand, was in no shape to look at it. But to have it. Maybe to show it to Charlie, so he would understand why I had to go to Portland.

I look down the empty beach, remembering last summer, hoping for just the briefest moment that a storm, like the one last summer, will appear, and descend on us, so I can stop thinking of that earlier, terrible time.

Rhamy stretches out her legs and leans back, resting on her elbows, looking toward the sky. The sun is full on her face, and her eyes are closed.

"Or," she says, "I might arrange it as a downhill scene, if I feel like my life is all uphill and hard. Like when Connor is off on a kayaking trip, and I don't hear from him for days on end because he's on some wild river. Or when I'm having problems at school: parents who insist their kid wouldn't cheat, or they want you to change a grade because 'he worked so hard on his paper.' Or when Madeleine is having problems, and I can't do anything to help her. Whatever strikes me. I probably arrange a new scene every month or so. Depends on what crisis I'm dealing with at the moment."

"You're visualizing how you want things to work out," I tell her.

She sighs, and lies back in the sand. I sit beside her, and the ocean is nudging toward us, and there is only the sound of the wind and the waves.

"Coming here," she says, "is like walking through a Zen garden."

The sun beats down on us, and she's quiet for a few moments.

"No, it's more than that," she continues. "It's like actually being in a Zen garden, spending time there, discovering the things that are important, and separating them from those that are not."

Back at the historic district, on our way to the Dungeness dock, we pause at the car graveyard. We've seen it before, several times, but it never fails to draw us in.

Spanish moss hangs from rusted roofs and hoods, vines grow out of engine and passenger compartments, fenders rust away, slowly returning to the base elements from which they were constructed. The single strand of rope that surrounds the site has been replaced since last year, I notice.

"Is it possible," I ask, "that the cars have sunk deeper into the ground since last summer?"

Rhamy shrugs. "Probably not. Well, maybe, an inch or two."

"How many years until they're completely gone? The old Model T on the end, I swear it's more tilted than it was before, like one side is sinking faster than the other."

What looked like a row of cars the year Charlie was with us has begun to look like rubble. A headlight hangs from its socket, a door is attached by a single hinge, a windshield has fallen across the dashboard. A seat has been reduced to corroded springs.

We leave the auto graveyard and walk up the seashell road. A park employee on a tractor approaches, and we step to the side to let him pass. He waves to us. We wave back. He pulls into a gravel parking area outside the carriage house and jumps down from the tractor. He lets the motor idle while he pushes open the double doors of the building. Back on the tractor, he revs the engine, then drives the tractor inside.

He closes the doors, then glances at Rhamy and me. We've crossed the road and are standing at the edge of the gravel, watching him.

His shift for the day is over. Evening is approaching; he's about to head to the house where he lives with other park employees. But there we are, standing by the road, yearning for a look inside.

He offers a tour of the carriage house.

"Madeleine should have come with us," Rhamy whispers. "He's hot."

"Hush," I tell her.

We accept his offer.

"I saw you looking at those old cars," he says. "They're quite a curiosity. People always want to know about them."

"My husband says one is a 1950 or 1951 Studebaker. He recognized the bullet nose. And the hood ornament."

He nods. "He's right. It's a Champion convertible. And they tell me it was in pristine condition when it was hauled out there."

He looks toward the live oaks that shelter the cars. "They've been there since the early '70s," he says. "That's when the Park Service pulled them out of the carriage house and lined them up under the trees. Two Model A's, a 1933-34 Ford, two 1939 Chevys, the Studebaker, and what old-timers tell me is a 1949 or 1950 Mopar."

"Mopar?"

"It's kind of an acronym. Short for 'motor parts.' Chrysler began building them in the '30s. They were customized, high-performance vehicles. Built to the customer's specifications." He laughs. "Only a Carnegie would have a car built exactly the way he wanted it, then abandon it on a deserted island."

Inside, the building has the feel of a barn, open to the rafters. The floor is painted gray concrete. The room is filled with machinery — a bushhog, mowers, chainsaws, tools of every kind — wrenches, shovels, vice grips, hammers, mallets, rolls of wire, lengths of rope. Above the ledge that runs along the side are shelves containing jars filled with nails, screws, and washers of every imaginable size. There are wooden shingles stacked against a wall, tires arranged along the side.

To our left is a partial second story, wooden steps leading up to it.

"We've stored a few of the old carriages up there," our guide tells us. "Some of them have been moved to a museum over on the mainland. Lucy Carnegie owned one called a Victoria carriage. Named for the Queen of England, the carriage was open on the sides, presumably so the queen could show off her finery when she went riding. We're in the process of restoring it now. We have some other carriages up in the loft — one called a mountain wagon that was used for transporting luggage and supplies. The back seat could be taken out for extra storage space."

When the tour is over, the three of us leave the building. The guide closes the door behind us, and we stand beside the road, gazing at the ruined automobiles.

"The owners could have come back and claimed them," he says, "anytime they wanted. No one would have stopped them. The Park Service didn't want them, had no use for them.

"There are other cars scattered around the island. They belonged to people who had signed their land over to the Park Service but had retained rights. When their rights expired, most of them abandoned whatever vehicle they'd brought over. I guess it was just too much trouble to ferry them back to the mainland. Charles Fraser left a bunch of construction equipment. The Park Service tried to locate the owners. Those they could find they asked to remove whatever they'd left behind. Mostly the owners just ignored the letters they got.

"The cars out there belonged to the Carnegie children and grandchildren," he continues. "They kept them here on the island so they'd have transportation when they came to visit. When the trust ended, and the heirs started selling off whatever portion they owned, it all became kind of murky. After the Park Service took over management of the island, they needed a maintenance building. They chose this. The cars had to go."

We thank him for the tour, take one last look at the auto graveyard, and head toward the dock.

23

On our last full day in the Golden Isles of Georgia, we head for Florida's Amelia Island. It's a familiar drive, down I-95, Rhamy at the wheel. I think Charlie is excited to be visiting a real-life juke joint, but he doesn't want to tell us that. It's his Irish heritage: never get too excited about something, or you're likely to be disappointed.

The island, when we arrive, is a disappointment. It doesn't feel like an island. If there's a moment when we leave the mainland and drive onto Amelia, it is lost in the confusion of gas stations, fast-food franchises, and car dealerships decorated with strings of triangular flags. There are bridges over wetlands, a Goodwill store, an electrical supply house, palm trees, and nurseries. We're in a town called Yulee, and then we're not. A welcome sign announces that we've arrived at Fernandina Beach.

"Where is the intracoastal waterway?" I ask Rhamy. "Did we cross it?"

"We went over a few bridges," she says. "But they weren't very big. Nothing like the one on the Torras Causeway."

We're on a two-lane highway, smooth and straight. There are concrete block houses, video stores, and fruit stands. It looks like every small town in Florida: buy a piece of property, build a house, open a business, put up a sign.

Could this be the place where Charles Fraser came when he left Cumberland Island? Was it like this when he bought the lower third of the island and began construction of the Amelia Island Plantation?

The unrestricted growth along Highway A1A ends abruptly, and we drive into the historical district. It's a different world. Live oak trees shade narrow streets. There are horse-drawn carriages, a restored railroad station, bistros, taverns, and art galleries. Planters filled with flowers surround outdoor cafes. Flags from the different countries that have laid claim to the island ripple in the breeze.

You can feel the age of the place. It's in the old churches, the second-story balconies hidden behind swaying ferns, the rocking chairs set out on verandas.

Amelia Island was once both an international seaport and a railroad terminus. Shipments of lumber, cotton, naval stores, and phosphate were transferred from railroad cars onto outgoing vessels. Ship captains paid off their crews here, knowing the money would be spent on whiskey and women, and the sailors would have to sign up for another tour.

Pirates once walked these streets, drank in the bars, slept in the hotels. Slaves newly arrived from Africa were warehoused on the island until they could be smuggled into Georgia. Carnegie guests bound for Dungeness arrived here by train. They waited at the Palace Saloon for someone to pick them up and ferry them back to Cumberland.

The Palace Saloon is on our right, at the corner of Centre and Second Street, the entrance guarded by a life-sized statue of a peg-legged buccaneer. I want to go in and order a beer. Rhamy wants to have coffee in one of the outdoor cafes. Charlie would like to check out the Clubhouse at the Amelia Plantation Resort.

"It's not a very big island," he says, "so it can't be far away. The clubhouse is world-famous. Built on a high dune with a view of the ocean. We can grab lunch there."

Rhamy and I exchange glances. We owe him this. We've gone off to Cumberland and left him alone on St. Simons too many times.

But the Palace Saloon is something I can't pass up. "When we come back," I tell him, "before we leave the island, we have to have a beer there. It's the oldest saloon in Florida. When will we ever have the chance to do it again? A bar that's forty feet long, swinging doors, women bartenders. The Carnegie sons used to hang out there."

"To meet girls?" Rhamy asks.

"What else?"

"To socialize," Charlie says. "When pickings were slim on Cumberland."

"What do you mean?"

"They didn't come looking for brides," he says.

"If you never had a job," I tell her, "and you live at home with your mother, and you're a healthy American boy, wouldn't you want to go someplace where she wasn't looking over your shoulder?"

Ten miles along the ocean, still on AIA, we enter the cool, perfectly landscaped Amelia Island Club Resort. Once a nearly deserted marshland, it is now a place of meticulously maintained golf courses, tennis courts, multi-million dollar homes, condos, restaurants, villas, shopping boutiques, spas, and salons.

No flower, no shrub, no tree is allowed to grow anywhere except where it was planted. Everyone who lives here is happy. They have everything anyone could ever want. Their children are beautiful and accomplished, their friends of the most desirable sort, their businesses thriving, their investment portfolios gaining value every day. They have their own little corner of heaven, and they are secure. There are gates to protect them.

We drive through the gates, slowly, taking it all in. When we reach the clubhouse, Rhamy parks the car. We can hear the ocean, but it is not yet visible.

The Clubhouse is spectacular. So spectacular, I worry that we're leaving sand on the polished floor. The ocean is visible through a wall of glass, and it is a mirror that reflects the sky. When the waves roll onto the beach, they do so gently, then retreat. There are no whitecaps.

The reception area is cold. Rhamy and I are wearing T-shirts, shorts, and sandals. Charlie is wearing a polo shirt and slacks.

At the Carnegie-owned Greyfield Inn on Cumberland Island, men are required to wear jackets to dinner. If they've neglected to pack the required evening wear, the management keeps a supply of suitable attire they may borrow.

We've come for lunch, not dinner. Rules are surely more relaxed here than at Greyfield. And it would never occur to Charlie that anyone would ever tell him he was inappropriately dressed.

There's a man behind the reception desk. I can feel him appraising us, deciding if we are the kind of people who belong in this place. His gaze shifts to Rhamy, and it lingers there a beat too long. She's wearing her "I'm on Island Time" T-shirt.

"The Ocean View dining room is rather full, I'm afraid," he tells Charlie. "May I suggest the Sea Oats Cafe. It's a lighter fare, but quite nice."

Charlie glances around the room. Not all the tables are occupied. He looks back at the man. "There are quite a few empty tables," he says.

"I'm sorry, sir. They're reserved."

Charlie stares at him, and I can hear the tick of an invisible clock.

"Maybe we'll come back another time," Charlie says, and he turns away.

There are dozens of places to eat in the historic district. On the way we'll stop at the American Beach. That's the thing that most interests Charlie — the chance to see a nightclub where black artists once performed.

24

American Beach is a deserted place of vacant houses, empty lots, roads half-buried in sand. The wind off the ocean is gentle; it rustles the sea oats that anchors the dunes, the dry weeds that grow rampant around the buildings, a street sign hanging lopsided from a post. It feels as if the last person who lived here threw down his broom, his hedge clippers, his paint brush, gathered his belongings, and drove away. Never to return.

Yet there are signs of life. A few blocks from where we parked is a house built by degrees: add a second story, then a third for a view of the ocean, an extra room on the side, a shed in back, a carport at the end of the driveway. Children's plastic toys are scattered about, the bright Fisher-Price reds, yellows, and blues fading in the merciless Florida sun. There is nothing not weathered in this blighted place.

Beside us, on a deeply rutted road that looks as if it leads straight into the ocean, is a historical marker that tells the history of American Beach. In 1935, Abraham Lincoln Lewis, owner of the Afro-American Life Insurance Company, bought two hundred acres with the intention of building a resort for his employees. It became one of the few places in the racially segregated South where blacks could swim in the ocean.

Opposite the sign is a two-story, flat-roofed building that must be the juke joint Charlie has come to see. The windows are boarded up, screens ripped from rotted frames, doors nailed shut and padlocked. Half-buried bits of trash litter the ground around the building.

"Evans's Rendezvous," Charlie says, and he's standing so still, gazing at the ruins of this ruined place, he might have been in a church.

"There were places like this all over the South," he muses. "That's what the Chitlin' Circuit was — a chain of clubs throughout the United States where blacks could perform. They weren't allowed in the big venues, places like New York and Chicago. And if they had been, there were no hotels where they could stay, no restaurants that would serve them. So they booked themselves into these out-of-the-way places. Juke joints."

I step off the road, into the weeds, to get a closer look. Rhamy does the same. Charlie follows.

The cracks between the boards are wide enough that we can see inside. There's a wooden staircase, half rotted, the bottom steps completely gone. Jars on shelves, the lids rusted, no telling what was once inside. Canned tomatoes? Peaches? Pigs' feet?

There are old barstools. A rusted hot-water heater. A metal folding chair, upright in the center of the room, the seat completely rusted through. A machine that would tell your weight and fortune for a penny. A gallon jug, partially filled with a tea-colored liquid. Broken glass and odd bits of lumber littering the floor.

If we walked around the building, might we find an open door or window?

A train whistle sounds, and Charlie looks toward the mainland, to determine where it's coming from, how far away it might be. It's an old habit.

When he was a boy, he gave up his bedroom so his grandmother could live with the family. Until he went away to college, he slept in an attic room, beneath ancient rafters and a slate roof. When it rained, it sounded as if each tile were a drum head, reverberating to the tapping of the raindrops. He didn't mind, nor did he object to the slanted walls or low ceiling, for in that high place he could better hear the train whistles from the Collinwood Railroad Yard where his grandfather once worked.

In the morning he woke to the sound of trains from the East Station beginning to huff, slowly at first, then picking up speed, faster and faster until the wheel drivers were whirling and the train was screeching down the tracks. The sun would be lighting the single window at the gable end of the house by then, and the local radio station he'd been listening to the night before would have given way to more sedate offerings.

Music was his escape from that house where lived a father who drank too much, a mother who never wanted children, a brother who shone like the morning sun, and a grandmother who believed she was living among strangers.

Once, long ago, Charlie showed me that room. He told me of the boy who had spent so many hours there, and how he struggled to learn to play the guitar, and to write songs that would one day be played on the radio stations he listened to at night.

Somehow, being in this place where children of slaves gathered to hear music, to dance, to get up on stage and perform, being here has brought it all back. Standing outside that ruined building, the ocean waves crashing behind us, Charlie talks about those years, and he says things I've never heard before.

With his grandfather's old radio muffled beneath the covers, Charlie listened to his favorite Cleveland disc jockey play the music his elders both hated and feared. He heard Dinah Washington plead for the "Soft Winds" to bring her lover home to her. He listened to Screamin' Jay Hawkins whose recording of the blues ballad, "I Put a Spell on You," was banned from most radio stations. He thrilled to Chuck Berry's cover version of the old western swing song, "Ida Red," that had morphed into the rocking, driving "Maybellene." He yearned to own the record so he could play it over and over again.

He found it at a downtown store called Record Rendezvous that had begun to stock these wailing, hammering recordings. To placate worried parents, the clerks were told to no longer refer to the music as "Rhythm and Blues." They were to call it "Rock and Roll."

Charlie's future was sealed. He would have a career in music. He didn't know how, but he was determined to find a way. No matter how hard he had to work, or what he had to do, he would one day join the ranks of those who created music as infectious and as emotionally charged as what he heard on his grandfather's radio.

Now we're at a place called Evans's Rendezvous that was once part of a chain of juke joints. The music was unsophisticated, sometimes racy, always down-to-earth, a river of sound that merged and yet retained elements of the blues, country, western, gospel, jazz, and folk music. These were the places where it was played and sung and danced to, and ultimately, given to the world. Duke Ellington played here, as did James Brown, Ray Charles, Louis Armstrong, Billie Daniels, and Cab Calloway. For Charlie, it is a hallowed moment.

Stepping carefully through the weeds and rubble, we move around to the ocean side of the building. There's a one-story addition we hadn't noticed. Rhamy motions for us to come look through one of the windows. Inside is a sign, upside down and partially hidden behind what was once a bar. She spells out the part that is visible: S-U-O-V-Z. Read it the other way, and it's the last five letters of *Rendezvous*.

This is surely Evans's Rendezvous.

"Rock and Roll came out of places like this," Charlie says, backing away from the window, leading the way around to the south side of the building. "There was a club like this in Ferriday, Louisiana, where Jerry Lee Lewis used to go when he was a kid. He'd sneak in the back door and hide under a table. Haney's Big House was the name of the place, and they booked in some of the best black musicians in the country. Jerry Lee always claimed that's where he learned to play the piano.

"They called it race music," he says. "But white kids, kids my age, we loved it. There was something about the beat, the raw sensuality, the combination of blues, jazz, gospel that was new, and different, and exciting. White entertainers began recording it, artists like Elvis Presley, Carl Perkins, and Bill Haley. They had huge hits.

"It didn't bother me at all when they gave my room to my grandmother," he says. "I actually liked being up on the third floor. There was no one to bother me. It was a place where I could escape. And I had that radio."

Rhamy is amazed. She's never heard any of this before. She looks at me, and it's clear she wants to ask if I knew these things about her father, but she doesn't want to interrupt. Charlie is in a place he has not visited for many years.

In truth, this is a Charlie who is new to me. I knew about the attic room and his love of trains, but I'd never made a connection between the sound of the trains heading out to unknown destinations and the songs that reverberated in his head from the night before. I remember the radio, and I knew he treasured it, but that he felt he had to hide it from his parents? No. I didn't know.

But I've always known his childhood was a tortured one.

The song he wrote for Rhamy the day she was born contained a promise; she would be treasured. As he had not been.

The first time I saw you / I knew I was hooked…

That's the father Rhamy has always known: songwriter, guitar player, occasional performer. As a man who wrote songs of love, of loss, and of regret.

I could tell her that no one achieves what her father has without pain, that most artists are driven to succeed because of pain. But not now. The time is not right. We are on an island, outside a building where black comedians, musicians, and singers came to get up on stage, to perfect their artistry, and to try to break through the color barrier.

A faded inscription on the front of the building, beside what might have been the main entrance, bears the legend:

> *THESE FACILITIES ARE*
> *FOR OUR CUSTOMERS ONLY*
> *NO FOOD, DRINKS OR PICNICING*
> *ALLOWED TO BE BROUGHT ON PREMISE*
> *Thanks for Cooperating, The Management.*

Something moves in the weeds beneath the sign. We step away and head for the safety of the road.

We might have left then, but there's the beach, at the end of that rutted road, and it calls to us. We climb over the dunes and walk out onto hard-packed sand. The shoreline curves off in both directions. To the north, the Ritz-Carlton Resort surrounded by high-rises and luxury homes. To the south, Fraser's Plantation. In the middle, the narrow strip of land that is American Beach.

Standing on the damp sand by the ocean, I turn to look at the once-famous nightclub. It is barely visible over the high dunes.

Who could believe there was a time, before Civil Rights legislation, when blacks were forbidden to swim in the ocean? They came to this place on Friday and Saturday nights from miles around to hear the music that echoed out over the waters, music that spoke of their yearnings, their joys, and their sorrows. They were sharecroppers, house servants, gardeners, and janitors. They brought banjos, harmonicas, guitars and fiddles. They came for companionship, a sense of community, and they came searching for love, or something that could pass for love, if only for a night.

Some among them would have looked across the waters and thought of the country where their ancestors had lived. A few, in sickness and despair, might have gone into the water and let the ocean carry them where it pleased.

Charlie, as he often does, pulls me back from such thoughts. "Juke joints like this one," he says, "they could be pretty rough places. Drinking, gambling, high-stakes card games, people crammed into small places, low ceilings, loud music, it was a recipe for some violent encounters. Knives, guns, broken bottles. Fights over women. Think of some of the crossroads bars out in the country, the fights that broke out on Saturday nights, the blood that got spilled, the local hospitals that stitched them up."

"But this is a part of music history that shouldn't be forgotten," I argue. "And look at what a contribution they made."

He nods. "I just wouldn't romanticize it too much," he says.

We turn to the north and begin to walk along the American Beach, eyeing the trash line for things that might have been deposited there during high tide. Beach-combers often find sharks' teeth in this place. On sunny days, the fossilized black ones are easily spotted. But none of us is willing to look too closely; who knows what unexpected things might lurk in those piles of detritus.

The sadness of that abandoned building has chilled us. Charlie's harsh assessment of juke joints and the reminder of his lost childhood have thrown a shadow over the sun.

A hundred years ago, the chained bodies of negroes thrown from slave ships often washed up on these beaches. The penalty for bringing slaves into the U.S., after the passage of Jefferson's Act Prohibiting Importation of Slaves in 1807, was death. Better to toss the human cargo overboard than risk capture by the U.S. Navy.

American Beach has a history like no other place on earth.

I take off my shoes and head toward the water. Rhamy does the same. Charlie hangs back for a time, but then he joins us. We're splashing through a warm pool of trapped water when we hear another train whistle. We stop to listen. It is a mournful sound.

25

We leave St. Simons early the next morning. Our vacation is over, our next visit to Cumberland a year away. It's a five-hour drive to the Birmingham airport.

We arrive with time to spare; Rhamy has an hour to wait for her flight. She insists we not hang around. "Go," she tells us. "It's already two o'clock in the afternoon, and you have a three-hour drive ahead of you."

We hug her goodbye and I don't tear up until after we've left the airport. We won't see her again until Thanksgiving, and maybe not until Christmas.

We're still trying to find our way out of the city when my phone rings. It's Rhamy: the airport officials won't let her board the plane.

"They took my Cumberland Island sand," she says, sounding both shocked and irritated. "The sand I scooped up when we were on the beach. They think it's heroin. They've called for heroin-sniffing dogs."

"We'll come back," I tell her.

"No," she says. "Let's just wait it out."

"You put a shell in the bag. Show them that."

"I did. They don't believe me."

"Show them your legs. Tell them how we sat on the beach, and the front of your legs got sunburned."

She sighs. "Heroin," she says. "Only in Birmingham."

"You don't look like an addict," I tell her. "Show them your library card. Addicts don't have library cards."

"Does heroin look like sand?" she asks.

"I have no idea. I'll Google it and let you know."

Ten minutes later Rhamy calls again. Airport officials have decided to let her board her plane, sand and all.

"Pure heroin is a white powder," I tell her. "There are pictures on the internet. It looks like sugar, but it has a bitter taste. On TV, when they want to know if something is heroin or not, they taste it. Did they do that?"

"No, and there weren't any heroin-sniffing dogs available. I think they just decided to believe that it was sand."

"Well, for future reference, street heroin can be just about any color. It depends on what the dealer used to cut it. If your supplier is from the UK or Holland, it'll be brown, and you'll have to dissolve it in something acidic, like lemon juice. But mostly it's white or off-white."

I hear her take a deep breath.

"There's something called black tar heroin, which you have to dissolve before you can inject it."

"TMI, Mom," she says. "I'm getting on the plane now."

"Why didn't they taste it? And what about the dogs? Did they just say that to scare you? Why would they have drug-sniffing dogs in a place like Birmingham? Bomb-sniffing, maybe."

"I'm boarding now," she says.

"Text me when you get to Dallas," I tell her.

I turn my phone off and slip it into my purse. I might as well have thrown it out the window. It never works again. The salesman from Sprint tells me, two days later, that my phone is ruined. "We ran a diagnostic on it," he says. "The technician opened it up, and it was full of sand."

"Sand? How is that possible? How would sand get inside a cell phone?"

He shrugs. "Maybe someone took it to the beach."

Luckily, I still have my old flip phone. They're able to transfer my data, so I'll be able to use that until the insurance company sends me a new one.

26

First the periscope emerges from the water. Then a cluster of antennae. Something that looks like a smokestack, but surely isn't. The tower comes into view, flat on top, trapezoidal in shape, fins protruding from the sides.

The passengers on the *Cumberland Queen* cluster in the back of the boat, Rhamy and I among them, looking at this thing coming up out of the water. It's so close, we can feel the disturbance beneath our feet.

"Submarine," a young boy says, and his voice is full of wonderment.

In the Cumberland Sound?

The hull emerges, breaking the surface of the water, looking like a huge, shiny, gray whale. Crowded on the back of our boat, we watch, hardly speaking, in awe of what we're seeing.

"It's surfacing," someone breathes.

"She's a big one," says another. "She must be over five hundred feet long."

Water cascades off the sides. The hull steams in the morning sun. It rises higher and higher until at least half of it is above the surface of the water.

I think of German U-Boats from World War II prowling the shipping lanes in the Atlantic, looking for troop ships they could torpedo and send to the bottom. Before the sinking of the two oil tankers in St. Simons Sound, a German submarine was spotted off the coast of Jekyll Island. Some in the War Department wondered if the enemy might be planning to sneak onto Jekyll and capture the industrialists who were wintering there. They could carry them back to Germany and hold them for ransom. Because there was no way to adequately protect the island and its inhabitants, government officials advised everyone to leave.

The Jekyll Island Club and cottages were abandoned.

Could this be a relic from that era? Like the Japanese soldiers discovered in caves in the Philippines, could this be an enemy submarine, somehow lost in a time warp?

We're fifteen minutes out of St. Marys, on our way to Cumberland. The submarine is behind us, but close enough that we can see the rivets on its hull.

"Trident submarine," an old man says. "She's heading back to the base. Naval Submarine Base at Kings Bay."

"He's surfaced for the ride up the North River," another passenger says. "They had to dredge it when they built the base. It was too shallow to accommodate submarines. Could be the river is silting up again."

I turn around, wondering about these men who seem to know so much. They stand in a group, four or five of them, all mature men, all with short hair, each one at least twenty pounds overweight. Old Navy men, I decide.

"It's a huge base," one of them says. "Covers something like sixteen thousand acres. They call it Jimmy Carter's gift to his home state. Right after he won the presidency, he decided to locate the base here, just a few miles north of St. Marys."

"The Navy has eighteen nuclear submarines armed with Trident missiles," says another. "They keep ten of them here, the other eight in Bangor, Washington. At any given moment, five of them are on patrol in either the Atlantic or the Pacific. Each one is capable of firing Trident ballistic missiles at whatever target they choose."

Rhamy grabs my arm. "Remember the year we got lost trying to get to St. Marys? The rental agent had given us terrible directions, and we ended up at a submarine base. That must be where we were, on that base. Remember?"

"There were gates across all the entrances," I answer, "and guard houses, and armed guards patrolling the entrances. Was it three years ago?"

"Three or four," she says. "I've lost count. We thought we were gonna miss the ferry."

The hatch atop the submarine opens. A figure emerges. Another. And another. They keep coming until there are at least twenty sailors standing on the boat, strung out along its length.

What an amazing thing to witness. We've seen it in movies, but this is real. We're close enough we could shout at the men standing on the submarine, and they might shout back.

They're dressed in various shades of blue, most of them wearing dark blue coveralls and lighter colored shirts.

"Daddy will never believe this," Rhamy says.

"He should have come with us. In your whole lifetime, how many times do you get a chance to see something like this?"

"It's a miracle. And it could only happen here."

That's not true, of course — that it could only happen here. Yet, in a way, it is. There are submarines that surface unexpectedly all around the world. If you're on a ferry, and you're near a submarine base, your chances of seeing one are higher than if you're in Nashville or Portland. But still, there's something about the Golden Isles, and Cumberland Island, and our pilgrimage here every year, that seems to put us in the way of the unexpected.

The sailors wave to us, and we wave back, and our boat moves slowly away from the submarine, or it from us. Then it is gone, either lost to distance or to a curve in the river. Or maybe it descended into the deep.

The Fates are not finished with us. Walking along the Atlantic beach, we see what looks like a tarp covering a mound in the distance.

"Oh, God, Mom," Rhamy says. "It's a horse. It's got to be a horse. What else could it be?"

I think of the old stallion that ate the apple out of Rhamy's hands. Is she wondering the same thing? I don't ask.

We could turn around, go back to Sea Camp, but we've come too far. We can't take a chance on missing the ferry back to St. Marys. The tarp and whatever it covers is close to the dunes, far enough away from the ocean that we'll be able to skirt around it, eyes averted.

Could the old stallion have survived the winters that have gone by since that day? Did he wait for us to come back? When we did not, or we came and he didn't see us, did he walk away from the band, and come to this place by the ocean, and lay himself down?

It is a fantasy. At any given time, there are well over a hundred horses on the island. It's been three years. He could not have survived that long.

Another hundred yards up the beach, and we know it isn't the stallion. Whatever is beneath the tarp is larger than a horse. Much larger. And in an advanced stage of decomposition. We pick up our pace, wanting to be beyond it, wanting to not have seen it, wanting for it not to have been there.

We can't go fast enough or far enough into the water to avoid the awful smell of rotting flesh, innards, and blubber. The thing on the beach is a whale. What we thought was a tarp is actually the skin of the whale, black and shiny in the sun. It is a huge animal, at least thirty feet long, partially buried beneath windblown sand, yet so big it rises up out of the dunes like a dune itself.

I look to the sky, wondering about scavenger birds. There are none.

"We know about it," the ranger at the Dungeness dock tells us several hours later. "It was a humpback. We think she was hit by a boat. Humpbacks tend to stay near the surface of the ocean, and they feed in the shallow waters close to shore. That puts them more at risk than other whales. Most of them we see have scars on them."

"Humpbacks are the ones that sing, aren't they?" Rhamy asks.

The ranger nods. "Scientists are studying them, trying to figure out what their songs mean. Their sounds carry for miles and miles in the oceans. Kind of eerie, but beautiful. They're great swimmers, too. We often see them leap clear out of the water — it's called breaching — then land with a great splash. It's possible they do it to clean pests off their skin, or maybe just to have fun. No one knows for sure.

"She'll be gone in a few days," the ranger says, and she turns away.

We sit at a picnic table beneath a tree to wait for the ferry. Three horses graze the open space near the Ice House. Rhamy looks around to be certain no one is watching. She tosses an apple. Two of the horses spook. The third one merely looks at the strange object that has landed in her pasture. She stretches out her neck, sniffs, takes a step forward, and picks up the apple. She bites into it, and there's a look of surprise on her face. She chews, and part of the apple drops to the ground. She finishes what's in her mouth, picks up the piece she dropped. Still chewing, she looks at us, and we can read her thoughts: *What is this wonderful thing you've thrown into my pasture, and do you have more?*

We do. Several more.

Rhamy doles them out, one by one, while I keep watch for the ranger, or anyone else who might report us for the crime we are committing.

Thoughts of the submarine and the whale, and of anything that speaks of war and death, are gone. This one mare who has eaten our apples and looked to us for more has reminded us of what we love about the island: the isolation, the naturalness, the freedom. It is a place where nature in all her beauty and her cruelty, can have her way.

There is a peacefulness here, and it washes over us, and we can only bow our heads in acceptance.

27

The live oaks on Cumberland have survived hurricanes, salt air, and assaults by men with chain saws. Now they are being threatened anew. The dunes are smothering the trees. They are filling up Lake Whitney, the largest freshwater lake on the island, home to brim and bass, alligators and cottonmouth moccasins.

It's because of the horses, environmentalists say. They graze on the sea oats that anchors the dunes, and it causes the dunes to migrate to places they've never been. The horses eat the spartina grass, reducing its density, decimating the habitat of fiddler crabs, leading to marsh erosion. They churn the soil and compress it, ultimately decreasing the size of the marsh. They create trails where nature never intended. They chew the bark off trees, browse the leaves, eat the saplings. They pull the Spanish moss from the trees. They gallop along the beaches, trample the shore birds, destroy the sea turtle nests.

They don't belong here, ecologists say. They are disrupting the fragile ecosystems on the island. They should be removed, or at the very least, their numbers controlled.

Yet the population of the herd has been stable for years.

Look at the death rate of the foals, animal scientists respond. Look at the mares, their skin conditions, their weight. Stallion castration is the only answer. Or birth control.

But they already tried that. Not castration. Birth control. They shot contraceptives into the mares. It was supposed to make them sterile for four months. It didn't work. Despite the promises of the pharmaceutical companies, veterinarians discovered you have to do booster shots every month. How is that possible with a herd this large, on an island this size?

Look at their feet, Rhamy would say. For horses that have never seen a farrier, they look amazingly good. She wishes her horse's feet looked so good.

She buys hoof hardeners to paint on Quest's hooves, special supplements to add to her grain. Her horse is pampered. The pasture is soft and lush. There are no stones to trim her hooves, to rasp away the excess growth.

Nursing mothers have special nutritional needs, veterinarians argue. Here, on the island, with pasture as poor as this, there's no way they can get what they need.

Yet the horses have been here for hundreds of years, and they've survived. Some years are kinder to the herd than others, but they've never gone extinct. Rhamy and I would argue they've adapted to the environment, and now they're a part of the ecosystem.

Once, on our way back from the ocean, we saw a foal near the Greene-Miller cemetery. There was no sign of his mother, but he looked as healthy as any foal we'd ever seen. Rhamy said he was as healthy as Quest when she was a baby.

It's not uncommon for horses in captivity to live thirty years, horse owners will tell you.

And then be sent to Mexico to be slaughtered, Rhamy would remind them. Better that they live here, on this island, where they are free.

But the damage to the environment…

The debate goes back and forth.

On this my seventh visit to the island, Rhamy's sixth, we have no expectations. We've crossed the high dunes that shield us from the ocean, and are now at the edge of the historic district. There's a shady spot behind the building where two years ago we sought shelter from a storm. It seems a good place to rest, and to take in whatever the island has to offer.

Grazing in the pasture between the Dungeness outbuildings and the dunes is the largest band of horses we've ever seen on the island. There must be at least twenty-five, moving around the pasture where the Carnegies once kept dairy cattle. There are bays and chestnuts, a few strawberry roans, at least two pintos, a chunky gray at the edge of the band. The pasture is littered with rocks, bits of tabby, tree branches, and discarded fence posts. Yet among the debris and bare spots the horses are finding plenty to eat.

"Castration wouldn't work, you know," Rhamy says. "You'd have to castrate all the stallions. If you missed a single one, he'd breed all the mares, and you'd have lost the genetic diversity of the herd. If you managed to castrate every single stallion on the island, you'd wipe out the herd. So it makes absolutely no sense."

"I wonder if that has occurred to them," I answer. "Or is that what they want to happen?"

"There's no laminitis, that I can see," Rhamy says. "Or colic. We had a horse colic in our barn a few months ago. The vet pulled him through, but horses that colic are likely to do it again. Last summer it was equine herpes virus. They quarantined all our horses for a month. No trail rides off the property, no horse shows, special procedures we had to follow every time we went into a stall, groomed our horses, took them outside to jump. It's just possible these horses are in some ways healthier than our domesticated ones."

"There have been outbreaks of equine encephalitis on the island," I remind her.

"Yes. There are mosquitoes here. A few horses have died. One just last year. I read that on a blog."

"So during the winter you read blogs from people who have been to Cumberland Island?"

"Sometimes," she says. "One equine veterinarian visited here a few years ago. He rented a house that belonged to a retained rights owner. He brought his family and spent a whole month here."

"Sounds like heaven."

"He thought the herd was in amazingly good shape, commented on how shiny their coats were. They tend to stay on the southern part of the island, he said, because this was where the cotton plantations were. There are more open fields, more places to graze. He noticed they often go out into the marshes in the evening, and he wondered why they don't get trapped there. He actually put on boots and went out himself, thinking he'd find remains, but he never did."

She raises her binoculars and gazes out at the band. They're milling, and occasionally nipping at one another, pinning their ears, but mostly they're contented.

"It's the rocky areas that keep their hooves worn down," Rhamy says. "That, and the seashells. Their hooves are longer than what you'd normally see on domestic horses. That would give them traction when they're climbing dunes or walking along the beach.

"The mares all look pregnant," she adds. "Either that, or they've had plenty to eat over the winter."

"Which one is the stallion?"

She raises her binoculars and scans the band. "I think it's the gray we noticed before." She leans forward to get a better view. "Except he seems to be missing the equipment he needs. He's a girl."

"Look at that black horse over by the rocks," I suggest. "I just saw him take a bite out of a horse that got too close. Maybe it was a mare trying to steal a clump of grass he had his eye on."

"I think the black is an alpha mare. The dominant mare in the band. Normally you'll find stallions at the edge of the band. I still think it's the gray."

"How could that be, if he's missing the things he needs most?"

"I could be wrong about that. It's hard to see. I can't really tell."

"Give me the binoculars."

She hands them to me. "The strawberry roan is a male," I tell her.

She takes the glasses back. "He might be the stallion," she says, but she sounds uncertain.

"Just look what we're doing, Rhamy. Connor would never believe it. Sitting here, trying to figure out which horses are stallions and which ones are mares. You'd think it would be obvious."

"It would be, if we were closer. Some of the males might be yearlings, still living with the band, not yet sexually mature."

She focuses on three horses at the far edge of the pasture, separate from the others, but still part of the band: stallion, mare, and yearling. "Could that be a family unit?" she wonders.

The largest group is grazing near the dunes. A third group of six horses has drifted toward the seashell road.

"What I think we have here," Rhamy says, and her voice is slow and deliberate, "is not one band, but three separate ones that are part of a herd."

"Bands?"

"Separate bands, each with a stallion and his mares and maybe a yearling or a foal. For some reason, they're all fairly close together, and it doesn't seem to be a problem. It's amazing."

"The black is an alpha mare," Rhamy continues. "I'm sure of it. She just pinned her ears at a juvenile who got too close, chased him back to his mother. Alpha mares are the ones in charge of discipline. But if it's three bands, there are others."

She gets up from the log where we're sitting and moves toward the herd. I watch, wanting to warn her to be careful. These are wild horses.

They pay her no mind. She keeps to the edges at first, moving slowly, talking to them, occasionally extending an upturned palm. Sometimes they move away from her. Other times they raise their heads, gaze at her, then go back to grazing. The horses on Cumberland are used to people walking their trails, frolicking on their beaches, traipsing through their meadows. After a while, I join her in the pasture. It seems the most natural thing in the world, to be in this place, among these horses.

The mares are big-bellied, the colts long-legged and frisky, the stallions fat and healthy. Their coats are shiny, their manes long and silky. It's been a good year: plentiful rain, sweet grass.

A white foal moves toward me, his head outstretched. His nose is pink, his mane short and feathery. He sniffs, turns and races back to his mother, a bay so dark she's almost black.

Rhamy has been watching. "Careful, Mom," she says. "Don't get between a mare and her baby. They can be more dangerous than a stallion. I've seen them go after owners, veterinarians, anyone who goes into their stalls."

"He just wanted to play," I tell her.

"The mare might not see it that way."

I back away, reluctantly, not really believing there could be any real danger, not here, not on this magic day, not in this place. Not when the island has offered up this chance to walk among the horses, which we do, for a time that seems without end.

The island has never failed to give some unexpected gift, and on this day, this is her gift to us. We accept it and store it away for days when skies are gloomy and troubles abound.

The horses on Cumberland are such a mixture of different strains, their genetic inheritance so diverse, it's impossible to look at any particular horse and assign to it a specific breed. There's a blue roan yearling with a delicate little head that looks Arabian to me. Does she have twenty-three vertebrae rather than the normal twenty-four? I have no idea. But that dished face and those fine hooves lead me to believe she's at least part Arabian.

Some of the larger horses surely carry the genes of the Tennessee Walker — majestic horses with long necks, long, straight heads, calm dispositions.

The strawberry roan I saw earlier; could he be the offspring of the old horse that ate the apple out of Rhamy's hands? He's grazing near the edge of the center band. Is he the band stallion? And if he is, what happened to the black stallion with the white stockings that led that band?

There's a chestnut so solidly built, so broad-chested with such well-rounded hind quarters, she has to be at least part Quarter Horse. The Pintos are small and chunky. Indians liked Pintos because they are such willing little ponies, tough and intelligent, easy to mount and ride into battle. Could they be descended from the wild mustangs rounded up by the Bureau of Land Management, loaded onto a boxcar in Arizona and shipped to Cumberland in 1921?

There are a number of Appaloosas — spotted horses like those brought to the island by the Spanish Conquistadors in the early 1500s. Do they carry the same bloodlines as the first horses known to live here? What remarkable animals they were, to survive sea journeys that lasted for months, to then walk off the ships and carry their owners into the wilderness. What of the work horses and the pleasure horses brought here by English settlers in the 1700s? They must have left traces of their genes.

When Robert Stafford established his cotton plantation on Cumberland in the early 1800s, there were as many as three hundred feral horses on the island.

For a time they were a cash crop; Stafford sold them to anyone willing to round them up and load them onto ferries bound for the mainland.

During the Civil War, Union soldiers captured and pressed them into service as cavalry mounts. Their numbers dwindled, but in the wild forests and marshes of Cumberland, some escaped, and they survived.

When the developers of the Jekyll Island Club needed a place to relocate the horses that roamed free on lands they wanted as hunting grounds for their members, they looked to Cumberland. Thomas Carnegie agreed to take them. In an effort to further improve the herd, he brought in more mustangs. Lucy's horses joined the wild horses of Cumberland after her death.

Still it continued, this inflow and outflow of Cumberland horses, the mixing of blood and genetics. The Bureau of Land Management sent a second group of horses to Cumberland in 1939. Residents brought pleasure horses to the island. On occasion these Thoroughbreds, Arabians, Paints, horses of mixed and various breeds broke free. At other times the owners simply turned them loose.

Lucy Ferguson, granddaughter of Thomas and Lucy Carnegie, sold hundreds of horses to buyers on the mainland during the 1950s. As recently as the early 1990s, a retained-rights resident released four Arabian horses into the wild.

Moving among the horses, I'm struck by how tall they are. The Chincoteague and Assateague ponies from Virginia and Maryland are small, their legs stubby, their coats wooly. Forced to drink brackish water and subsist on salt marsh plants and brush, their growth has been stunted.

The Cumberland horses stand fourteen and fifteen hands, nearly as big as Rhamy's Quest. The black mare I noticed earlier is even taller, Thoroughbred tall, lean and athletic, black eyes surveying me, intelligent and curious but without fear, taking me in as I move closer to her. Her muscles ripple beneath a coat so smooth and velvety I want to reach out and touch her.

Fresh water abounds on Cumberland Island: numerous ponds and creeks, the artesian well at Dungeness, Lake Whitney in the north, Lake Retta in the south. The horses graze in the marshes and in the dunes by the ocean. They eat the broad leaf grasses and clover that grows in the cleared areas around Dungeness. They feed on the natural grasses that have replaced the cotton.

A gust of wind off the ocean ruffles their manes and their tails, and what beautiful creatures they are. I am in love with each and every one of them.

The wind picks up, and I can feel the sand against my skin. I look up. At the very top of the dune three horses are standing, silhouettes against the sky, looking down on us. One is a buckskin, his coat so pale he might be lost in the clouds, if not for his black mane and tail. The other two are either sorrels or light bays.

We've seen the buckskin before. Rhamy took pictures of him on the beach this morning.

I catch her attention and motion for her to look up.

"It's the bachelors," she says. "The ones we saw earlier."

They begin to move toward us, sliding in the soft sand, going sideways at times, weaving around dead tree stumps, thickets of brush, disappearing from sight when they descend into gullies, reappearing, moving inexorably downward, toward the herd.

Bachelors are always looking to pick up a stray mare, a filly forced out of a band, or a mare not properly guarded. On occasion, they'll challenge a harem stallion. It's time for Rhamy and me to retreat.

Seated once again in the shade of the machine shed, it's immediately obvious to us which are the harem stallions. The gray at the edge of the pasture is suddenly alert, his head high, his body tense as he watches the progress of the three bachelors. The red sorrel by the seashell road is nervous, his ears alternately perked and flattened. The palomino stallion in the center group, closest to where we sit, paws the ground and snorts. He circles his band, herding them away from the dunes, closer to where we sit.

I hadn't noticed the palomino before. Now I look closely, and I see the marks of battles won and lost, a scar from an old bite wound near his jaw, an injury on his hindquarter that has not yet healed. Yet he is still a powerful stallion.

Rhamy has her eye on the three bachelors. "The buckskin is too young to try anything," she says. "He'll never challenge a stallion as powerful as that palomino. The same for the other two. They're all too young, too inexperienced. Nothing to worry about," Rhamy says.

But she keeps watching.

The white foal has once again strayed from his mother. He's racing around the edge of the band, kicking up his heels, sparring with a yearling, then running off to find another playmate. He collides with the palomino, who herds him back to his mother. Properly chastised, the foal begins to nurse, and his mother turns to groom him.

Watching the foal, I'm reminded of a documentary I saw a year ago about a band of wild mustangs in the Arrowroot Mountains of Montana. Ginger Kathrens, the documentarian, filmed a white foal shortly after he was born. Because of his coloring, she named him Cloud. Over the next fifteen years she watched him grow, join a band of bachelors, and years later acquire mares of his own.

In one of the episodes, Cloud steals a filly named Velvet from a rival band. He'd known her since she was a foal; they'd once been playmates. He was a mature stallion by then, seven or eight years old. When he saw Velvet, he was smitten. He moved in, separated her from her band, and herded her away.

When Cloud and Velvet got back to where Cloud had left his band, they were gone, stolen by another mustang. A short time later the mares came back to Cloud; they'd waited for their chance, and when they saw it, they left that thieving stallion and made their way back to Cloud.

Another story in the series did not end so happily. The Bureau of Land Management conducts annual roundups in order to reduce the size of the herds. In 2006, hundreds of mustangs were targeted for removal from their ancestral homes. Cloud had been caught in at least one previous roundup and released because of his unusual coloring. This time was different. Led by a Judas horse and chased for miles by a helicopter, Cloud and his entire band were captured. Cloud and several of his mares were ultimately released, but four members of his family were marked for adoption. For fifteen minutes this remarkable horse "snaked" the remaining members of his band. Ears pinned, head lowered, he tried to turn them, force them back to the pens so they could free his lost mares. He was finally forced to give up.

When the three Cumberland bachelors reach the pasture, they break into a gallop, dashing across the field, racing this way and that, kicking up their hind legs. The buckskin approaches the palomino, and the stallion rears up, shrieking, front legs flailing. The buckskin races off, as if it was all in fun, *we didn't mean anything, we were just hassling you.*

"Bachelors are always testing the limits," Rhamy says. "It serves a purpose, though. They're actually developing skills they'll need when they're old enough and strong enough to challenge a harem stallion."

"Send me that picture you took of the buckskin on the beach this morning. I'm gonna change out the wallpaper on my computer screen. Imagine, seeing that horse grazing in the dunes every morning when I turn it on."

"It would be like being on Cumberland every single day, wouldn't it," she says.

The shadows created by the trees and the building behind us are lengthening. The band led by the red sorrel begins to drift off toward the marsh beyond the Greene-Miller cemetery. In the melee created by the marauding bachelors, the gray stallion with his mare and yearling have disappeared. The remaining band, the largest of the three, is moving into the woods behind where the Carnegie barn once stood.

Our water bottles are empty. It's time to head back to the ferry, but still we linger. It's hard to think of leaving. For each of the last two years we've seen only a handful of horses. This year, for whatever reason, has been different.

"Think of it, Mom," Rhamy says, "to see three bands, maybe four, all grazing this close together. When I get back to Portland, I have to get a book on herd dynamics, try to figure out what's going on. Normally a stallion will mark his territory, and other bands will respect it."

"We could watch those Cloud documentaries after dinner tonight," I tell her. "Remember? You're the one who told me about them: *Cloud: Wild Stallion of the Rockies*. I've forgotten the names of the others, but there are at least three of them. They're on PBS, so we might be able to find them on Charlie's iPad."

"The white foal," she says. "I was thinking the same thing. He looks like Cloud."

The park ranger in charge of counting passengers as they arrive at the Dungeness dock is on her walkie-talkie, talking to another ranger. The male voice on the other end of the line is scratchy. It fades in and out, but we're close enough to make out both sides of the conversation.

"Two kids have gone missing," he says. "They were supposed to meet their parents at the dock at 3:45 p.m. They didn't show. It's nearly 4:30. The parents are on their way to Sea Camp, hoping the kids will turn up there. I'm heading there now."

"It happens every year, doesn't it," she answers. "You'd think parents would keep a closer eye on their kids."

"They're boys, aged ten and twelve," is the response. "One of them is wearing cut-off jeans and a Star Wars T-shirt, the other one khaki shorts and a blue, T-Rex tank top. The older kid is about five feet, the younger one just a few inches shorter. They're blonde with hazel eyes."

The ranger looks out over the water. "Could they have gone to the beach?" she asks, and the tone of her voice has changed.

Two kids drowned in the ocean across from Sea Camp several years ago. Rescuers found the bodies in shallow water, near the spot where they were swimming. The parents sued the Park Service. The case is still working its way through the courts.

"That's where they were heading," the man replies. "The parents told them not to go in the water, warned them about undertows, and they promised they wouldn't. But you know kids."

The ranger sighs and walks toward the picnic tables. She checks the restrooms, scans the surrounding area, looks up and down the road. The kids are nowhere in sight.

"If they show up, I'll let you know," she says. She mashes a button on her radio and returns to the dock. In the distance we see a boat heading in our direction, but it's too far away to see if it's the *Cumberland Queen*.

A crowd of about thirty passengers have gathered, some in the sheltered area, others standing along the dock railing. Rhamy and I sit on one of the benches.

The ranger walks to the far end of the dock and stands by the opening to the gangplank. She's a formidable woman in every way: ramrod straight, dark hair pulled back in a tight pony tail, hat worn low over her eyes.

Everyone beneath the shelter is silent. The conversation, when it begins, is slow and halting.

"Why on earth would parents let two kids that young go off by themselves?" a woman asks.

A pause.

"Anything could have happened to them," the woman continues. "They might have been bitten by a snake, gotten lost, anything."

"Or drowned," someone says.

Another pause.

"Surely they'll show up."

"If they miss the ferry, how will they get back to St. Marys?"

"They'll have to charter a boat." This from a heavy-set man, arms crossed over his ample belly.

"But there are no boats. I haven't seen a single one since I've been here. Just the ferry."

"Maybe one of the rangers can take them back?"

"They'll have to spend the night. Aren't there benches on the porch at Sea Camp? Maybe the family can all sleep there."

"The important thing is to find the kids. The rangers will have to go out looking for them, if they don't turn up. Nothing else to do but start searching the island."

"But it's twenty miles long. It's just not possible, not before it gets dark."

"The parents should never have let them go off on their own."

"There's a bed and breakfast on the island, run by one of the Carnegie descendants. Maybe they could go there. From Sea Camp it's only about three miles."

Rhamy glances at me. We know about the Greyfield Inn. But we don't volunteer anything. Back in January we visited the Greyfield website to check availabilities. Our idea was to take the ferry to Sea Camp, rent bicycles, ride up the main road to the inn, spend the night, and return to St. Marys the next day. The cost of a double room ranged from $425 to $695 a night, and there was a two-night minimum.

Luckily, Greyfield was booked for the nights we might have been able to stay. But one day we'll do it, Charlie and I, Rhamy and Connor. Charlie will need some convincing. It's an obscene amount of money, he'll say. And he won't like being told he has to wear a dinner jacket.

But when in our whole lives will we ever again have the chance to sleep in a bed that might once have belonged to Lucy Carnegie? The price is exorbitant, but it's all inclusive: gourmet dinners, picnic lunches, naturalist-led Jeep tours of the island, bicycles, cocktails and hors d'oeuvres. We can drive to Fernandina Beach, park our car, board the *Lucy R. Ferguson* for the trip up the Cumberland Sound to Greyfield. There's even a shuttle from the Jacksonville airport, if we fly instead of drive from Nashville.

I think I'll be able to convince Charlie. When you do something like that, you remember the experience, not how much it cost. That's what he said to me once when he wanted to buy first-class tickets on the *City of New Orleans*, the Amtrak train that runs from Chicago to the Gulf of Mexico.

It was a wonderful trip, but it might not have been. The coach sections of the train were filled to near capacity. If there was air conditioning, it was not working. Many of the passengers were from Canada. They'd been on the train for a long time, and they had another nineteen hours to go. There were no showers.

First-class accommodations gave us climate-controlled passenger cars, roomy seats, a separate dining car, lounge, and a dome car complete with seats that swiveled. I promised Charlie I would never again question his judgment. I try to keep that promise. Sometimes I'm successful.

The ferry that will take us back to St. Marys appears on the horizon. When it reaches the dock and crew members have secured the boat, the ranger removes the rope that blocks the entrance to the gangplank. The passengers begin to board. After one last look around the pasture, the marsh, the seashell road, and the forest beyond, the ranger follows the last of the passengers down the gangplank.

Her walkie-talkie beeps just as she steps onto the boat. The boys have been found. They're at Sea Camp with their parents. They were having such a good time they totally forgot they were supposed to meet their parents at Dungeness. They saw horses, an armadillo, a wild pig, deer, a flock of turkeys, and some black birds they thought were buzzards. They want to come back tomorrow to swim in the ocean.

Ten minutes later we dock at Sea Camp. The boys are the first to board. There's a tussle as they fight to be the first to climb the stairs to the top deck. Their parents, looking tired and sunburned, find seats along the side.

We never leave the island that we don't ask about the latest herd count. The rangers always know the numbers — many of them volunteer for the two-day count held each year in late March. They're always happy to share the information.

Now that the boys have been found, and our ranger is not faced with the prospect of having to search for them into the night, she's lost some of her severity. The hat is gone, her hair disheveled. She's concentrating on the wake behind the boat, the birds that are following and overtaking us, dropping back, veering off.

A motorboat is coming up behind us, its bow high in the air. As it nears the ferry, the driver cuts sharply to the right and roars past.

"One hundred and thirty-six horses," she says in response to Rhamy's question. "There were 111 adults, 22 yearlings, and three foals."

"Just three foals?"

"It's early," she says, grabbing onto the railing as the ferry rocks its way through waves and troughs caused by the speed boat. "Most of them haven't been born yet, so you can probably add another fifty to that number. There's no way you can count every horse. We do it over a period of two days, and we follow the same routes. But some horses are gonna get counted twice, and some are gonna get missed. We can usually eliminate the duplicates, but how many we miss is anyone's guess."

"It's up from last year, isn't it?"

"The population has held pretty steady between 120 and 140 horses for the last ten years," she says.

The water smooths and the ferry plows into it, splitting it apart, leaving a ditch of foam in our wake. The wind is gentle, the sun pleasantly warm. The three of us stand in the back of the boat, watching the waters churn behind us. The conversation turns from island horses to the mustang roundups in the West, the Bureau of Land Management, the holding pens where the captured horses are kept, the controversy about whether the mustangs are native. Because horses went extinct in America some ten thousand years ago, many argue that the mustangs should be considered an invasive species. Ranchers want nothing less than the complete removal of the wild horses from land where the herds have lived for five hundred years, and before that, for tens of thousands of years.

The ranger works for the National Park Service, and she's careful what she says. But she knows the statistics. There are currently 25,000 wild horses on 31 million acres of public land in ten Western states. Twelve million cattle and sheep graze on these lands, as well as on an additional 245 million acres of public lands. For every single horse, there are nearly 500 food animals.

The ranchers are not satisfied. They believe the horses compete with their livestock for forage. They want them gone.

"The 25,000 are luckier than they realize," the ranger says. "At least they are free. There are 50,000 in holding pens. Some will be euthanized because of the brutality of the roundups, the helicopters that force them to run for miles. A few will be adopted. None will be released. They will either be sent to slaughter houses or die in the pens."

She puts her hat back on her head and stares into the water. Birds wheel above us, cutting this way and that, choosing a flight plan and changing it mid-air. Each of us standing there needs some time to reflect on what the ranger has just said, and what it means.

Among those 25,000 mustangs, she tells us, are horses directly descended from those brought by the Spanish to the West Indies, Florida, and Mexico in the late fifteenth and sixteenth centuries. To protect the horses during those long trips across the Atlantic, the Spanish constructed slings for the most valuable animals, to take the weight off their feet and to allow the animals to swing with the roll of the ships. Other, less valuable horses were confined to dark, damp holds. Those that sickened or died en route were thrown overboard.

When the ships reached their destinations, the surviving horses were blindfolded, raised from below deck, and led off the ships. In the ensuing years in this land where their ancestors had once lived, some escaped. They became feral. And they thrived.

There's a herd in the Arrowroot Mountains that have been directly, genetically linked to horses brought across the Atlantic in slings. In their veins runs the blood of Barb horses from Northern Africa, Andalusians from the Iberian Peninsula, and Arabians from the Middle East.

"Some of those pureblood Spanish horses are here, on this island," the ranger says. "I can't prove it, but I believe it."

"And they're safe here, aren't they?" Rhamy asks.

"For the moment," she says, and she leans against the railing. The water behind us is churning, tumbling, roiling in its attempt to close the ditch our passing has caused. White-tipped waves wash across it, and far behind us it becomes smooth again.

28

Charlie refuses to commit. No matter what I say, how many times I ask, how many different ways I find to bring up the subject, he won't tell me if he plans to come to Cumberland Island in the spring. He's seen the pictures of the beachfront condo we've rented on St. Simons, and he thinks it'll be wonderful; he's as tired of our gray January skies as I am. But about Cumberland, he just won't say.

I tell him I've reserved three spots on the Cumberland Island van tour and three seats on the early ferry. I already sent the money, I tell him. They won't refund it. You have to book early because the tours fill up. They run the van tours rain or shine. They have to. When the Carnegies deeded Plum Orchard to the Park Service, it was with the stipulation that the mansion be kept in good repair and open to the public. The "good repair" part cost the Park Service about seven million dollars.

"It'll be a trip through unspoiled wilderness," I tell him. "Never to be forgotten. So much better than the boat tours they used to run. Visitors never liked the boat tours. So the Park Service started these Lands and Legacies Tours — six hours up the main road with stops at all the historical places along the way. This is only the second year they've been running them, and they're wildly popular. We'll bring our lunches and find a picnic spot under the trees at Plum Orchard."

Plum Orchard, I remind him, is the twenty-two room mansion Lucy Carnegie built for her son George, who married Margaret Thaw, who was the younger sister of Harry Thaw, who shot the architect Stanford White, who was having an affair with Harry's wife, Evelyn Nesbit.

"There's a movie about that," Charlie says, and I know I've hit on something that might just persuade him.

"*The Girl in the Red Velvet Swing,*" he says. "Joan Collins and Ray Milland. I saw it when I was a kid."

"I can't believe your parents let you see a movie like that. The story is absolutely scandalous."

"Maybe I was a little older," he admits.

"It was in black and white, I remember. Harry Thaw shot Stanford White in cold blood on the rooftop garden theatre of Madison Square Garden, a building White had designed. There were hundreds of eye witnesses. The press called it 'The Trial of the Century.' It had everything: a lecherous old man, a beautiful young chorus girl, a jealous husband. Harry Thaw's mother spent a chunk of the family fortune trying to get him off."

"There were actually two trials," Charlie reminds me. "The first one deadlocked. In the second trial, Harry pleaded not guilty by reason of insanity. The jury sent him off to a mental institution."

"Evelyn Nesbit might have visited Plum Orchard," I tell him. "Harry could have brought her there. It was his sister's home, after all, and the Thaws spent a lot of time on Cumberland. Maybe in one of the bedrooms there'll be a swing made of red velvet."

"And the walls and ceiling will be completely covered with mirrors," Charlie says.

"I don't remember that. Is it in the movie?"

He shrugs. "I think so. Or maybe I read it somewhere. Stanford White had a room in his apartment furnished like that. Red velvet swing, green velvet couch, and mirrors everywhere."

"It sounds like he had a thing for velvet."

"And young girls. Evelyn Nesbit was sixteen when he supposedly seduced her. He was in his late forties."

I think Charlie is beginning to come around. But just in case he needs more convincing, I continue: "Here's another connection you might not know about. When Harry Thaw's mother announced the engagement of her daughter, Alice, to the Earl of Yarmouth, guess where the Thaws were staying?"

"Plum Orchard?"

"So you have to come with us."

He doesn't answer. But later that night he asks what I think they mean when they describe the tour as "strenuous." I'm surprised. He's obviously done an internet search. How else would he know that? I would never have told him such a thing.

"How strenuous can it be," I answer, "when you're riding in a van for most of the trip? This is the National Park Service. The vans will be air conditioned, state-of-the-art. There'll be plenty of stops along the way, bathroom breaks, chances to get out, walk around, take pictures. We'll get to see Stafford Plantation, the Chimneys, visit the church where John F. Kennedy, Jr., and Carolyn Bessette were married."

In truth, I care less about the First African Baptist Church than I do about the cabin next door where naturalist Carol Ruckdeschel lives.

Charlie would never admit it, but he relies on me to take him places he would never otherwise go. Or, at the very least, he is grateful for the adventures we've had, and he understands that, on his own, he'd never attempt some of the things we've done. Won't his life be richer when he hears the story of Carol Ruckdeschel? Surely he'll be thrilled to see the cabin belonging to the woman who allegedly sent a shotgun blast through the door, killing the man who had once been her lover.

But now is not the time to tell him about the island naturalist. Let him think about Harry Thaw and Evelyn Nesbit and Stanford White for a while.

Three months later, after I've read accounts of the death of Louis McKee written by Will Harlan, Art Eulenfeld, Charles Seabrook, Lary Dilsaver, Robert Coram, and others, and we're heading into the mess that is downtown Atlanta, I tell him how it happened, as best I can put it all together.

McKee must have been an angry man when he went to Carol Ruckdeschel's cabin that April day in 1980. When she heard him at the back door, she jumped up from the table where she'd been sitting with the backpacker she'd invited to stay with her. She locked the door and grabbed the sawed-off shotgun she kept for protection. Louis beat on the door. He beat harder, until he knocked out the center panel. Carol raised the gun, aimed, and fired. The buckshot hit him in the chest, all nine pellets entering his body on the left side, just above the heart. The area where he was hit was so small you could cover it with one hand, authorities said later. She must have been awfully close to him when she fired, they deduced. With the center panel gone, she would likely have been looking directly at him.

By the time Park Service rangers got to the cabin, McKee had been dead for several hours. Officials from the Camden County Sheriff's Department did not arrive until nearly midnight. They had to fly to the airstrip on the south end of the island, borrow a pickup from Greyfield, and make their way north to the Ruckdeschel residence.

Park Service personnel placed the body in the bed of the vehicle and began the journey to the Sea Camp dock. From there it was loaded onto a Park Service launch for transport to St. Marys.

Until the previous December, Louis McKee had been co-owner of the cabin where Ruckdeschel lived. The sawed-off shotgun Carol used that day once belonged to Louis. Inside the cabin were a number of his possessions.

McKee had bought the shack six years earlier for $6,000. He helped Carol refurbish it, level the floors, and repair the roof. During the Christmas holidays in 1979, he quitclaimed the property to her, and she began to negotiate with the Park Service. Three months later she sold it to the agency for $45,000 with a retained right that would allow her to live there for the rest of her life.

Carol and the hiker who was inside the cabin at the time of the shooting, Peter DiLorenzo, accompanied the body to the Dungeness dock, then on to St. Marys. Rather than sleep in the sheriff's office or the jail, they chose to spend what was left of the night under a tree in front of the courthouse.

County officials held an inquest the next morning. McKee came onto her porch and was beating on her door, Carol stated. Though she couldn't remember what he said, his tone was threatening. In the past she'd been assaulted by McKee, and she was terrified.

DiLorenzo collaborated her story. He'd heard the man yelling, saw him break through the door panel.

Twenty minutes after the inquest began, it was over. There'd been no mention of the $45,000 Carol received from the Park Service, no suggestion that McKee might have felt he had a right to a portion of the money.

Carol and DiLorenzo were released without charges. They made their way back to Cumberland Island.

Through my whole story, Charlie has been silent. Normally, he'd be reading the road signs and telling me when to change lanes. Driving through Atlanta is a nightmare. But I've done it so many times I must be getting used to the tangle of interstates that intersect, crawl over, dig under, and come at you from the side. I've made all the right lane changes, and surely now Charlie is as excited about going to the north end of the island as I am.

"Get in the right lane," Charlie says. "The turnoff to the airport is coming up."

I see a plane off to my left, coming in low. There are sections of I-75 that are directly beneath one of the flight paths. The plane casts a shadow over our car, so close we can hear the roar of its engines.

"She keeps horses and pigs and at least one blue-eyed Abyssinian cat," I tell him, "so she must be a nice person. Maybe a little eccentric. In a separate building she calls the Cumberland Island Museum, she stores preserved remains of logger-head turtles, snakes, horses, birds, deer, and other animals that come her way. There are whole skeletons, skulls, even alligator hatchlings preserved in Mason jars."

I turn onto the airport's Loop Road and we begin looking for Rhamy.

Charlie wouldn't be interested in Carol's museum. But I think he might like to catch a glimpse of the woman who lent the Kennedy party an oil lantern to help light up the church for the evening ceremony. Not wanting to miss such a historic event, Ruckdeschel watched from her backyard while the Kennedy-Bessette wedding was taking place.

When we get to the place where Ruckdeschel lives, I'll be looking for that door, wondering what she used to replace the panel McKee had smashed. And did the police keep that illegal sawed-off shotgun, or did they return it to her?

I hope they gave it back. There are dangerous animals on Cumberland, and if I lived there, I'd want something to defend myself.

Charlie never really commits. But two days later when we're on the balcony of our St. Simons condo, Rhamy calls from the kitchen to ask if he wants cheese on his turkey sandwich. He says yes, he'd like two slices, some lettuce, but no mayo. We take that to mean he's coming with us.

I take a sip of my Pinnacle vodka and cranberry juice, and I wonder if I might be able to arrange for a submarine to rise up out of the waters of the Sound when we're passing through. Would it be possible to have a white stallion and his harem of mares greet us when we dock at Sea Camp? I promised Charlie an air-conditioned van, but I'd prefer an open vehicle, a Jeep perhaps, for our ride up Grand Avenue to the north end of the island. Maybe, on some future trip, we can borrow one from Greyfield.

29

I t shouldn't be this cold. In all the years we've been coming to Cumberland, there's never been a year when it's been this cold. The trip down the St. Marys River and up the Cumberland Sound is always chilly, and we often bring sweaters or jackets. This year, we need coats, hats, scarves, and maybe even gloves.

Charlie, Rhamy, and I get off the boat at Sea Camp and crowd into the ranger station. Campers, bikers, and day-trippers are waiting there, along with twenty-two people who plan to go on the Lands and Legacies Tour. There's room for twenty. The two extras don't have reservations, but the ranger at the St. Marys Visitor Center sent them on; there might be cancellations or no-shows.

Daniel, our guide for the day, gathers his ten passengers and shuffles us out to his van, leaving the rangers inside to sort out the rest. He's a tall man with graying hair, muscular and tanned. As we board, he hands each of us a receiver complete with ear bud. Rhamy slides into the front-row seat and motions for me to sit next to her, Charlie to grab the one behind. She's taken her seventh and eighth graders on enough field trips to have learned a few tricks. Those who sit close to the driver have the best view. Microphones and PA systems are notoriously bad. If you sit in front, you are less likely to miss what the guide is saying.

When we're all on board, Daniel climbs into the driver's seat and introduces himself. He doesn't normally do the Lands and Legacies Tours, he says, but the regular guide is on vacation. Daniel has been a volunteer on the island for a few years, and he promises to do the best he can. If we have questions, he'll try to answer them.

The keys to the van are missing. They're not in the ignition, the center compartment, or above the visor. Daniel looks toward the ranger station.

The two extras are standing by the door of our van, gazing in at us, anxious looks on their faces.

"I'm sorry," Daniel tells them, exiting the van. "We have a full load. There's no place for you to sit."

Still they linger, a tall man and his equally tall wife.

Daniel hesitates. "It's a rough road," he says, "and there's just no way we can take you. I'm sorry. Maybe they can arrange for a third vehicle to make the trip. Why don't you ask one of the rangers inside? Or maybe you could come back another day?"

They shake their heads, and slowly, sorrowfully, walk toward the other van. Daniel goes inside to try to locate the missing keys. Five minutes later he emerges from the building, holding the keys high in the air, jiggling them in victory. "I found them," he says, and though he's thirty feet away, we hear him perfectly through our earbuds. The sound system is crisp and clear.

Heading north on Grand Avenue, known to locals as Interstate Zero, Daniel gives a brief history of the island. He tells of the Timucuan Indians who lived here for over three thousand years. "They stood seven feet tall and left oyster shell middens on the island," he says. "When the Spanish arrived in the sixteenth century, they attempted, without much success, to convert the Indians to Christianity. There followed years of conflict between the Spanish and the British over ownership of Georgia and the Golden Isles. The Spanish were finally defeated at the Battle of Bloody Marsh in 1742. Shortly thereafter, Spain ceded control of most of Florida, Georgia, and parts of South Carolina to the British."

The van rattles over a series of deep ridges in the road. In an attempt to find smoother going, Daniel veers to the left. Tree branches and Spanish moss scrape the sides of the van.

"Catherine Greene," he continues, "wife of the Revolutionary War hero, Nathaniel Greene, built the first Dungeness mansion in 1803. She harvested lumber and grew cotton. One of the largest plantations on the island belonged to a man named Robert Stafford. In 1860, he held title to over eight thousand acres and owned three hundred and fifty slaves. Sea Island cotton brought premium prices, and he became a rich man. Then came the Civil War. Yankees captured the island and moved into Dungeness mansion. A short time later it burned to the ground."

He glances in the rearview mirror at his passengers.

No one objects; it must be okay to call the invaders "Yankees."

Rhamy and I exchange looks. We like this guide.

Daniel goes on with his story: "The Emancipation Proclamation freed all of Stafford's slaves. He was an old man by then, but he stayed on the plantation until he died. We'll be stopping there shortly," he says.

A shouted question from the back of the van: "So he's left with an eight thousand-acre plantation and no one to work it?"

"There may have been a few who stayed," Daniel says.

He slows the van and points to a narrow lane that branches off to the right. "There are five houses just beyond the trees," he says. "They're owned by members of the Carnegie/Rockefeller families."

"That's the ocean just beyond the houses?" Rhamy asks.

He nods.

"And they're retained rights?"

"No, those are privately owned," he says. "Retained rights refers to people who sold their properties to the Park Service, but they have the right to live in their houses until a specific time when they have to leave. In some cases that might be thirty years, or until the death of the owner, or the death of the heirs. The contracts were all negotiated separately, so each case is different.

"As you might imagine," he continues, "a number of these retained rights people are reluctant to leave. You can't blame them. Most of them have been here for years. They've vacationed here, their children and grandchildren have spent time on the island. They're attached to it."

He stops to allow two horses to cross the road in front of us. They're in no hurry.

"Some residents," he says, "like the owners of Greyfield, never negotiated with the Park Service. They're called inholders. They actually have the right to develop their land, if they choose to do it."

"Would they ever do that?" I ask. "Considering how important the island has been to the family, how much it meant to Lucy and Thomas Carnegie?"

He shrugs, pulls back onto the road and accelerates.

I can see only a portion of his face in the mirror, and I can't read his expression. I sit back in my seat and open the map I picked up at the ranger station. Greyfield is off to the right, but Daniel doesn't mention it, and if the turnoff is marked, I miss it. The Greyfield Inn is not a part of the Lands and Legacies Tour.

Our first stop is beside an open field. A number of horses are grazing in the distance, but they're so far away, we can barely make them out. Ahead of us is Stafford House, the mansion built by Lucy Carnegie in 1903 for her son, William Coleman, and his wife, Martha Ely.

Outside the van, the wind is fierce.

"This used to be a cotton field," Daniel tells us. "It belonged to Robert Stafford. Back when I first came to the island, one of my jobs was to mow it. It took five days."

He takes a map from the center compartment of the van and tries to unroll it, but the wind threatens to tear it out of his hands. We move to the opposite side of the van where we're somewhat protected.

It's not a map at all, but an artist's rendition of what Stafford Plantation once looked like. The most imposing structure is the plantation house, surrounded by trees and gardens. Smoke rises from chimneys at each end of the house. The slave quarters are spaced so that each family had room for a garden, a hen house, and a pig pen. The fields are carefully cultivated, the rows straight and even. Nothing is out of place.

Daniel points eastward, toward the Atlantic. "You can just barely see them — the chimneys. That's all that's left."

"Everything is gone?" I ask. "The plantation house? Everything?"

"The chimneys are all that remain," he says. "And the hearths. The land actually belongs to the Park Service, but until the retained rights expire, we have no right to go onto the property. The people who live there, Carnegie descendants, have been very cooperative. They've allowed us to repair some of the structures that were in danger of falling down. Altogether there are twenty-four chimneys. That's all that's left of the slave quarters."

"We can't just walk across the field and go look at it?" I ask. "It can't be that far."

Daniel shakes his head. "It's a lot farther than you realize."

"He burned the cabins, didn't he? Robert Stafford? I read that when the slaves were freed, they refused to work for him, so he burned their cabins and everything in them. 'If you won't work, you're no good to me,' he supposedly said. Some of the freed slaves went to the mainland, but many ended up on the north end of the island."

"The Settlement," he says, nodding. "There's a graveyard up there where many of them are buried. Most took their former owner's name, so they're practically all Staffords."

He looks across the field toward the chimneys. "Archeologists from the Park Service have done a number of digs," he says, "and they can find no evidence that the cabins were ever burned. No ashes, nothing charred, nothing to indicate they were destroyed by fire. But the story persists."

He begins rolling up the drawing. "The plantation house is gone too; it burned around 1900, after Lucy had bought the estate from the Stafford heirs."

"Did it really take five days to mow?"

"It really did," he says.

I take one last, long, lingering look at the chimneys. They're nearly lost in the mist that rises from the ocean and sweeps onto the island, and it seems somehow fitting.

"Robert Stafford is buried close by," Daniel says, and he leads us into the nearby woods to a small graveyard enclosed by a wall of tabby. It's a lonely place, untended and overgrown with weeds and tangles of vine. Daniel points out Stafford's grave: "As you can see, he was born on the island in 1790. He died at the age of 87." He looks off into the woods, then adds: "He fathered six children with a slave woman, but he never married."

He points to a headstone that marks the grave of Thomas Hutchison, a young man brought over from Scotland to lay out a golf course for Lucy's son, William Coleman Carnegie. "Shortly after Hutchison arrived on the island," Daniel tells us, "he was thrown from his horse. He landed headfirst on a stump and died the next day." He pauses, then adds: "William sent for Thomas's brother to finish the golf course."

The only other marked graves are those of Stafford's mother, Lucy Spalding, and his sister, Susan. They're buried in box graves covered with flat ledger stones.

The graves are clustered near the back wall of the enclosure. If there are others, they are unmarked. The tabby walls are low. We could step over them, if we wanted to read the dates and inscriptions, but no one does.

Daniel moves around to the opening into the graveyard. His voice carries to the edges of the clearing and into the greenery that surrounds us: "Most of the plantation owners left the island after their slaves were freed," he says, "but Stafford stayed. The economy was in ruins. With the slaves gone and no one to work the land, the fields that once yielded cotton, rice, and indigo lay dormant. Shortly before the war ended, Stafford learned that, by order of General Sherman, his lands were to be confiscated. His plantation would be divided into forty-acre plots and given to black families who had once belonged to him. Still he stayed on.

"When he was well over 70 years old, a reporter from the *New York Times* visited him in his plantation house. Except for an elderly negress, a decanter of brandy, and thirty-four dogs, Stafford was alone. Even at that advanced age, he was still 'as tall as a chimney (with) a voice like a trip-hammer,' the reporter wrote. 'He fairly made the chairs move when he spoke.'"

Someone on the fringe of the group asks if the elderly negress could have been the slave woman who bore him six children.

"Elizabeth Bernardey was her name," Daniel responds. "They called her Zabette. It's not likely she'd have been with Stafford at that point. Before the war broke out, he sent her north, with the children. He bought a house for them in Connecticut, and he visited there fairly often. He evidently cared for her, and the children, and though she belonged to him, he wanted the children to one day be free.

"She'd grown up at Plum Orchard," he continues, "the illegitimate daughter of a French planter and a house servant. She was educated as if she were white. Somewhere along the line she was given some medical training, and historians believe Stafford hired her to care for his mother and sister the summer of 1836.

"They both died of yellow fever," he tells us, indicating their graves. "His sister in July, his mother in August. A few years later Zabette bore the first of Stafford's children. Their relationship lasted for nearly forty years, but it did not end well. After the war, Zabette came back to Cumberland, only to discover that Stafford had taken a new mistress. No one knows what happened to her after that," Daniel says. "But it's unlikely she'd have stayed on the plantation."

The story ended, we make out way out of the woods toward the cotton field. The horses we saw earlier have moved closer to the road. Two stallions, both chestnuts, are posturing, their heads touching, nostrils flared, tails arched. Charlie grabs his camera from inside the van and focuses. One of the stallions bounds away, then circles the other horse, who swivels. They eye one another, each looking for an opportunity to land a blow or sink teeth into some fleshy part of the other horse.

In the end, it amounts to nothing. The smaller horse tosses his head, turns, and runs off.

"It's a ritual," Rhamy says. "One horse will challenge another, but it's like they're both aware of how serious it can get, so one will almost invariably back off. Like that horse just did."

"And if he doesn't? What happens then?"

She glances at Charlie before she answers. "Sometimes they'll fight to the death," she says. "Rearing, legs flailing, both horses pounding each other with their hooves, shrieking, snorting, taking hunks out of each other's manes. If one of the horses goes down, the other will stomp him. Legs get broken, ribs smashed. The mares just stand and watch, as if they had nothing to do with it."

Charlie puts the lens protector on his camera and climbs into the van.

"You know about horses?" Daniel asks.

"I have a Hanoverian/Thoroughbred back in Portland," Rhamy says. "She's a hunter/jumper. Her name is Quest. We do shows in the summer, when I'm not teaching. This is my mom, and that's my dad in the van. They bought me my first horse when I was nine."

"You win ribbons?"

"I do. She's a pretty horse."

"And you come to Cumberland because of the horses."

"It's what first drew us here. We've been coming for years now, every spring break. It's hard to say exactly why. The wilderness, I guess. The beach. The freedom. The fact that it's all so unspoiled. To realize that humans have lived here for five thousand years that we know of, and each time civilization tries to conquer her, the island I mean, she fights back."

The wind blows a strand of hair across her face, and she pushes it behind her ears. "I guess, for me, the horses symbolize that freedom, that ability to adapt to whatever happens on the island. Poachers from the mainland come and take them away. Union soldiers capture them and turn them into war horses. Lucy Ferguson rounds them up by the hundreds and sells them. But look at them, grazing out there, totally free. And happy."

"There are fewer of them than last year," Daniel says, and there's a tone of somberness in his voice.

"You've already done the annual count?"

He nods. "Last weekend. There were only 108."

"Why?" Rhamy asks. "Why would the count be down so drastically? It was over 130 last year."

"Maybe because of the rain. We had rain off and on both days, Saturday and Sunday. We used the same people, walked the same routes. We note the coloring, the sex, estimated age, location, and habitat of each horse. It's all put into a database so we can compare with previous years and look at long-term trends."

He hesitates before continuing. "To go from 130 down to 108 is pretty dramatic."

"They might have been holed up under trees," Rhamy says. "Horses don't like nasty weather. They'll find some place to hide out."

"It's possible. Disease could be a factor. Or malnutrition. The island sizes the herd. If food is scarce, the numbers decline. But this is the lowest it's been since I've been volunteering."

"You hear a lot about how they're trampling the marshes and causing the dunes to migrate, and they should either be removed or their numbers controlled."

"Or restricted to the southern part of the island," he says.

"You'd like for them to be free, wouldn't you? Live the way horses have lived for tens of thousands of years."

"They've been here a long time," he answers.

The farther north we go, the rougher the road. Daniel tries to pick the smoothest parts, but it's a hard task. The passengers in the back of the van are mostly silent, with only an occasional complaint.

A red pickup truck rounds a bend, heading toward us. Two vehicles cannot possibly pass on this narrow road, and there's no place to pull off. Daniel slows and moves as far to the right as he can. We cringe, waiting for the sound of metal against metal.

The woman in the pickup is fearless. She waves to Daniel as she drives past, hardly slowing though our vehicles are inches apart.

Daniel pulls back onto the road. "Retained rights owner," he says.

The jostling and the jarring bumps must be worse in the back of the van. "Is it gonna be like this the whole way?" someone calls out.

Daniel doesn't answer. But he slows, and the bouncing isn't quite as bad. "The Park Service scrapes the road," he says, "and when they're done, it's no better than before. You wonder why they keep doing it."

Since leaving Stafford Place, the terrain has gradually changed. The live oaks and saw palmetto have given way to a pine forest, more open, undergrowth grazed to the point where it would actually be possible to go for a walk in the woods.

The van bounces over a particularly rough section of washboarded road, and we in the van bounce along with it. Then we hit a fairly smooth stretch.

"We'll be stopping at Plum Orchard shortly," Daniel announces. "We'll tour the mansion, then have lunch. There are restrooms inside, and faucets outside where you can fill your water bottles."

He turns onto a side road, and this one is more narrow than the last. A quarter of a mile farther on the forest opens up. Ahead of us is Plum Orchard, a sprawling mansion set down where it has no right to be. Above it, a cloudless blue sky. To the left, the Brickhill River, calm in the late morning sun. All around us, manicured lawns bordered by woods and shoreline.

Four white columns support the main section of the house; wide verandas stretch out on both sides; tall windows are topped with fanlights; intricately carved woodwork edges the roof and the cornices below.

This is the "cottage" Lucy built for George and his wife Margaret. The con-
nections among the people who lived in the mansion or were guests there are amazing. Margaret was the sister of Harry Thaw, deranged killer of architect Stanford
White. Thaw was married to Evelyn Nesbit, model, chorus girl, sex goddess, and
the woman at the center of the triangle. Alice Thaw, younger sister of Margaret
and Harry, was given in marriage by Harry to George Seymour, the Earl of Yarmouth. Nancy Carnegie, George's little sister, was a bridesmaid at Alice's unfor-
tunate wedding. The infamous earl, also known as "The Countess," was visiting
Plum Orchard when Alice Thaw's mother announced the engagement of Alice
and the Earl of Yarmouth.

I gaze upwards, wondering which bedroom he slept in, and if he ever donned
women's clothing while he was here.

Charlie knows all these things. He's had to listen to me talk about the adventures Rhamy and I have had on the island, the things we've learned, the books
we've read. And because he's only visited Cumberland that one time, and the
Lands and Legacies Tour will take him to places he's never been, and because it
was so important to me that he come with us this year, back in the winter we
rented a copy of *The Girl in the Red Velvet Swing*. Charlie is a movie aficionado,
so it wasn't hard to get him to watch it again.

He's many other things, as well. A history enthusiast, with a special interest in
the Great Depression, World War I, the Gilded Age, and the Progressive Era. A
student of how all these things intersected. He reads a lot of books about Holly-
wood, too. He knew *The Girl in the Red Velvet Swing* was made in 1955, and that
Joan Collins played the leading role. He didn't know that Evelyn Nesbit, hired as
a consultant, disapproved; she thought Joan was too British and too bosomy. She
would have much preferred Marilyn Monroe.

I have to smile, remembering the look on Charlie's face when I told him of
Evelyn's disapproval of Joan Collins. He wouldn't admit it and I didn't ask, but I
knew he was mentally comparing bosom size.

It was so long ago when Charlie first saw the movie, he'd forgotten most of
the story, disremembered much of it, gotten some of it wrong. So it was fun to sit
in our living room in the dead of winter and watch it. He had his iPad at the ready
so he could Google anything he wondered about. He loved pointing out how the

screenwriters twisted themselves into knots trying to convey the story of sixteen-year-old Evelyn's seduction by the forty-seven-year-old architect, and do it in a way that the Legion of Decency did not come down on them.

In 1955, the Legion was a powerful force. Catholics recited a pledge once a year at Sunday services to never go to an objectionable movie. Further, they promised to boycott any movie theater that even showed a film the Legion considered immoral. Married couples in movies and on TV retired for the night in separate beds, if not separate bedrooms. Lucille Ball and Desi Arnaz slept in twin beds. The word *pregnancy* was never uttered. Women in that delicate condition were hidden from view.

The story of the rooftop murder of Stanford White and the trial that followed is salacious, to say the least, but especially so with the commentary Charlie gleaned from the internet. We'd hardly begun watching the movie when he hit the pause button. He'd found a description of White's apartment at 22 West 24th Street, and he wanted to read it to me.

The first floor contained White's studio, a spectacular room filled with antique furniture, paintings, and tapestries. Climb to the second floor and enter a forest green room filled with White's sketches and paintings. At the far end of the room hung the infamous swing, its red velvet ropes entwined with green foliage. Bearskin rugs were scattered about the floor. There was a fireplace into which White would throw chemicals that produced a rainbow of colors amid the flames.

At Stanford's urging, Evelyn would climb onto the swing, and he would push her higher and higher, until she could touch the Japanese parasol he'd suspended from the ceiling. A room on the third floor was completely paneled with mirrors. It was to this room that White led Evelyn. On the bedside table he'd placed a bottle of champagne and a glass. Evelyn had never tasted champagne before. She drank several glasses. At some point, she changed into a yellow silk kimono.

When she awoke the next morning, White was beside her. There were bloodstains on Evelyn's legs and on the sheets. The kimono was on the floor.

Eventually, White tired of Evelyn, though they remained friends until his death.

Charlie resumed the movie, but he was only half-watching by then. He paused it again to show me a picture of Harry Thaw, behind bars, enjoying his Delmonico's catered dinner. Several of Thaw's suits hung from the bars of his brass bed.

He found a site that contained dozens of pictures of Evelyn: Evelyn dressed as *The Little Butterfly*, asleep on a bearskin rug. Evelyn her body draped in a diaphanous fabric. Evelyn wearing a crown of flowers. Evelyn in a feathered hat and fur stole. Evelyn wearing a black velvet choker, her hair piled on top of her head, spilling down in careful disarray. On a darker site he found a portrait of a seminude Evelyn, her breasts small, her shoulders thin and delicate.

Among all these photos of the nubile Evelyn was one of Stanford White. Charlie read the caption: *Stanford White was the owner of the greatest mustache ever grown*. He handed me the iPad, and I looked at the picture. I couldn't disagree. It was a veritable forest, completely covering his upper lip, extending so far out even his cheeks were obscured. He's looking straight at the camera, his eyes large and fearless. His eyebrows are bushy, but nothing like the mustache.

"He could never have kissed a girl," I said. "Not with a mess like that on his face."

When Joan Collins took the witness stand, I realized they'd completely skipped the first trial. We didn't get to see Thaw's angry outburst at the jury for not understanding that when he shot White, he was striking a blow for all the innocent girls the architect had victimized.

Charlie was busy reading headlines from the *New York Times*:

June 26, 1906: *"Thaw Kills Stanford White on Roof Garden! Shoots Architect in Back as He Sits Talking to Woman: Slayer, Captured, Gives Police False Name, But Is Immediately Recognized"*

June 27, 1906: *"Murderers' Row Gets Harry Thaw"*
"All Watching Thaw to See How He Acts"

June 28, 1906: *"Thaw May Plead He Was Justified"*

June 29, 1906: *"Emotional Insanity the Thaw Defense"*

Feb. 2, 1908: *"Thaw Insane: He is Found Not Guilty of Murdering White Because He Was Crazy"*

In the end, Thaw was sentenced to incarceration for life in a hospital for the criminally insane. He was released seven years later.

February. 23, 1947: *"Harry K. Thaw, 76, Is Dead in Florida"*

Jan. 19, 1967: *"Evelyn Nesbit, 82, Dies in California"*

We sat in our living room, and the credits rolled across the screen. We hardly knew what to make of the film. If it was true, what White's friend Augustus Saint-Gaudens said of Evelyn, that "she had the face of an angel and the heart of a snake," the film we just watched must be about another girl. Evelyn seated in the red velvet swing is an innocent child who is betrayed, mistreated, thrust into a media circus for which she is ill-prepared. When she can be of no further use to the Thaw family, she is tossed aside. Harry Thaw is a chivalrous man intent on protecting the world from a lecherous man who had love nests all over the city.

"Harry Thaw was a nut," Charlie said. "When he was arrested, he said his name was John Smith and he was a student. Everyone knew who he was. Then he gave the policeman some money and told him to 'get Carnegie on the phone and tell him I'm in trouble.' How much sense does that make?"

"Which Carnegie?"

"Andrew, I would imagine. He was the more famous of the brothers. Besides, Thomas would have been dead by then, wouldn't he?"

"He might have meant his brother-in-law, George Lauder Carnegie. He'd been to Cumberland, spent time at Plum Orchard."

"Well, he was a nut."

I might have told Charlie about the disloyal Carnegie descendants who bring up the history of insanity in the Thaw family, and that they point out, somewhat snidely, that Lucy was related to the Thaws. They say that Lucy herself sometimes acted strangely. That she often disappeared into her Dungeness tower and refused to come out for long periods of time. That she spent time in a psychiatric hospital near Boston.

But such things are only rumors, and no one knows if they are true.

Daniel pulls into the parking area below the mansion and we exit the van. The group from the other van is on the porch, waiting to go inside. Somehow, they've passed us.

"There probably weren't any horses in that cotton field when they came through," Rhamy says, "so they drove right on by."

"And they didn't get to see the two stallions having their little disagreement," I add.

"There's water around the side of the building," Daniel tells the group, "if you want to fill your water bottles. Restrooms are inside. We'll wait here until the other group has moved farther into the house."

While Charlie is checking the video he shot of the horses, Rhamy and I roam the grounds. What used to be a working plantation has been reduced to the few landscaped acres. Wilderness has reclaimed the rest. If there was once a plum orchard, it is gone.

When the Carnegies lived here, they could send over to Dungeness for fresh fruit, milk, vegetables, whatever they needed. But in earlier days, plantations as remote as this one had to be self-sufficient. There would have been gardens, fruit trees, cotton fields, slave quarters, support buildings. I imagine cultivated fields, slaves turning the soil and planting in the spring, chopping weeds in the summer, picking the cotton bolls in the fall. There would have been pastures for the horses and cattle, pig pens, and chicken houses. Elizabeth "Zabette" Bernardey would likely have been born in one of the slave cabins. This is where she lived until she became the common-law wife of Robert Stafford.

Attracted by the water, Rhamy and I drift over to the dock. The river runs clear and calm, with only a slight breeze ruffling the surface. We sit on the bench, enjoying the warmth of the sun, the sound of the gently lapping water, the occasional splash of a fish jumping. A bird flies over, low in the sky, his wingspan so large he casts a shadow over us.

"An osprey," I tell Rhamy. "Looking for a meal."

We watch him disappear.

"Daddy's waving," Rhamy says. "Let's go join the group."

Daniel climbs the stairs to the porch, opens the front door, and steps back to wait for us to enter. As if it's his home. Which it was, for five years.

While Rhamy and I were wandering around the mansion and lounging on the dock, Charlie spent some time with our tour leader. There's something about my husband that makes people want to tell him their stories.

In 2001, Charlie tells us, Daniel took early retirement from his job as a wireless engineer at a technology firm in New Jersey. He'd spent thirty-seven years working for the company, and he was ready for a change. He'd always wanted to do community service. Having no idea what to expect, he volunteered on Cumberland Island.

At first he lived in a dormitory and did carpentry work for the Park Service. His experience as an amateur handyman was wide and varied, and he was good at whatever job they gave him.

The Park Service, having just begun the work of restoring Plum Orchard, asked if he'd like to work as a caretaker at the mansion. When the Carnegies donated it to the Park Service in 1972, it had been vacant for thirty years. Hurricanes, high humidity, frequent rain, and salt air had taken a toll. The mansion was in desperate need of a new roof, new electrical wiring, and a fire suppression system. There was extensive termite damage, cracked plaster walls, rusted support beams. Asbestos and lead paint needed to be removed. Wallpaper was peeling and floors buckling.

With the gift of the mansion, the Carnegie family included a check for $50,000, an endowment of sorts, but added a stipulation that the mansion be preserved, maintained, and open to the public.

Fifty grand would hardly make a dent. The renovations would cost millions.

Daniel agreed to try it for a year. He moved from his dormitory into the 22,000-square-foot mansion and set to work.

On occasion, day hikers would show up at his door, and he'd set aside his tools to show them through the mansion. Sometimes people came by boat, and Daniel would invite them inside, accompany them as they walked through the rooms, and offer what commentary he could. It was his way of honoring the commitment the Park Service had made to the Carnegies. And it was good to have company, if only for an hour.

He learned a lot about the house in those first few months. Sometimes the visitors told him things he didn't know. These cabinets were probably meant for storing ammunition. There are elevators like this at the Biltmore — the Vanderbilt mansion in North Carolina. One of the Carnegie daughters was married to a doctor. The bottles randomly tossed on a shelf in an alcove off the library were probably filled with medicines at one time.

Daniel knew little of the Carnegies, but he listened, and over the years he learned a lot about the people who had lived there. Yet it was the house that intrigued him most. At night, when he was tired from his labors, he explored the different rooms and levels of the house, wanting to learn its secrets. And because he lived there, and he was both caretaker and host, the house became, in many ways, his house.

When Laura joined him — Laura had been an administrative assistant at the firm for thirty-four years — it became a home.

Daniel had already begun the job of clearing the debris that had accumulated around the mansion. Now, with Laura by his side, the work became a pleasure. They spent months restoring the grounds to some semblance of what it once was. Inside the house they removed trash, scraped paint off walls, replaced rotten timbers, cleaned and repaired, always careful to save what could be saved. Laura used a toothbrush to remove encrusted dirt from intricately carved woodwork.

Once a week they drove to Sea Camp dock where they took the ferry or a Park Service boat to St. Marys for supplies. Anything that was forgotten had to wait for the following week.

On occasion park rangers visited, sometimes coming by the main road, sometimes by boat up the Brickhill River. Mostly, the two were alone, and life was good.

When their work was done, they hiked the island, fished the streams, carried picnic lunches outside to enjoy on the verandas or under the live oaks.

They live on the mainland now, but when Daniel talks of the five years he and Laura spent at Plum Orchard and of the three-room apartment on the second floor they called their home, you know he misses his life on the island.

There's a single piece of furniture in the grand entry room: an antique mahogany table. A silver tray holding a crystal decanter and matching glasses sits atop the table. The tray and its contents are centered beneath a Tiffany lamp that casts muted blues and greens onto the table and the parquet floor beneath. Is this the table, I wonder, where Charles Fraser laid out his maps and land plats showing how he planned to develop Cumberland Island?

Daniel is in deep conversation with a man who has just come into the house, so I can't ask him.

On the far wall is a fireplace with built-in benches on both sides. The curved stairway rises around and above the fireplace. Stenciled burlap wallpaper covers the walls. To our right is the dining room, the table set with what I imagine is Carnegie china, crystal, and silver.

From the entry room, Daniel leads us into the gallery, pointing out the alcove where Marius Johnston, Nancy Carnegie's second husband, kept his medical supplies. Beyond that, the library, and finally, in one of the two wings added in 1906, the drawing room which also served as a gentlemen's salon and a gun room. Two Tiffany lamps hang there, the largest I've ever seen. They are the focus of the room. Magazine articles written about the mansion have valued them at well over a million dollars each.

"The Carnegie family commissioned Tiffany & Co. to make the lamps," Daniel tells us. "Notice how the panes are designed to look like the back of a loggerhead turtle."

We gaze at the lamps, and then scatter around the room, snapping pictures, admiring the wall fixtures.

George Lauder Carnegie died in 1928, and Margaret Thaw remarried. Her new husband, a French count, had furnishings, bathroom fixtures, books, and guns shipped off to auction houses in New York. Someone, perhaps Margaret's new husband, a member of the moving crew, maybe Margaret herself, forgot to pack the lamps. They stayed in the drawing room. Presumably now they belong to the Park Service.

Daniel shows us the built-in cupboards to the right of the double doors — dozens of drawers and compartments, some meant for storing guns, others for different caliber ammunition.

"Pocket doors," he announces, pulling one of the doors out of the wall. "They were installed in 1906 when the two wings were added. They still work perfectly," he adds, pushing the door back into its pocket.

Beneath one of the lamps is a grand piano. Daniel invites any of us who play to sit down and try it out. I look at Charlie. Though guitar is his instrument, he's been taking piano lessons for a year. I can tell he's tempted. Does he dare?

Do it, I want to tell him, and I hope my raised eyebrows and the tilt of my head conveys the message.

He hesitates.

I bring my hands together as if in prayer.

For a long moment he's on the brink, but then he shakes his head.

Aren't we, all of us on the tour, yearning for Daniel to lead us up that winding stairway to the second floor? Now that we've seen the grand entry hall, dining room, library, gallery, and gentlemen's salon, don't we want to see the bedrooms where they slept, the dressing rooms, the bathrooms? Isn't Charlie dying to see the bed believed to have been the one Lucy slept in at Dungeness? The bed Nancy Carnegie Hever Johnston brought to Plum Orchard to replace the one shipped off to a New York auction house by the impoverished French count?

Instead, Daniel leads us down a narrow stairway to the basement. It smells of dust, mildew, and things both rusty and earthy. As we descend, so does the temperature. When we reach the bottom, it's icy cold.

We file along narrow, stone hallways, past empty rooms, gaze into spaces half-filled with broken furniture, discarded tools and items unidentifiable in their antiquity. Beams of light from unexpected openings in the foundation find their way into dark enclosures. We step into and out of rooms full of ancient and monstrously complicated machinery whose purpose no one knows. Except Daniel. He has plumbed the depths of this house. He knows her secrets.

"Coal was brought in through that chute over there," he says, and he points to the furnace in the room opposite. "This is the hydraulic Otis elevator that carried occupants from the basement to the second floor. Here is one of the first refrigerators ever made, and it would still work, if we cranked it up. It actually made ice cubes. The Carnegies could sit out on the veranda, drink mint juleps, and hear the sound of ice clinking in their glasses."

He moves on. "This is the Koehler generator that supplied electricity to the house. Originally it had gas lighting, but it was converted in 1905. For a house to have electricity at that time would have been unusual, especially for one as remote as this."

He points out electrical wiring wrapped in what appears to be cloth. "This would be some of the oldest wiring, dating from when the house was first electrified," Daniel says. "It's been disconnected, of course. The house has been rewired twice since it was built."

"Very few homes had electricity until the late 1920s," says an old man. "You heated your house with coal and you had an ice box on the back porch. The ice man brought blocks of ice once a week. A twenty-five-pound block cost you fifteen cents. Two blocks for a quarter."

At the far end of the last room is a narrow, winding staircase. We climb to the top and enter the butler's pantry, then the kitchen. Daniel points out the wall of cupboards that once held place settings for four hundred people, a Thanksgiving menu from 1910, a recipe for Spun Sugar Chocolate Sauce.

Someone asks if it's true that the Carnegies often served cold meals to show off their refrigeration, but Daniel is already heading up the stairs to the second floor. Opening off a long hallway are bedrooms connecting with sitting rooms, dressing rooms, and bathrooms with heated towel racks and knobs that dispense both hot and cold water.

Lucy's bed is a sleigh bed, odd-looking with its identical headboard and footboard. Made of dark mahogany, it's shorter than a modern bed. The sides are trimmed with gold scroll work; Roman soldiers standing in golden chariots lash the winged horses who pull them. The bed is dwarfed by the enormous size of the room and the scarcity of furniture.

There's a coldness, an emptiness in the room that makes us not want to linger.

Daniel ushers us on to the squash court and indoor swimming pool, the last stops on the tour.

We pick a spot on the veranda for our lunch; egg salad sandwiches are, by now, a deeply entrenched tradition. And it feels right, to be vegetarian in this place that is so respectful of all living things. Daniel joins us, and he entertains us with tales of his time at Plum Orchard.

He tells of the first night he spent in that decrepit house with its leaky roof and termite-infested timbers. He was sleeping in a room on the second floor when he heard someone open the front door. A few minutes later, he heard the door close. Then footsteps, soft, muffled, hesitating, and intermittent. Someone was in the house. He wondered if he'd forgotten to lock the door. Had someone, thinking the house was deserted, simply wandered in? Could it be a hiker seeking shelter for the night? Someone staying in one of the retained rights houses wanting to look around?

Or was it more nefarious than that? Dungeness, it was widely believed, had been set afire by a poacher from the mainland who had a grudge against the Carnegies. Family members living at Plum Orchard had seen the blaze over the treetops. They watched as the fire consumed the mansion and burned on through the night.

Thoughts come uncensored on dark nights. Thoughts unreasonable, brought up from some mammalian part of our brains. So it must have been with Daniel that night. Alone in that long-abandoned place, miles from the ranger station, hidden in a room where servants had once lived, Daniel chose not to investigate. He would wait.

The sounds did not cease until well into the night.

When morning came, he crept down the stairs, careful to make no noise. He found nothing. The front door was as before, windows shut tight and locked. He went outside. No shutters banging, no tree branches scraping against the sides of the house. Nothing.

The next night, before he went to bed, he set a glass atop the doorknob. If anyone should try to come in, if they should even turn the knob, the glass would crash to the floor.

In the morning the glass was still there. Undisturbed.

We wait for the story to go on, but Daniel is watching an armadillo out near the van. The animal is moving through the grass, stopping occasionally to root for a morsel of food.

"They didn't used to be here," Daniel says. "Now they're all over the island. Biologists think they swam across from the mainland. They have no predators, so their population is exploding."

The armadillo disappears into the woods, and Daniel launches into a story of visitors from Atlanta. "Ghost hunters," he says. "And they were absolutely loaded down with paranormal detection equipment."

They'd heard about the mansion and the enormous wealth of the Carnegie family, he continues. Did Daniel have reason to believe, they wondered, in the light of the history of the island — slavery, miscegenation, plantation owners selling their half-white daughters to men who took a fancy to them — was it possible that Plum Orchard might be haunted?

Daniel invited them in. They set up their equipment throughout the house: motion sensors, electromagnetic field meters, infrared thermometers, and electronic voice recorders.

By morning, they'd found nothing. They declared Plum Orchard free of ghosts. As they prepared to leave, Daniel suggested they visit a site nearby where a mass burial had reportedly taken place.

One of the paranormal investigators walked to the area Daniel indicated. He stepped gingerly, perhaps sensing something odd. There had been a number of outbreaks of yellow fever on the island. One that occurred in the early 1800s was particularly virulent, sweeping through the slave quarters, felling young and old alike. No one knew how many had been buried in mass graves.

The ghost hunters dragged their equipment out to the mound, and Daniel went back to his labors. Twenty minutes later they were scrambling to get their paraphernalia packed into their van. The mound had caused their EMF meter to spike, their EVP recorder to emit strange sounds, the thermometer to register heat signatures they'd never seen before. The house might be free of ghosts, but the grounds were not.

But Daniel was not a man to leap to conclusions. Who knew if there was a connection between the yellow fever epidemic and the activity at the mound.

Rhamy offers him a Sunrise energy bar. He refuses. The same with Charlie's bag of Fritos. Laura, back on the mainland, is planning an early dinner, he says. He looks at his watch, and we know he's anxious to go on with the tour. If there's time at the end, some in our group want to visit Dungeness. Others would like to walk to the ocean. We finish our lunches, pack up our trash, and head for the van.

It would have been indelicate to ask him why he left Plum Orchard. He and Laura were getting older, of course. They might have needed to be closer to medical facilities. Perhaps they had grandchildren back in New Jersey. They might have begun to yearn for friends, family, social gatherings, phone service, libraries, the laughter of children, the sound of traffic.

What is clear is that Daniel loves the place, and if he could come back, he would.

"There are volunteer positions available," he tells us. "If you can commit to three months, the Park Service would love to have you. They're always looking for volunteers. Use your time to write a book, paint, whatever. Your only job is to greet visitors and show them through the house."

It's a tempting proposal.

Back on that narrow road of sand, I'm disappointed. Daniel promised to show us what he called "Laura's Porch." Located just off the rooms where they lived, Laura liked to sit there in the evening when their work was done. He'd forgotten.

Lucy Carnegie often sat in her tower above Dungeness, and she was the empress of all that she saw. Laura sitting on her porch after her day's work was done, Daniel beside her, the two in silent communication as the sun set over the river and the sky darkened, seems a different thing. There is about this Laura a gentleness, a sense of accomplishment despite tired muscles and ruined fingernails and work-hardened hands.

Daniel had forgotten to point out Laura's porch. Or the carriage house where the Carnegies had kept their buggies and later their cars.

I'd wanted to see the garden where Nancy Carnegie Johnston grew her prize-winning flowers. Is the sand mound still visible, all these years later? What of the grave of Peter Bernardey, owner of the plantation where Zabette grew up, and presumably her father?

Charlie has at least some of the answers. While Rhamy and I were setting out our lunches, he'd overheard one of our fellow passengers ask about the remains of the old plantation house.

Retained rights, Daniel told them. The Bernardey graveyard, the foundation of the original tabby house, and the Plum Orchard garden are all covered by agreements the Park Service made with owners years ago. When the Carnegies turned over Plum Orchard, they included only twelve acres of the original estate. The boundary line was drawn just beyond the freshwater pond in back of the house. Someday, it will belong to the Park Service. Until then, we have to respect the rights of the property owners.

"How many years?" I ask.

Charlie only shrugs.

30

From Plum Orchard we pull out onto the main road and once again head
north. Daniel narrates as we bounce along.

"Sections of the road we're traveling on show up on maps drawn as
early as 1802," he tells us. "The island was practically uninhabited then, but fifty
years later there were 455 black slaves living here and about fifty white plantation
owners and small farmers. They needed a way to get their products to market, so
they carved this road out of the wilderness. By 1870, it was thirteen miles long and
pretty much the same as it is today. It linked the various plantations, primarily
Dungeness, Stafford Plantation, and Plum Orchard.

"After the Civil War," he continues, "many of the freed blacks settled at the
north end of the island. They built shanties out of scrap lumber and roofed them
with palmetto fronds. In the 1880s the area began to develop as a resort. Investors
envisioned hotels, cottages, hunting lodges, stables, even a bowling alley. They
hired blacks as construction workers, and later as gardeners, housekeepers, waiters,
and cooks.

"Because Georgia law required racial segregation in housing, one of the investors in the Cumberland Hotel and Resort, Mason Burbank, purchased five acres
in the Half Moon Bluff area. He divided it into fifty-by-hundred-foot lots separated by roads ten feet wide. He sold the lots to blacks, thereby insuring a ready
supply of workers for the hotel and resort. No longer would blacks have to leave
the island in search of work. Pride of ownership would keep them here. The area
became known as the Settlement.

"It's our next stop."

The First African Baptist Church where John F. Kennedy, Jr., was married
sits at the end of the main road. There's a sandy area in front of the church where
the Lands and Legacies vans can park.

If they painted the church for the Kennedy-Bessette wedding in 1996, the harsh conditions on Cumberland have undone their work. The red paint on the double doors is peeling, as is the paint on the clapboard siding and the tin roof.

The building sits on concrete pilings. There's a small opening to the right of the main entrance, animal door or coal chute, except there would have been no coal deliveries when the original church was built in 1893, nor would anyone have wanted to provide a door for animals.

Three wooden steps lead up to the double doors.

On each side of the center aisle are narrow pews, five on one side, four on the other, two beneath the windows near the front of the church. The seats are narrow. Some are varnished, some not. One is made of raw wood. All are mismatched.

It's hard to imagine the Kennedy clan gathering here, forty guests secretly ferried or flown to Cumberland, then driven from the Greyfield Inn to the church. Carolyn Bessette had trouble getting into her $40,000 zipperless dress, and she was hours late for the wedding. When she finally arrived, the dress was perfect, as were her beaded sandals and her lily-of-the-valley bouquet. Her hair was styled in a bun at the nape of her neck, and she was stunningly beautiful.

It was an evening ceremony, the church lit with a single candle and a borrowed kerosene lamp, decorated with local greenery and wildflowers. The couple stood beneath an arch and said their vows.

Now, in the harsh light of day, it all looks so different. The floor boards beneath the threadbare pieces of carpet are of various woods, widths, and lengths. There's a broom propped against the wall in a corner of the church. The ceiling is shedding paint chips, as are the walls. A small table in the pulpit holds a wooden cross made of sticks secured by a twisted vine. In front of the cross, an open Bible. I'm drawn to it.

The Settlement is mostly gone, the inhabitants moved on, the church a remnant of the past. But someone cares about the things that were said here, preached about, inveighed against. Ecclesiastes 4:1 is marked with a thin red ribbon:

> *Then I looked again at all the acts of oppression which*
> *were being done under the sun.*

And behold I saw the tears of the oppressed and they had
no one to comfort them;

Another ribbon, another verse: Proverbs 10:27:

The fear of the Lord prolongs life,
But the years of the wicked will be shortened.

I look up. Charlie is sitting in one of the pews, his head bowed. Rhamy is reading a brochure she found in the back of the church. I check to be certain the ribbons are as before, and I step down from the pulpit.

All things on Cumberland deteriorate. So too the church. When it was rebuilt in 1937, the children and grandchildren of slaves used whatever wood they could find. Their jobs at High Point were gone by then. The Cumberland Hotel and Resort had closed. St. Simons Island had developed the King and Prince as a resort. With a causeway and bridge over the intracoastal waterway, the facilities there were more accessible than here on Cumberland.

We leave the church and step down into loose sand, weeds, stray bits of wood, saw palmetto bushes.

Seeing the church as it is now, I begin to understand why JFK, Jr., chose to be married here. It was his father who proposed legislation that outlawed discrimination based on race, ethnicity, and religion. John F. Kennedy was dead when his signature Civil Rights legislation passed, but he, more than anyone else, was responsible for ending segregation in schools, in the workplace, and in housing.

We buried our slain president on the occasion of his son's third birthday, and America fell in love with the little boy wearing short pants and a jacket. When he stepped forward and saluted the casket, we turned away in anguish. We watched him grow up, following his every move, wondering when he would go into politics.

No matter where he went or what he did, there were photographers. *People* magazine named him "America's Most Eligible Bachelor." When he went on a date, the cameras were flashing. When he failed the bar exam, the headlines were brutal. When he and Carolyn had a public disagreement, their pictures filled the racks at grocery store checkout lanes across the nation.

Cumberland was one of the few places where he could be free of the paparazzi. From the time he was a teenager, he sought refuge here.

Daniel is leaning against the fender of his van when we walk out into the parking lot. I ask him if it's true that JFK, Jr., purchased land from Charles Fraser when Fraser was trying to develop the island.

He's heard the rumor but has no idea if it's true.

"He wouldn't have done it in his name," I add. "He'd have used an agent."

Daniel will neither confirm nor deny.

"I read somewhere that he was friends with one of the Rockefellers whose family owned a vacation house on the island. They met at Brown University. Probably one of those houses you mentioned this morning. On the ocean. He used to come here a lot."

"He might have stayed at Greyfield," Daniel says. "He and Gogo Ferguson were friends, I understand."

"Gogo Ferguson: she planned the wedding. She hosted the reception at Greyfield."

He nods, scuffs a shoe in the sand, and says no more.

The thriving village where ex-slaves and their descendants once lived is gone. The cemetery is still there, and the First African Baptist Church with its newfound notoriety. The Beulah Alberty house, directly across from the church, has been restored and is maintained by the Park Service. Beside it sits the ramshackle shanty and outbuildings belonging to Carol Ruckdeschel, island naturalist, fierce defender of Cumberland's loggerhead turtles, opponent of the Lands and Legacies Tours, and the woman who used a sawed-off shotgun to kill her ex-lover.

Louis McKee bought the three-room cabin from the descendants of a freed slave. Together he and Carol removed the exterior boards and turned them to hide the pink paint and to give the house a more rustic look. They reinforced the chimney and replaced sagging floor joists. Then he signed the property over to her.

Louis's friends believe he wanted his share of the money Carol had collected from the Park Service, and that he went there to confront her. He never made it past the back door. Minutes after the shooting, the backpacker, Peter DiLorenzo, ventured out onto the porch. McKee was dead. He and Carol had to step over the body to walk to High Point, a mile away, to use the radio-telephone to notify authorities.

Later that night Carol and DiLorenzo went with the sheriff to the Camden County Seat in Woodbine. In the morning they wrote out their statements and signed them.

No charges were filed. There was no autopsy. They were free to return to the island.

Carol's friends are an illustrious group. When she was younger, she roamed the state of Georgia with Sam Candler, great-grandson of Asa Candler of Coca-Cola fame. At one time the Candler family owned several thousand acres at High Point on Cumberland. In 1982 they sold most of their holdings to the National Park Service. The Candlers are now retained rights holders of the hotel complex and the surrounding thirty-four acres.

Carol rowed Christmas Creek with Jimmy Carter, governor of Georgia and later president of the United States. Carter was a frequent visitor to Cumberland, believing it to be one of the most beautiful spots on earth. There was talk of locating a Southern White House on the island, should Carter win a second term.

Gogo Ferguson was one of Carol's best friends, until the two women disagreed on the future of Plum Orchard. Gogo wanted the mansion turned into a retreat for artists. Carol wanted the island to retain its wilderness designation with tight restrictions on access and development. The disagreement turned rancorous, their friendship to bitter enmity.

In a 1973 profile of Ruckdeschel in the *New Yorker*, essayist John McPhee told of Carol picking up road kill, including possums and snakes, and of cooking and eating them. She admitted to sleeping in church graveyards; she liked them because they were both quiet and private. A slim, attractive woman with long braids, she had an affinity for animals, at times exhibiting great tenderness toward them. Yet she could cut into a turtle and remove its organs, all the while talking to the butchered animal as if it were still alive. She would separate the edible parts and put them in a Ziploc bag to be eaten later, throw the inedible pieces into a nearby pond, and remove the eggs so she could bury them in sand to hatch.

Robert Coram in a piece in the *Atlanta Weekly* in 1981 told of seeing her astride an island horse in the middle of a stampeding herd. She was naked and holding onto the horse's mane with one hand, a bottle of Jack Daniels in the other.

This is a woman I'd like to meet. But there's the issue of her opposition to the Lands and Legacies Tours. Carol Ruckdeschel is not interested in meeting visitors who come to her part of the island. She'd like to see the church moved to somewhere near Dungeness. She wants the main road once again designated as part of the wilderness area. She would like to stop Greyfield vehicles from driving on the beach, taking guests out into wilderness areas, disturbing the balance that nature strives to maintain.

Carol might have prevailed. But in 2004, Georgia Congressman Charles Kingston attached a rider to a spending bill that removed the road from the Wilderness designation. Without that rider, the Lands and Legacies Tours might never have been. The road which brought us here would be, in the words of the original Wilderness Act of 1982, "an area where the earth and its community of life are untrammeled by man, where man himself is a visitor who does not remain." Infrastructure development, commercial activities, motorized uses of any kind would be prohibited. There would be no chainsaws, tractors, gasoline-powered mowers. Park Service vans filled with tourists would be banished. I would not be here with my reluctant husband and enthusiastic daughter.

Carol's horses crop grass in the fenced pasture that borders the parking area. Rhamy, our lover of horses, walks toward the chestnut mare that is closest to us. The horse lifts her head to gaze at us, and then goes back to eating. Extending a hand, Rhamy moves closer, her voice a whisper of endearments.

A vulture watches from a tree limb that hangs over the enclosure. He makes a hissing sound, deep and guttural. Another is perched on a post at the far side of the pasture. A third one sits on a high branch. Fat feathered bodies, grey heads, so still they could be statues.

Rhamy, eyeing the vultures, moves back from the fence.

A cat sleeps in a sunny spot on the cabin porch. This is the place where McKee was shot. I wonder if the door has been replaced. When Carol raised the gun and aimed, did she, in that split second before she pulled the trigger, look into his eyes? I wonder if his blood soaked the boards, and if they had to be turned so they were not a reminder of what happened.

To the left of Carol's house stands the plain, plywood building that is the Cumberland Island Museum. It is not open to the public, so we have no hope of entering. But I have some idea of what's inside. For nearly thirty years Carol has been driving along the beaches of Cumberland Island in search of sea turtles, marine mammals, and birds. She saves those she can, and she collects the dead. DOBs, she calls them. Dead on the Beach.

She loads their bodies or body parts into her all-terrain vehicle and brings them back to her laboratory. She necropsies them, documents her findings, cleans the bones, labels them, and looks for a place to store them. They are shelved, stacked, put in boxes, barrels, placed in the attic or on the porch. There are jars containing snakes, preserved frogs, stomach contents of birds.

The most important, most valuable items in the museum are grocery bags containing the bones of sea turtles. Someday, she believes, this collection will yield valuable information on environmental issues we have not yet begun to study.

When she drives along the Atlantic, she finds other things washed up on the beach, and she loads them onto her vehicle. When she returns to her compound, she finds homes for these found things. She leans them against the fences, sets them beside buildings, places them on rough shelves. There are buckets, plastic and metal, scraps of lumber, a computer monitor, window sashes, pots, vessels of unknown origin and use, poles, posts, tubs, ladders, fencing, bits of wire, scraps of iron, wooden barrels, rusted iron hoops, dishes, metal rods, sticks, window screens, old shoes, rubber boots, ragged bits of clothing, strings and cord, plastic dishes, rusted enamel pans, wrinkled sheets of tin, other items unidentifiable and of no use to anyone, but Carol.

The vultures that hang around the cluster of buildings where Carol lives are nature's clean-up crew. When the necropsies are done, the bones must be cleaned, then dried in the sun. The vultures know this. They only have to wait. Dinner will come to them.

Newspaper accounts of the Kennedy-Bessette wedding say Carol Ruckdeschel sat on a milk crate outside her house, eating popcorn while the ceremony was taking place. Except for the wild creatures on the island, she may have been the only uninvited guest.

She was dressed as she always dresses: baggy pants, loose shirt, floppy hat, tall boots, hair in pigtails. Wedding finery is not Carol's thing.

It had drizzled for much of the day, but the rain was gone by the time the wedding party and their guests arrived at the church. The fourteen-mile drive from Greyfield up the narrow road had been a challenge. They'd had to stop for horses, armadillos, other creatures who claimed ownership of the road.

The double doors of the church were kept open during the ceremony. The light from the single candle and the borrowed lamp sent a warm glow out into the night. There was music: gospel songs performed a cappella by a gospel singer from Florida: "Will the Circle Be Unbroken" and "Amazing Grace."

Carolyn and John waited inside the church until their guests had left the building. The bride descended the three wooden steps, and cameras flashed. She placed one jeweled sandal and then the other onto a piece of tin — placed there to keep her stiletto heels from sinking into the sand — before turning to embrace her new husband. The guests cheered and offered congratulations to the new bride and groom. They had pulled it off. Those in the media who'd gotten hints of what was happening were stranded on the mainland. Gogo Ferguson, Greyfield owner and wedding planner, had managed to get the couple and their guests to the island and to the church, and there was not a reporter in sight.

The friends and relatives of the newlyweds talked and milled about and took stock of this lonely place as they waited for the vans and pickups that would take them back to Greyfield for the reception. What must they have thought of that cluttered compound where Carol Ruckdeschel has lived since 1975? And what did the vultures think of them?

Carol Ruckdeschel's cabin sits just beyond the pasture. To the right of the cabin, a cluster of weathered sheds, one of which likely houses her pigs. Another, the chickens. A small garden, gone to seed. Propped against the sides of buildings, leaning against every available surface, such a collection of miscellany, such a hodgepodge of items, such an assortment of junk, it is hard to discern individual objects. And harder yet, in that dim light, to imagine a purpose for them.

Herein lives a woman who is off the grid, and happily so. When she dies, much of what she has collected will sink into the earth. This place where newly freed blacks lived in the shadow of enormous wealth, entitlement, and privilege, will again become pristine wilderness.

The road loops around the Settlement and we head south once again. The day is nearly gone, the sun slanting into the side windows of the van.

"Will there be time to go to Dungeness?" someone in the back of the van asks.

Daniel shakes his head. "I'm sorry. The day has gotten away from us. There might be time to walk to the ocean, though. When we get to Sea Camp, take the trail through the campsite area, over the dunes. There should be time for that."

"Will we miss the boat back to St. Marys if we go to Dungeness? Just a quick run-through?"

"The ferry will leave on schedule," Daniel says.

Come back again, I want to tell them. Once is not enough. Ten times is not enough. There is always more to see, more to contemplate. The old cars will sink farther and farther into the ground. Stallions will steal mares away from established bands and foals will be born. Carol Ruckdeschel will be laid to rest in the plot she purchased in High Point Cemetery. Her house will sag, and it will fall, and the lumber will disintegrate into the elements from which it was created. The loggerhead turtles will come out of the sea and lay their eggs and return to the sea. The last of the retained-rights contracts will expire, and the island will begin to heal from all that has been done to her.

But what of Greyfield?

"What will happen to Greyfield?" I ask Daniel. "When all the retained rights expire, the Carnegie descendants, Gogo Ferguson and her husband, they'll still own a chunk of the island. They never entered into any kind of agreement with the Park Service."

"There are several inholders," he says. "Not just the Carnegies."

"So what will happen? Will they be allowed to keep their land?"

He shrugs.

"The Park Service could condemn it, couldn't they? Eminent domain?"

"It's a five-star hotel," Daniel answers. "The property fronts on the intracoastal waterway. They bring their guests by boat from Fernandina. It's not likely any of that is going to change, at least not in the near future."

"But when all the retained rights expire, and other inholders sell their land to the Park Service, and you have just this one commercial property smack in the middle of the island, what then?"

Daniel edges to the side of the road to avoid a series of deep ruts, and for a long time he does not answer. This is a very careful man, I decide.

"I suppose," he begins, "if the Park Service is ever going to get title to the Greyfield land—it's about two hundred acres—the easiest way would be to negotiate with the owners. One thing that has always been important to the Carnegies is they'd like their impact on the island, their preservation of it, to be part of the historical record. They want the things they built to be preserved. When they deeded Plum Orchard to the Park Service, they did it with the stipulation that it be preserved and open to the public. They hated it that the Park Service let the recreation building fall down, that their cars were pulled out of the carriage house and parked under a tree."

We round a gentle curve and come upon a horse, directly in front of us, walking down the center of the road. Daniel stops the van and we wait for her to decide where she wants to go. When she finally moves to the side, we ease past.

I lean forward in my seat. "So what you're saying is that the Carnegies want to be part of the legacy. They want their names and the things they did here to live on into the future. There should be museums full of their belongings, their clothes, their cars, their china."

"There's one in St. Marys," he reminds me. "It's got furniture and carriages. All kinds of things."

"I've never been," I tell him.

Rhamy has been listening. "Next time we come to Cumberland," she says. "We'll check it out." And she settles back into her seat.

Somewhere between Stafford House and Dungeness is an intersection. If you take the road to the left, you'll arrive at the Atlantic Ocean. To the right, the Greyfield Inn. I missed it on the way to the north end of the island, and I miss it on our way back.

Traffic is sparse. Only Park Service employees and retained-rights holders are allowed to drive on these roads. Carol Ruckdeschel and the Candlers at the north end of the island are retained-rights holders. Gogo Ferguson and her family at Greyfield are inholders. They, and the others whose properties are unencumbered, have no obligation to ever leave the island. They can drive on the roads and on the beaches. They can rent out their properties, improve their houses, build new ones, sell off portions of their land.

If we'd come here during the final years of the nineteenth century, we might have heard the sounds of construction at Plum Orchard, Lucy Carnegie's present to her son George. There would have been shipments of materials from the mainland and from across the globe, many landing at the dock at Dungeness. They would have been loaded onto wagons for transport up the main road to the site of the mansion. Some supplies would have been brought up the intracoastal waterway to the dock on Brickhill River.

The site was handpicked by Retta Carnegie's husband, Oliver Ricketson. He needed a port deep enough to accommodate his seventy-foot schooner.

When fire destroyed the Stafford plantation house where William Coleman Carnegie lived with his wife Gertrude in 1901, Lucy began construction of a new one.

No matter the cost, Lucy would keep her children close. Yet they drifted away, one by one. Of all her children and grandchildren, only one chose to make Cumberland her permanent home. Lucy Ricketson, daughter of Retta and Oliver, opened Greyfield to the public in 1962. She lived there until her death in 1989.

Now her granddaughter, Gogo Ferguson, continues the tradition.

It doesn't matter that I've missed the turnoff for Greyfield. From the main road there would have been nothing to see. It's a secluded place.

Charlie is busy packing up his cameras. Rhamy is looking off to the side, memorizing all that she sees, storing it away for the winter months.

"One day, I'll book rooms for the four of us at Greyfield," I tell her.

She reaches across the aisle, takes my hand and squeezes it. "Thanks, Mommy," she says.

"We'll be able to sit on the porch and watch the sun setting over the marsh. Can you imagine anything more wonderful? We'll spend time in the parlor, sipping wine from stemware or bourbon from old-fashioned glasses. We'll walk through every room in the house, studying portraits of Carnegie ancestors. We'll peruse the books in the library. We'll walk beneath the ancient oaks, listen to the murmur of the river, the call of birds in flight, the rustling sound of saw palmetto fronds moving in the breeze. We'll eat by candlelight, Charlie and Connor wearing borrowed jackets. We'll walk to the ocean, and if we're lucky, we might catch sight of Carol Ruckdeschel on her weekly beach patrol, stopping her ATV to pick up the dead things that have washed ashore."

Charlie is sitting next to me, scrolling through the pictures he took. He has no comment. Was he even listening?

We pull into Sea Camp. Daniel cuts the motor and exits the van.

"How far to the ocean?" someone asks.

"Or," Rhamy says, "if we had a month, we could rent one of the vacation homes. Remember the ones Daniel pointed out? By the ocean?"

"We'd have to do it in June. During your summer vacation."

"We'd be able to see things we haven't seen before," she says.

"The Carnegie graveyard. Lucy's grave. We could go there. Daniel promised to show us where it is, if there was time."

The last of the passengers have climbed out of the van. Daniel has disappeared inside the park headquarters.

"There's never enough time," Rhamy says. "But if we came for a whole month…"

Teachers are used to thinking ahead, planning things down to the last detail. "We could bring dried beans and brown rice," she says. "Bags of apples and carrots, jars of peanut butter, and we could survive. Coffee. Canned milk. We could rent bicycles from the Visitor Center and ride to Greyfield if we wanted fresh eggs or orange juice. We could learn to fish and catch oysters. Ride to the north end of the island and ask Carol if she'll show us inside her museum."

Charlie is sitting on one of the benches outside the Visitor Center, and he's listening to every word.

I take a seat next to him. "If we ran out of food," I tell him, "we could take the ferry to St. Marys, buy groceries, and bring them back."

He shows me the video he took of me standing in front of the table in the First African Baptist Church, reading from the open Bible, sun streaming in the side windows.

"If we find a house to rent on the island," I ask, "will you come? Will you spend a month on Cumberland? Do all these crazy things we have planned?"

It's a long time before he answers. When he does, his words are slow and careful. "It's an interesting proposition," he says.

I look at Rhamy. She's beaming.

31

Cumberland never fails us. If we have our hearts set on a particular adventure, and it turns out to be impossible, the island will offer up something else that is equally wonderful. A year after our van tour to the north, it's a wedding.

We first see the bride when she emerges from the Visitor Center at St. Marys and walks toward the dock where the *Cumberland Queen* is tied up. She's wearing a long, white-beaded dress. The bouquet she carries is a mixture of pink roses, spike lavender, and baby's breath, the stems secured with a lavender ribbon. Her shoes are the flimsiest of sandals. A single strap holds them on her feet.

The groom walks beside her, dark suit, blue-striped tie blowing in the wind. Behind the couple, a photographer, a giant of a man wearing a Hawaiian shirt and shorts. He's carrying a shoulder bag and a camera with the longest lens I've ever seen. A lens so long he could surely take closeup pictures of the dark side of the moon.

Rhamy and I try not to stare, but we've never seen anything like this before. Could this couple be going to Cumberland to be married?

She's not young, but she's pretty, long blonde hair caught up in an elaborate coiffure studded with pearls. Her figure is full, her dress sleeveless and low-cut. Her skin is winter white. It's a perfect day for a wedding; the sun in this semi-tropical land is already sending showers of heat down on us.

"I hope she's wearing sunblock," Rhamy says.

"We could offer her some," I answer.

"No, it might stain her dress. Besides, she probably slathered on SPF 45 before she got dressed this morning. Well, maybe not slathered."

The groom leads his bride to a seat under the pavilion which offers some protection from the sun. The photographer follows. Backpackers and campers make room.

"It's too early for mosquitoes and no-see-ums," I tell Rhamy, "so she probably won't need bug spray. But Adidas would be nice. Not as pretty as her sandals, but they would protect her from piles of horse manure. And maybe snakebites."

Rhamy wrinkles her nose. "No bride should have to wear bug spray," she says.

The water laps against the shore, and the ferry strains against the ropes that hold it. Pelicans perch on high pilings, seagulls squawk and explode into flight. Out on the river the waves swell and heave. They lift the ferry and drop it down again.

The ranger from the Visitor Center unhooks the rope at the top of the ramp, and the passengers step forward. One by one they hand him their tickets and start down the gangplank. There are campers carrying huge bags of camping gear, and there are tourists with power bars and water bottles. A few are like Rhamy and me, day-trippers come to mark the changes that have occurred in our absence, to see how the wild horses have fared over the winter, to be open to whatever gifts the island has to offer us.

The bridal couple and the photographer are the last to board. The groom holds his bride's arm as they start down the ramp.

They step onto the boat and move along the side toward a group of empty seats. I notice that the zipper on her dress is not zipped all the way up. I wonder if I could approach her at some point, touch her arm, tell her about the zipper, offer to zip it up. But the fabric is already strained, and the photographer will not be taking pictures of her back. If he does, it's his place to tell her, not mine.

Something about that unzipped zipper makes me hope this wedding, and all that comes after it, is as wonderful as she wants it to be.

Our goal for this trip, Rhamy's and mine, is to find the Carnegie graveyard. As many times as we've been to the island, it has eluded us. We know it's here, somewhere. Over the winter we've done our homework. We've studied maps, and though they are far from perfect, they show the graveyard just off the main road, between Sea Camp and Dungeness.

As Lucy grew older and heavier, so heavy she needed an electric car to get around the island, she saw the need for a Carnegie cemetery. Cumberland was her home by then, and she wanted to be buried on her beloved island. The remains of her youngest son, Coleman, who had reportedly died of pneumonia at age thirty, would be moved from the Greene-Miller cemetery into the new cemetery when it was completed.

The site was selected, cleared, and work begun. The cemetery walls, made of concrete, seashells, and sand, were built high enough to discourage deer and free-roaming cattle. Gates that included in their design the year the Carnegies bought Dungeness, 1881, were installed.

Lucy Carnegie was in poor health the last years of her life. She entered McLean Hospital in Belmont, Massachusetts, in 1915, and died the following January. Her daughter Nancy was by her side. Lucy's remains were brought to Cumberland for burial.

Surely we'll be able to find it. The distance between Sea Camp and Dungeness is not great. We'll simply walk the seashell road until we find it.

We've left the dock and are nearing the main road when we see a sign pointing to something called the Duck Pond. It's the opposite direction from where we want to go, but this is something we've never seen before. Could the Park Service have cut a road that leads to some newly discovered attraction?

We take the turn and head down the road.

At the end is a large, irregularly-shaped pool, fallen into disrepair, though still pleasing. The water is dark, but it's easy to imagine a fountain spraying fresh water into the air, ducks and geese stopping to rest and feed before continuing on their journeys. This might once have been a favorite stopover for migrating birds.

There are cement planters in the center of the pool and a bridge that crosses to the other side. We walk along the edge, then cross over. Out in an open pasture now, we explore several buildings that are close by. The door to the largest one is padlocked, but we stand on tiptoe and peek in the windows. Junk. Nothing of interest.

In the pasture opposite the buildings four horses are grazing. These are the first we've seen on this trip. And we are drawn to them.

"It's a family group," Rhamy says, and she points them out: stallion, mare, yearling, and foal.

Close by is a family group of another kind: a tall, loose-jointed man, a woman who is even taller, and a teenaged boy. They are like horses we've seen on Cumberland in years past when food was scarce: jutting bones, faces long and angular, no trace of fat anywhere on their bodies.

The three of them are busy snapping pictures of the horses. The boy gets so close to the foal, I wonder if we should warn him to keep a safe distance. But the mare is grazing peacefully beside the stallion, and we say nothing.

Rhamy points to the foal: "Look at her shoulders. See how narrow they are? Now compare that with the yearling. His are filled out, more square. Narrow shoulders make for easier births."

The three tourists drift near us. Greenhorns, we judge. But potential islomanes. The father asks Rhamy if she knows about horses, and she regales them with her observations, pointing out the stallion and mare, speculating on how pregnant the mare might be, identifying the coloring of each of the horses: gray stallion, black mare, flea-bitten yearling, and flea-bitten foal.

"Flea-bitten?" the woman asks. "Why do you call that little one flea-bitten, when he's clearly white?"

Rhamy talks of genetics and herd dynamics, and of coloring that changes as horses age. They nod, but their body language says they are not convinced.

Not islomanes, we decide. Too closed-minded. Too stuffy. Too set in a belief system that allows for no deviation.

We part.

At the far edge of the clearing stand the remains of Dungeness, but it's a different Dungeness from the one we've seen before. The fence that once surrounded the ruins is gone. Also gone are the signs warning of rattlesnakes.

The palm trees, the vines, the bushes that threatened to obliterate what was left of the mansion have all been removed. Resurrection ferns rooted in crevices have been pulled away. The rocks that littered the grand stairway have been removed. In order to stabilize what are now free-standing walls, steel braces have been bolted into place. What is left are clean walls, gaping window openings, and jutting chimneys. For the first time since we've been coming to Cumberland, we can see the actual bones of the structure. We're able to walk up to the mansion, touch the stone walls, look through the bars into the ground level interior. If we wanted, we could climb the stairs to the first floor of the mansion. Gates at the top of the stairs block further entry, but they are flimsy, no heavier than garden gates.

"Scalable," I tell Rhamy.

"Easily," she answers.

We could go inside the mansion. Walk where Lucy once walked. Sit on the porch where she sat. Visit the rooms where the family gathered, where food was prepared, where guests partied and the clamor could be heard as far away as the Georgia mainland.

"McLean Hospital is a mental institution," Rhamy says. "Sylvia Plath was a patient there."

"Are you serious? How do you know?"

"I read *The Bell Jar* when I was in college," she says, stepping onto the concrete apron at the bottom of the main staircase. "It's Plath's account of the time she spent at McLean. When I was in grad school, I had a professor who loved Plath. He talked a lot about her life, her husband, her suicide. She was such a tragic figure."

She sits on the low wall that curves around the bottom of the stairs and lifts her face to the sun. The day is as perfect as any could ever be.

"When I read about Lucy being taken to McLean," she continues, "I Googled it. There are tons of famous people who have been patients there. Susanna Kaysen, for one. The woman who wrote *Girl Interrupted*. She overdosed on pills when she was a teenager, spent nearly two years there. James Taylor, treated for depression when he was in high school. David Foster Wallace, the writer, depression and substance abuse. John Nash, the mathematician. Steven Tyler from Aerosmith. The hospital has been around since the early 1800s. It used to be called the McLean Asylum for the Insane."

I take a deep breath and let it out slowly. "Why Lucy Carnegie?" I ask. "She had everything a woman could want."

"Maybe not," Rhamy says. "Six sons and three daughters, children she tried very hard to keep on the island with her. Sons who got up every morning with nothing to do but figure out how to fill the day: should they go hunting, fishing, or sailing?"

"They could go picnicking on the beach," I answer. "Have the servants prepare a nice picnic lunch. Or ask the stable boys to saddle up one of Lucy's polo ponies and go riding."

"Or they could go carousing," Rhamy says. "Some of them were pretty heavy drinkers. 'Margaritaville' hadn't been written yet, so they didn't have to wait until 5 o'clock to have their first drink."

"Wrong song," I tell her. "You're thinking of 'It's Five O'Clock Somewhere.' 'Margaritaville' is the one about 'wasting away.'"

"Wasting away," she repeats, drawing the words out as if in replication of the process. "Don't you imagine that's the way their lives must have been? They could have had whiskey with their bacon and eggs in the morning."

Lucy must have realized, we speculate, that her sons were destined to accomplish nothing in their lives. There was nothing of their father or their uncle in them, none of the immigrant's drive to climb up out of poverty, to build something, to leave something for future generations. Andrew Carnegie often visited here; what must he have thought of his dead brother's children? Lucy had raised them to live a life of leisure. And when they were grown, and they lived in the world she had created for them, water all around, her health failing, she might have begun to realize that their lives were a waste. She had done that to them.

"At some point she would have realized, too, that the money wouldn't last forever," I tell Rhamy. "But those are regrets. It's not insanity."

"Maybe *depressed* is a better word," Rhamy says. "Maybe it was a deep, heartbreaking depression. She couldn't ride horses anymore, couldn't go fishing and hunting, couldn't do many of the things she used to do. The Gilded Age had ended, replaced with the Progressive Era. The great industrialists were losing their grip. The power they once wielded over their workers was under attack. Their fortunes were being assailed from all directions."

A cooling breeze rustles the trees around us. The horses have moved close to where we sit, so close we can hear them cropping the grass, see the puffs of dust stirred up by their footfalls. In the distance, we hear muted voices.

If we ever seriously thought of climbing over the gate and going into the mansion, we've lost our chance. There's a ranger heading our way, leading a group of about twenty tourists. Inside the main entrance gates she stops long enough to warn them to watch where they step, and to keep a safe distance from the horses.

Then she leads them toward the mansion. When she's no more than fifteen feet away, she nods to us, turns to address the group. We listen as she recounts the stories of the Indians who once inhabited the island, the hunting lodge General Oglethorpe built here, Catherine Greene's tabby mansion, the fire that destroyed it, and the Carnegie mansion also destroyed by fire. She tells of the Park Service plan to allow people to actually go inside the mansion. "The plan has been shelved for the time being," she says, "because of safety issues and concern about further deterioration to the structure."

"But there's hope," she adds. "Maybe next year."

We're hooked. When the group moves around to the back of the mansion, we tag along, listening to the ranger talk about the Carnegies, how women in that long-ago time protected their skin from the Georgia sun, of afternoon promenades in the shaded pergola. She points out the remnants of the tower where Lucy spent hour after hour, missing meals, having to be coaxed down to join the family; the weddings that took place at the mansion; the touching desire of some of the Carnegie children to rebuild after the fire in 1959.

The ranger leads her group down the seashell road toward the ocean, pointing into the woods where the Carnegie children once had a treehouse, the ruins of the recreation building, the pool that could even now be filled with water if the gravel were removed, the remains of the greenhouse where servants gathered flowers for the mansion.

Farther down the road she points out the carriage house on the right, laundry facilities on the left.

I stop and look around, confused. Where are the cars? They should be here, just down from the carriage house. Isn't this where they were a year ago? What happened to them? Aren't these the live oak trees that sheltered them? Where is the rope that surrounded the car graveyard, the wooden posts to which the ropes were attached?

"What happened to the cars?" I ask. "Have they been taken away?"

The ranger glances at me, then at the empty area beneath the trees. "They were removed," she says, in a voice so quiet, I wonder if she hopes no one in the group will hear her.

"When?" I ask. "And why?"

"A few weeks ago," she says, stepping away from the group. "The goal of the Park Service, the thing we're mandated by law to do, is to protect the natural resources of the island and to allow it to revert to its natural state. As money becomes available, and we're able to do things we need to do toward that end, we move closer and closer to accomplishing that goal.

"Certain structures of historical value will be preserved. Dungeness mansion, Plum Orchard, the First African Baptist Church on the north end of the island, certain buildings we've converted for use by the Park Service. The decision was made to remove the cars," she says, and there's a finality in her voice that forbids further comment.

Some among the group have been to the island before. They've seen the cars, tried to identify make and model from what remains, marveled at how they have deteriorated, remembered cars that once belonged to ancestors. There is grumbling. Unhappiness. Muted anger, though anger kept in check. There must be a reason for this violation of our island.

The reason, of course, is the master plan. When the Park Service took over Cumberland, there were junk piles all over the island. Families who lived here all had dumps, hidden away, out of sight of their houses. As the Park Service acquired properties and leased them back to the owners, and the leases expired, the issue arose of what to do with the things people had left behind. There were cars, tin cans, bottles, building materials, tools, weed and brush killer, machinery, medicine bottles. Once a thing was brought to the island, it was, more often than not, left on the island.

The Park Service considered bringing in heavy equipment and burying the accumulated waste of a hundred years, but there was fear of contaminating the water supply. A master plan was put forth, and adopted. It called for the removal of all the things people left on the island. The refuse of an elite society that once inhabited this place would be loaded onto barges and taken to landfills on the mainland.

Rhamy and I move closer to the car graveyard that is no more. What had sunk into the ground has been dug up and removed. Saw palmetto is taking over. Behind the live oaks is the pasture where we've often seen horses grazing. Today it is empty.

If the Park Service can remove the cars, what about the horses? Will someone decide, at some future point, to end the debate among environmentalists, ecologists, and conservationists? Will they declare the horses an invasive species, round them up and ship them to holding pens somewhere on the mainland, where they can live out the rest of their lives?

The tour goes on, heading down to the Greene-Miller cemetery, but Rhamy and I do not go with them. Instead, we head for the picnic tables in front of the laundry building. In our backpacks, we have sandwiches, dried apricots, Cowboy Bark chocolate, and apples, halved and cored. Wild horses are more likely to eat apples if they can smell the aroma from a fresh cut, we've learned.

We spread napkins on the table and begin to divvy up the food. The wind has picked up, and we anchor the corners of our napkins with our food and water bottles.

"Nature could have done it on her own," Rhamy says. "She didn't need the Park Service to intervene."

"It would have taken a long time. The tires, especially."

Her sandwich lies untouched on her napkin. She's quiet for long moments, until finally she speaks. "I think we've lost something important," she says. "The cars are gone now, and we're the poorer for it. The lessons we might have learned are forever lost to us."

Another long silence, and when she looks up at me, her face is brighter. The wind pushes her hair across her face, and she sweeps it back.

"Let's do Greyfield next summer," she says. "Never mind what it costs, let's do it. Someday Greyfield will be either sold to the Park Service or condemned. Taken by eminent domain. Not for a while, not while the Carnegies are still such a political force, but it will happen, sooner or later. Let's not wait. Let's do it next summer."

"With or without our husbands?"

She shrugs. "We'll invite them," she says. And she picks up her sandwich.

When we've finished our lunch, we begin the walk back to the main road, taking detours when we see something that catches our eye. From the debris still scattered around, we try to determine where the dormitories for black and white servants might have been, the chicken houses, the kennel, the dairy. But it's mostly guesswork. Termites have been busy, as have the storms that rake the island, the salt air that abrades every exposed surface of every structure.

We explore the remains of a schoolhouse Lucy built for her grandchildren. Rhamy steps it off: twenty-four by twenty-seven feet. All that is left are the foundation stones, chimney, and shreds of tin roof that still cling to the chimney.

The temperature has risen, but the breeze is steady, and when we're not in direct sunlight, it's pleasant. We see no horses, no animals of any kind. We walk past the mansion and have turned onto the main road when a Park Service van pulls up beside us. Behind the wheel is the ranger who conducted the tour. She opens her window and asks if we'd like a ride. I glance at Rhamy, she at me, and of course we accept. The ranger will know where the Carnegie graveyard is.

We climb into the van and ask.

"It's not far," she says. "Just past the turnoff to the dock."

"Will you show us?"

"I'll drop you off, if you want. But you won't be able to see much. The actual cemetery is back from the road, behind a chain-link fence. There's no access; you can't go inside. It's private property, owned in perpetuity by the Carnegie family. And it's still an active cemetery. There was a burial there just last year."

A half mile or so down the road, she stops the van in front of the main cemetery gates. They are chained and padlocked. To the right of the center post, attached to the top of the gate, there's a weathered sign. Four words have been carved into two wooden plaques.

Private

Cemetery

Please Honor

"All the Carnegies are buried here," the ranger tells us. "Lucy, Thomas, and eight of her nine children. Only Nancy is buried elsewhere, up in Kentucky, with her husband Marius."

"Thomas? Wasn't he buried in Pittsburgh?"

"They moved his body here after the graveyard was finished. His remains were placed in a vault next to where Lucy would be buried. She lies between her husband and Coleman, her youngest son. He died of syphilis. Thomas on her right, Coleman on her left."

"I thought it was pneumonia."

She shrugs. "Maybe. It was a long time ago. If you walk along the road, you might be able to see some of the monuments. It's pretty overgrown. Someone tends the graveyard, but they leave the perimeter as a buffer zone. It shields the graveyard from public view."

We climb out of the van and close the door, but the ranger is reluctant to go. "His obituary mentions an accident in New York City," she says. "Coleman Carnegie evidently hit two pedestrians. They sued, and they got a judgment against him, but the court was never able to collect the money. The article says he was being paid a salary of $125,000 a year. And that he'd been in ill health for some time."

"You read his obituary?" I ask.

"They encourage us to learn as much as we can about the island and the people who used to live here. Back at the ranger station there are volumes of oral histories. They're pretty interesting."

"Pneumonia was the cause of death of lots of people back then," I tell her. "They used to call it 'the old people's friend.'"

She nods. "And influenza. But neither one drags on for long periods of time. Coleman's health declined over a period of years."

She puts the van into a forward gear, but there's more she wants to say. "At one time," she continues, "Andrew Carnegie planned to make Coleman his protégé. Take him into the firm, teach him everything he needed to know. But the boy's health was delicate. His doctors advised a milder climate."

"And there's a connection? The people he hit with his car in New York City couldn't collect because he was here, on Cumberland Island?"

She shrugs. "It was a long time ago," she repeats. And with a wave, she pulls away.

Through the double gates we can see the sandy road that leads into the cemetery. Indentations in the road bed tell us it is used with some regularity. Stretching out from the gates in both directions is a chain-link fence, six feet high, with three strands of barbed wire atop it. Through the wire and between the center posts of the gate we catch glimpses of the tabby walls that surround the actual graveyard. The bronze gates Lucy had designed for the cemetery are hidden from view.

We walk some distance up the road, toward Sea Camp, hoping for a better view, but the undergrowth is such a tangled mass, entry would be impossible. In places the chain-link fence is totally obscured. We retrace our steps, hoping to find a path, an animal trail, something that will give us a view into the cemetery.

The undergrowth thins out somewhat when we near the northwest corner, but we're reluctant to step into such a thicket of brush, brambles, and matted vegetation. Islands can be places of unexpected danger. Safety from without, but danger from within.

Rhamy points out that there are eighteen species of snakes on Cumberland Island. "Only three are venomous," she adds.

I step off the road, into a grassy area. "Tell me when we're on the ferry."

"All three are pit vipers, and they mostly hunt at night."

"So we're not likely to run into one. That's a relief."

"Diamondback rattlesnakes will run away from you, if they can."

"Let's make lots of noise, so they know we're here."

"They don't have ears. They respond to vibrations."

"So we'll stomp the ground really hard when we walk."

"Then there are canebrakes, but they're very rare. Mostly you find them on the mainland."

"Enough about snakes."

"Cottonmouths, too, but probably not here. They like to hang out near water."

"Like the Duck Pond? You could have told me earlier."

"There are lots of black racers, too, but they're good snakes. They eat other snakes."

Nice conversation, when we're about to claw our way into a jungle. Which we fully intend to do. Miraculously, we come upon a section where someone has cleared a narrow swath that veers to within twenty feet of the chain-link fence. This is our best chance.

I lead the way, and Rhamy follows, both of us watching where we put our feet, stepping on springy piles of dying palm fronds, wondering what might be underneath.

We reach the fence, but our view is still obscured. All we can see are small sections of graveyard wall, thirty feet away, and two concrete columns topped with globes. The columns are joined by a low wall.

"Could they be headstones?" I ask.

"There's no way to tell."

"They look like giant bedposts," Rhamy says. "Like the bed we saw in Plum Orchard, the one the guide said might have been Lucy's. These are bigger, and made out of concrete instead of mahogany. But they look the same."

If only we could get closer. We consider going back to the main entrance. Maybe there's room to fit between the two sections of gate. But the space was small, and the posts were chained and padlocked. It is hopeless.

We retreat to the cleared section and, with great relief, step into a clear pasture. We walk along the edge until the fence is once again lost in the undergrowth.

"This is as close as we'll ever get," I tell Rhamy.

We leave the pasture and cut back onto the main road, heading for Sea Camp.

"Are you disappointed?" she asks.

"In a way," I answer. "But maybe we've seen enough. They have a right to their privacy."

We're walking along the trail on our way to the ocean when we come upon the wedding party. Bride, groom, and photographer are having lunch at one of the picnic tables in the Sea Camp campgrounds.

The table is covered with a white cloth, corners anchored with camera, lenses, other photography equipment. There are pink napkins and champagne in fluted glasses.

"We saw you on the ferry," Rhamy exclaims. "Are you married?"

"We are," the bride says, and she looks at her husband, and the look is so adoring, we feel like intruders. "We were married in a little church on the north end of the island."

"The First African Baptist Church! We've been there," I tell her. "It's where John F. Kennedy, Jr., was married."

She looks confused. Is it possible she doesn't know about the Kennedy-Bessette wedding?

"We took the Lands and Legacies Tour last year, and it's one of the places we stopped," Rhamy says. "It's a beautiful church. I'll bet it was a wonderful ceremony. Congratulations."

"Thank you," she answers. "It was lovely. My dream come true. Our dream," she corrects herself, and she turns to her husband. She tilts her head up to him, inviting his kiss. He reddens, but he obliges, and the kiss is long and lingering. The photographer busies himself looking through the digital files of the pictures he's taken.

A gust of wind picks up a corner of the tablecloth, tipping one of the champagne glasses. It rolls off the table, onto the ground. The groom rushes to pick it up.

"You couldn't have picked a more beautiful spot, for your wedding, or for your lunch," Rhamy says. "Could I take a picture? Would you mind?"

They pose, and she snaps the photograph with her iPhone, and we go on.

More sand has tumbled into the campgrounds since we were last here. It has piled up against the trees, burying some that once stood on solid ground. The scramble up the hill at the edge of the forest is more difficult than ever, the loose

sand so slippery we despair of reaching the top. When I gain a foothold I reach
out to Rhamy, and she to me, and together, we make it.

Out in the open, away from the protection of the trees, we're suddenly cata-
pulted into bright sunlight and a wind so strong it stings our flesh. It carries with
it the sound of the ocean. It is in white turmoil, sloshing against the shore, with-
drawing, and sloshing again.

"Did you see where their lunches were from?" Rhamy asks. "Spencer's Bed
and Breakfast in St. Marys. That's the place where we got box lunches the first
time we came to the island. They gave us apples, and I fed them to the horses.
Remember?"

"I do. Gala apples. I remember the rocking chairs on the porch. Hanging ferns
and a lilac bush in the yard. Turkey sandwiches and chocolate chip cookies. And
a white tablecloth like the one on the newlyweds' table."

The wind and the sand it carries makes conversation difficult. We trudge on,
heads lowered, careful of our footfalls. Sections of the boardwalk are so weathered
we wonder if the boards might break through.

When we finally reach the ocean, we stand in awe of it, that vast expanse of
water that is so troubled, yet so predictable. The waves roll up onto the shore with
a furious roar, depositing their flotsam on the farthest reaches of the beach and
sweeping whatever they can carry back out to the ocean. Beneath the waters are
currents strong enough to wash us out to sea. We stay well away from them, never
venturing more than a few feet into the turbulent waters.

But what a glorious few feet they are. How refreshing, the salt spray that wets
our clothes and cools our bodies, the sand the squishes under our feet, the receding
waters that pull it from beneath us, and we scramble onto higher ground, not
knowing how deep we might sink.

Far to the north Rhamy sees what she thinks might be horses. In the summertime, they like to hang out by the ocean, the salt spray offering relief from the heat,
the flies, and other biting insects. We walk toward them, knowing we can't reach
them. The distance is too great, the time too short. We need to head back to Sea
Camp.

The newlyweds and their photographer have just finished packing up when we return from the ocean. We walk with them back to Sea Camp.

"Do you have friends who might be upset that they weren't invited?" Rhamy asks.

"I would have liked for my daughter to have been here," the groom says, "but she had other plans." His blue tie is tucked between the buttons of his shirt, but still the wind tugs at it.

"How old is she?"

"Nineteen."

"And she won't approve?"

He shakes his head. "I don't think she will."

We walk in silence, bride and groom directly behind us, photographer bringing up the rear. The canopy above us is nearly impenetrable, and if a cloud has moved across the sun, we would hardly know. A pall has descended over us. Mention of the daughter has taken some of the joy out of the occasion.

"We've been together for nine years," the bride says. "I always wanted to come to Cumberland Island. I can't remember where I first heard about it. But from the time I was little, I wanted to come here. When we decided to get married, I thought, why not do something really different, and special, come to a place where we've never been, just the two of us."

"You're not from the South?"

"No. We live in upstate New York."

"Amazing, that you'd end up here. And that you were able to arrange everything from so far away."

"I found a judge who lives on the island," she explains. "He said he'd be happy to marry us. That there was a church here, too, and we could have the ceremony there. So we set the date, and here we are. So far, it's all worked out perfectly."

"How did you get from the ferry to the church? That's seventeen miles up a dirt road."

"The judge," she answers. "He picked us up at the dock and drove us."

"In a pickup truck," the groom interjects, and he's smiling at the memory. "It was a tight fit," he adds.

"The judge performed the ceremony and then drove us back, dropped us off at the campgrounds trail. From there we walked to the picnic site."

"Where are you going on your honeymoon?" Rhamy asks.

"We're staying at a bed and breakfast in St. Marys. We'll be there tonight and tomorrow night, then head back."

"Never mind about your daughter," I tell the groom. "She'll get used to it. You have the right to marry whomever you want."

"Your bride is beautiful," Rhamy says. "That she would plan something like this, something so daring, so adventurous, the rest of your life is going to be such fun. She's a treasure."

They've been walking hand in hand. Now he moves closer to her and slips his arm around her waist.

The area around the ranger station at Sea Camp is crowded with people waiting for the ferry. The wind has become fierce, and Park Rangers have decided that docking at Dungeness is too risky. The dock itself is moving in the current, and there is concern the whole structure might break away.

They're using the Lands and Legacies vans to shuttle day trippers to Sea Camp. Some have chosen to walk; they arrive in groups of two or three, clutching their belongings, windblown and out of breath.

Crossing to St. Marys will be a rough one, the rangers warn us.

Rhamy, expecting the worst, takes a Dramamine. She offers one to me, but I refuse. We've never before experienced wind this strong, and this is a tidal channel. It can't be that bad.

The seats inside the ferry fill up quickly, as do the benches along the sides. By the time we board, our only choice is to climb to the open deck on top of the ferry.

The captain hugs the shore until we pass the deserted Dungeness dock. We look for horses along the beach, but there are none. The chimneys of Dungeness tower above the forest, and then they are gone.

Another year will go by before we return to Cumberland. And when we do, will the wild horses still be here? Or will they have been rounded up by the Bureau of Land Management, taken off the island and trucked to holding pens out West where they will spend the rest of their lives?

The bride and groom are standing in the back of the boat, holding hands, watching the wake, the birds, the distant land masses.

"Why do you think they chose an island they knew nothing about for their wedding?" I ask.

"She's an islomane," Rhamy says. "She doesn't know it, but she was born on an island. In a previous life. Or she read about Cumberland, and it awakened something in her. She has some attachment to islands, and it's there, inside her, and it will never leave her. Did you hear what she said? That this was her dream? That she'd always wanted to come here? She needs to come to a place like this in order to center herself."

"And maybe to get away from that nasty step-daughter?"

"That too," Rhamy says, smiling. But then her smile vanishes. "Do you think they'll take the horses away? And if they do, will we still come back?"

"I think it's almost inevitable; too many environmentalists are weighing in, saying the horses don't belong here. If they can take away the cars, it's only a matter of time until they decide the horses have to go. Then maybe the church where the bride and groom said their vows. And the shack where Carol Ruckdeschel lives. And her museum full of turtle bones. And the old graveyards. Not for a long time, but inevitably, it will all go."

There is no discernible moment when the winds lessen and the rough waters subside. At some point we leave the intracoastal waterway and begin to travel up the St. Marys River, and the winds are not so fierce, and the water not so turbulent.

By the time we reach St. Marys, we are in smooth waters.

Epilogue

One year later, against all odds, Rhamy and I are riding bicycles up the seashell road of Cumberland Island, and we're thrilled. When we checked into the St. Marys Visitor Center to pick up our ferry tickets, the ranger told us the bicycles were all rented. "We only have a limited number," she said, "and they've been reserved."

"All twenty of them?" Rhamy asked. "Are you sure?"

Yes, she was sure. The bicycles were gone.

But the ranger at Sea Camp wasn't so certain. He looked through the paperwork on his desk, glanced at the bike rack outside the window, then at the clock on the opposite wall. "Two people reserved bicycles, but they haven't shown," he said. "You can have them."

"How much?" Rhamy asked. I was already reaching for the credit card I'd had the foresight to bring along.

How is it possible we could be this lucky? Twenty minutes ago, on the ferry, Rhamy wondered if this might be our last trip to Cumberland. For years we've been coming to this island. We've visited her mansions, picnicked on her beaches, and hiked her river trails. We traveled north to the Settlement and sat in the church built by former slaves. We climbed the dunes and waded into the marshes. The sun has burnt our skin, the wind chafed our cheeks, the rain drenched our hair and our clothing. When we stood outside the gates of the Carnegie graveyard last year, didn't we both feel a sense of finality? What was left?

The Carnegies were a family that wanted to own an island. The island, in the end, would not be owned. The cars they brought onto her shores are gone. Some of the things they built will be preserved, but most will go the way of the cars.

At some point, the horses will likely be removed. But today they are here. And two people who reserved bicycles for the day did not show up.

Seats adjusted, brakes tested, and handlebars lowered, we're biking along Grand Avenue. The bicycles have only one speed, but it's fast enough. You have to pedal backward to apply the brakes, like we did when we were kids, but we can get used to that. The sand in the wheel tracks is smooth and hard, the pedaling easy. It might be possible to bike all the way to the north end of the island. There are side roads, and we resolve to take every single one of them, just to see where they go. We can visit the Rockefeller vacation homes by the ocean. We'll ride to Greyfield. We've always wanted to see it. Today we will.

We've hardly gone a quarter of a mile when it begins to rain. But it's April, and we've been rained on before. We have Ziploc bags for our phones. We pedal on, and as quickly as the rain began, it ends.

There's a surprising amount of traffic on the road: Park Service vehicles, pickup trucks, tourists sauntering along. The tourists look at us with envy; we're going so much faster than they are, and we're doing it with such ease. They wave, and we wave back.

We're riding bicycles on Cumberland Island, something we've dreamed of doing. We're passing hikers, weaving from side to side, steering into the woods to make way for oncoming vehicles.

Most of the side roads lead to the ocean, a few to the marsh. Some come to an abrupt end in a tangle of undergrowth. We've biked for several miles when a white pickup truck noses out of a side road and turns in our direction. We pull to the side and wait for it to pass.

The driver is a middle-aged man wearing a baseball cap. There's a decal on the side of the truck. *Greyfield Inn*. When he is far down the road, out of sight, we turn into the lane from which he emerged.

A short distance farther on, we come upon two columns, standing like sentinels on each side of the road. There is no chain between them. The sign suffices:

Greyfield Inn

Private

Guests Only

The mansion turned bed and breakfast that has eluded us for so long is directly in front of us, partially obscured by the ubiquitous live oaks. Like Dungeness, there's a tall, above-ground basement, an elaborate staircase leading to the main floor, a wide porch shaded by the floor above. Behind it, Cumberland Sound.

Wild turkeys walk across the lawn, pecking for food. Two horses graze in the pasture to our right. To our left, a small, red-roofed building that must be one of the cottages they rent out. Another at the far edge of the pasture.

Despite the "Private, Guests Only" sign, we consider riding up to the front door. We could ask for a drink of water. Tell them we've lost our way; could they direct us to Sea Camp? We could ask if they serve lunch.

Would we be welcome? If we're rebuffed, our perfect day would not be so perfect.

We turn our bikes around and head back to the main road. On to Stafford House and the Settlement.

On Cumberland, there's always more to see, more to learn, more to do. We've never biked on Grand Avenue before. Rhamy wants a picture. We approach a group of people. They're happy to oblige. She hands them her iPhone.

The man takes several shots and returns the phone to Rhamy. We're barely back on the road when we see an ATV coming toward us. We pull to the side and wait.

The driver is wearing a slouch hat, flannel shirt, and baggy pants. She comes closer, and we see her sun-browned face and her long, grey flecked braids. She waves to us. We wave back. She passes. We turn to watch. Is this the woman we think it is?

On the back of her four-wheeler is a silver toolbox. Several black plastic bags filled with something unidentifiable. The sound of the motor fades. The blue-tinged exhaust dissipates.

"Gogo Ferguson," says the man who took our pictures. "She's one of the Carnegies. Lives at Greyfield. She makes jewelry out of animal bones."

He's wrong. It's not Gogo Ferguson. It's Carol Ruckdeschel. The uninvited guest at the Kennedy-Bessette wedding. The woman who rides wild horses and fights for the island and for all the creatures who live here.

We get back on our bikes and pedal north, and for a long time we do not speak. We've seen Carol Ruckdeschel. She lives. She's still collecting things that wash up on the beach. She drives an ATV, and it spews out blue smoke.

About the Author

Rita Welty Bourke is the author of *Kylie's Ark: The Making of a Veterinarian.* She's a regular contributor to literary magazines, including *The Southwest Review, The Potomac Review, Shenandoah, Black Warrior Review,* and *The North American Review.* Married to songwriter Rory M. Bourke, she's the mother of three daughters. She lives in Nashville, Tennessee, and visits Cumberland Island whenever she can.

Visit her website at RitaWeltyBourke.com

Bibliography

Barefoot, Patricia. *Images of America, Cumberland Island*. Charleston, SC: Arcadia Publishing, 2004.

Barr, Nevada. *Endangered Species*. New York, NY: Harper Collins Publishers, 1998.

Bullard, M. R. and Ehrenhard, John E. *An Abandoned Black Settlement on Cumberland Island, Georgia*. DeLeon Springs, FL: E.O, Painter Printing Co., 1982.

Bullard, Mary. *Cumberland Island: A History*. Athens, GA: University of Georgia Press, 2003.

Bullard, Mary. *Robert Stafford of Cumberland Island: Growth of a Planter*. Athens, GA: University of Georgia Press, 1995.

Coram, Robert, "Life and Death on Cumberland Island," *Atlanta Weekly*, July 5, 1981.

Dilsaver, Lary M. *Cumberland Island National Seashore: A History of Conservation Conflict*. Charlottesville, VA: University of Virginia Press, 2004.

Durrell, Lawrence. *Prospero's Cell and Reflections on a Marine Venus*. New York, NY: Dutton Publishing, 1960.

Eulenfeld, Art L. *Lebensraum (Living Space)*. New York: Carlton Press, 1993.

Harlan, Will. *Untamed: The Wildest Woman in America and the Fight for Cumberland Island*. New York, NY: Grove Press, 2014.

Imes, Birney. *Juke Joint*. Oxford, MS: University Press of Mississippi, 1990.

LaBastille, Annie. *Women and Wilderness*. San Francisco, CA: Sierra Club Books, 1980.

Lauterbach, Preston. *Chitlin' Circuit and the Road to Rock 'n' Roll*. New York, NY: W. W. Norton & Company, 2011.

Lawson, Wendy. "Tour Plum Orchard Mansion on Cumberland Island." *Travel News*, Amelia Island, FL: March 3, 2011.

Lessard, Suzannah. *The Architect of Desire: Beauty and Danger in the Stanford White Family*. New York, NY: The Dial Press, 1996.

Lewis, Jeoffrey. *Celestial Navigations; Horses*. http://ravenstrom.livejournal.com/4666.html.

McPhee, John. *Encounters with the Archdruid*. New York: Farrar, Straus and Giroux, 1971.

McPhee, John. "Travels in Georgia." *The New Yorker*: April 28, 1973.

Monks, Millicent. *Songs of Three Islands*. New York, NY: Atlas & Company, 2012.

Nickens, T. Edward. "The Bone Collectors." *Smithsonian Magazine*: February, 2001.

Pheltz, Marsha Dean. *An American Beach for African Americans*. Gainesville, FL: University Press of Florida, 1997.

Rockefeller, Nancy Carnegie. *The Carnegies & Cumberland Island*. Limited edition, 1993.

Ryden, Hope. *Wild Horses I Have Known*. New York, NY: Clarion Books, 1999.Seabrook, Charles. *Cumberland Island: Strong Women, Wild Horses*. Winston-Salem, NC: John F. Blair, 2002.

Uruburu, Paula. *American Eve: Evelyn Nesbit, Stanford White, The Birth of the "It" Girl and the Crime of the Century*. New York, NY: Riverhead Books Inc., 2008.

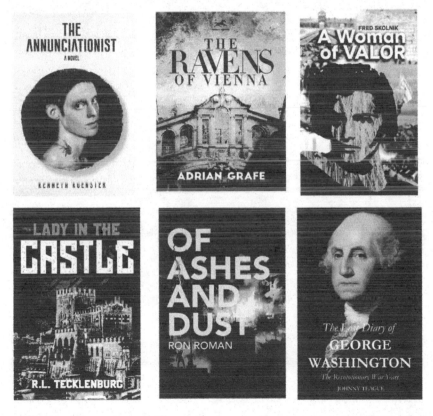